The King Of Hearts

Part 4 of the Red Dog Conspiracy

Patricia Loofbourrow

Praise for the

Red Dog Conspiracy

"This was the first steampunk book that I've read that I actually really loved."

— GABBY'S HONEST BOOK REVIEWS

"This is definitely noir, including the traditional breaking of the narrative timeline. People are doing nasty things for sometimes known, and sometimes not yet uncovered, reasons. It's what makes the world turn for the Families, who are in an uneasy alliance with shifting loyalties, cease fires, and outright aggression."

— MARGARET FISK, Tales To Tide You Over

"Patricia Loofbourrow has created a world of family intrigue combined with feuding households across the four quadrants of Bridges."

— JUNE LORRAINE ROBERTS, Murder In Common

"… a good read for anyone who likes mystery and suspense mixed with science fiction."

— IVORY MORTON, Beautyful Word

"… a mystery story of the first order in the best tradition of Sherlock Holmes."

— CLABE POLK

"… the political intrigue in this story is unrivaled …"

— TANGO WITH TEXT

"Beautifully written."

— GABRIEL CLASON

For more reviews, visit JacqOfSpades.com

FICTION BY PATRICIA LOOFBOURROW

RED DOG CONSPIRACY
Part 1: *The Jacq of Spades*
Part 2: *The Queen of Diamonds*
Part 3: *The Ace of Clubs*

PREQUELS
Gutshot: The Catastrophe
The Alcatraz Coup
Vulnerable

Foreword

This is the fourth chapter of a thirteen-part story. There will be no foolish maps or silly appendices in this book. If you need to know how Bridges is arranged, or what the Four Families are, or any other such detail, I refer you to my preceding books. There is also extensive information on JacqOfSpades.com

Buckle your seat belt, Dorothy, 'cause Kansas is going bye-bye.

To those struggling to break free from their cages.

You're not alone.

The Arraignment

"Wake up."

Someone pushed my shoulder.

Or was I dreaming?

"Get up!" Urgent, demanding.

A charcoal fog. I couldn't feel my right arm.

This is gonna hurt.

"Young lady, you get up this instant!"

My mother-in-law, Molly.

I'd never dreamed of Molly before.

Or was I awake?

My arm began to tingle in a nauseating way. My left shoulder was grabbed tightly, shaken. My head throbbed. My mouth was so dry I couldn't speak.

What happened? Where was Tony? Why was his mother here?

Then I remembered where I was: the bottom front room of my apartments on 33 1/3rd Street, Spadros quadrant.

I remembered why I was here: I was under house arrest.

I remembered why I left Spadros Manor: to flee Bridges with Joseph Kerr, the only man I had ever loved.

And Joe was dead.

"Jacqueline Spadros," Molly snapped, "if you don't get up right now, I'll call Roy."

I rolled off my arm, which tingled furiously. I squeezed my eyes shut, fighting pain, grief, despair. "Call him, then. Maybe he'll kill me, and this nightmare'll be over with."

An angry stomp of footsteps retreating.

My beloved Joe was gone.

Holding hands as we walked in a late summer's golden light … kissing in the moonlight … that one night of love before they stole me from him … the passion in his face as he held me in my lamp-lit study … his last words: *but we have no time.*

He'd been right. What was I thinking? The instant Joe said we might leave, I should have done so. What could have possibly been more important?

The footsteps returned, more slowly this time.

I killed him.

I killed Joe, just as surely as whoever pulled the trigger.

A cold shock!

I sat up, dripping wet. "What the hell?"

Molly stood in front of me, pitcher in hand. "You're due at the courthouse on Market Center in an hour for your arraignment hearing. Yet here you are in bed! What's wrong with you?"

My lady's maid Amelia cowered in the corner, hands to her mouth, fear in her eyes. "You wouldn't wake up, mum."

Molly grabbed my right arm, and I cried out as the numb tingling nausea returned full force.

The room wavered. How many bottles did I drink last night?

Molly snapped at Amelia, "You, get over here."

They stripped off the clothes Regina Clubb gave me at her hotel two days earlier as fast as they could.

No, wait, I thought, that couldn't be right. I left the hotel on Thursday. Wasn't this Saturday? Why would we go to the courthouse today? "A hearing? How was I supposed to —"

Molly glared at me. "The notice."

A sealed envelope sat on my dresser. Was it there when I arrived? I couldn't remember.

What day was this?

Clubb Hotel had been a nightmare all its own. The way that woman laughed …

I felt sick to my stomach.

Molly pulled me naked towards the tub. "This is going to be

the fastest bath ever. Gods, you stink of booze."

The water was cold!

Hands forced me under, pulled me out, water spraying across the room. They threw towels around me, rushed me into clothes, shoved me into a chair by my mirror.

Dripping thick curls, standing every which way, makeup smeared. Combs pulled my head this way and that.

Molly got out scissors. "These tangles must go."

I clasped my head, horrified. "No!"

She began snipping. "It's just the ends, dear." She set the scissors down, dipped a soft cloth in cold cream, wiped my face. "We'll do your hair in the carriage."

Amelia winced as she knelt before me, tying my right boot.

Empty bottles littered the floor. A crow cawed in the middle of the empty street. Panicked dread hit me. "My bird!"

Pushing past Amelia, I rushed to its cage. My poor clawed bird lay bound in its bandages, eyes closed, panting.

A flood of relieved gratitude: it was alive! "Bring water, Amelia." I dribbled some into its mouth, and it drank greedily.

Remorse struck. How had it survived?

Amelia took something from her pocket and put it into mine. "Your tenants' money. I collected it whilst you were gone."

I'd never considered it. "That was kind of you, Amelia." Especially after the way I'd treated her.

Molly let out a snort of derision, grabbed my arm, dragged me out to the navy blue carriage, and thrust me inside.

Just like Ma did when she sent me away …. I blinked away tears as I pictured Ma pulling me from my bed. Shoving me into that carriage. The disgust on her face as she turned away.

Amelia had followed. Molly snapped, "Get the room in order."

Amelia curtsied low. "Yes, mum, right away."

"And give my bird more water, please," I called out as we drove away.

This wasn't my carriage. Where was my carriage? The thin black curtains were pulled, which left us sitting in dim light as the carriage barreled along.

Molly snapped, "**Why** did you tell him?"

"Tell who what?"

My head yanked backwards. Molly hissed in my ear. "How dare you tell my son his marriage was a sham! And in a letter from the hand of a servant! What has he **ever** done for you to hurt him so?"

She let go, and I faced her. "I told him the truth. No one else was going to." All those years of pain and terror had been for nothing. Joe was dead! "I couldn't live like that anymore."

Molly pulled at my hair again, but only to braid it. "You do things without thinking, then you leave others to clean the mess."

No, I'd considered the matter ever since Ma shoved me into that carriage six years earlier. I had Tony buy my bird when we married so I'd never forget I lived in a cage. I knew there would be no way out unless I made one.

Tony deserved the truth. I even **told** him the plan in my letter!

But Joe had the tickets, and he never arrived at the station.

Molly opened a hatbox which sat across from us. Inside lay my forest green velvet hat Madame Biltcliffe made for the Grand Ball.

Madame. Another person hurt because of me.

"Come on," Molly said as she took out the hat, but her tone was kind. "We're almost there."

The carriage slowed. A man shouted, "Make way!"

The crowd roared. How many people were **out** there?

Molly's face was grim. "I can't be seen with you."

After an instant of confusion, I realized why. In leaving Tony, I betrayed the Spadros crime syndicate. If his parents were seen helping me, they could lose the quadrant. "I understand."

Molly patted my shoulder. "Good girl." She pulled a thick veil over her face, shrinking back as the door opened.

A man dressed in the navy blue livery of the Court extended his hand. His polished silver buttons bore the patina of long use.

Real silver on livery, I thought. These must be trusted men!

Beyond him, people filled the area as far as I could see. As I emerged, the roar increased; cameras flashed by the dozens. A sea of banners denouncing me danced atop the close-packed throng. My hair dripped down the back of my neck; the air felt chill.

The way to the courthouse was clear, six feet wide. Police lined my path on both sides, their shoulders touching as the crowd surged against them. Here and there one stumbled, an enraged group pushing against the weight of his body.

A guard on each side took my arm as if they did this every day. Ten armed members of the Court surrounded us, pistols drawn, scanning the crowds, the rooftops.

None of the men near me spoke, not that any of them could have been heard through the screaming.

"Pot rag whore!"

"Murderess!"

"Betrayer!"

A rock flew past to shatter on the ground in front of me.

I focused upon the Courthouse: sandstone walls, white marble steps. Four pillars of white stone supporting a wide overhang.

A crowd of police kept people back from the doors. Once the doors closed behind me, the vast hall fell eerily silent.

The hall had sandstone walls and ceiling with walnut banisters, the floor tiled in a grayish tan. I'd just been inside it the week prior to give the testimony which seemed to have doomed me.

But instead of going to the Family box upstairs, I was taken across the hall and along a long passage to my right, to a door marked "Room A."

This room, mostly empty, had many pew seats facing towards a small railing which came to my hip. The wood in this room was of a golden stain, darker than the oak the Clubb Family used.

The rows with their wide aisles reminded me a bit of the Cathedral where I grew up, although this room was much smaller. Men dressed in Court livery stood at intervals along the walls holding rifles, the butts of their weapons on the floor.

To my right, ten rows before the small railing, Master Jonathan Diamond and Mr. Charles Hart sat beside each other. Both were dressed for the street, their black top hats resting on either side. Jon's tight-coiled black and Mr. Hart's stiff-straight silvery-red hair still held the faint imprint of their hats.

Jonathan was a welcome sight, and not entirely unexpected. He was Keeper of the Court, after all, as well as my best friend. Charles Hart's presence, though, was a mystery. What possible interest might the Hart Patriarch have in this?

Beyond the railing, one long table lay on either side. A black-robed man sat upon a raised area, the seal of the Merca Federal Union upon it. At floor level on one side of the judge, a man sat with a contraption resembling a typewriter perched on its stand. A middle-aged uniformed man stood on the other side holding a thick staff. Beside him, a shotgun rested on its stand.

The tables at the front of the room were full. To my left, District Attorney Chase Freezout, a tanned, white-haired man in his sixties, sat in the middle of his table, several men on both sides.

To my right, the Spadros attorney Mr. Primero Trevisane sat, leaving the end seat near me empty. My husband Tony sat at the far end, his straight black hair disheveled.

When my guard opened a small gate in the railing, Tony jerked round towards me, his dark blue eyes stunned and disbelieving. A bandage lay on the side of his face.

What happened to Tony?

Ten Hogan, Molly's nephew, who the men called Sawbuck, loomed beside Tony, glaring at me.

Once I sat, the judge took a wooden hammer and rapped a wooden block, which made a surprisingly loud sound. "Case Number CF-1899-903, the People vs Jacqueline Spadros. Mrs. Spadros, please rise." The judge took up a paper. "Jacqueline Kaplan Spadros, you're charged with the destruction of Travelers' Federation Flight A26; two hundred fifteen counts of murder; sixteen counts of forgery; four counts of perjury; and one charge of criminal fraud. How do you plead?"

"I did none of this!"

Mr. Trevisane said, "Your Honor, the defendant pleads not guilty to all charges."

"So entered," the judge said. "I take it then, Mr. Trevisane, that you plan to be this woman's defender?"

Mr. Trevisane said, "The Spadros Family drops the charge of fraud, raised when the defendant's location was in question."

The judge said, "Very well. I —"

I blurted out, "Doyle Pike will represent me."

Everyone in the room turned to stare.

The judge peered at me. "This is most irregular." Then he called out, "Get Pike in here."

A man scrambled to obey.

The judge said, "Mrs. Spadros, is Mr. Pike aware you wish him to represent you?"

"Mr. Pike is already my lawyer. I was unaware of this meeting until an hour ago. Perhaps he wasn't notified either."

Tony stared at me with horror. Very few knew about his son Roland, and I was sure he now regretted ever telling me. I would never tell Mr. Pike about the boy, but Tony didn't know that.

"This court will recess for one hour." The judge banged his small hammer, and everyone rose as he walked out.

I stood there not knowing what to do. My head hurt, and I felt weary. Looking back, I'm pretty sure I was still drunk.

At the far end of the table, Tony argued with Mr. Trevisane. Past them, Sawbuck's hate-filled eyes bored into mine. To my left, Mr. Freezout stood, arms crossed, a smug smile on his face.

I sat.

Joseph Kerr and Nicholas Bryce had died to free me from the Spadros Family. So I couldn't see any reason for Mr. Trevisane — a Spadros Family lawyer — to represent me.

But I already owed Doyle Pike an inordinate amount of money. *Pike can fucking bill me.*

Tony stormed around the front of the table. On the bandage beside his face, blood seeped through a teardrop-shaped spot.

Alarm spiked inside when I saw the blood. What happened?

Tony said, "Get up." He winced when he spoke. When I didn't move, he grabbed my upper arms, dragging me to my feet. "What do you think you're doing? Do you **want** to die?"

"What are **you** so angry about?"

He scoffed, releasing his grip a bit. "As if you don't know. Doyle Pike's not getting one dime from me, you hear? Not one."

"I don't want your money. I want nothing to do with you."

His grip on my arms tightened. "You're going to stop this nonsense right now. My father's forbidden anyone to kill you —"

Oh?

"— so you needn't fear returning. You'll tell them you made a mistake. You don't want Mr. Pike. Then we're returning to Spadros Manor, and this whoring will stop. Do you understand?"

Whoring? I felt bitter. "I was never a whore until I married you."

Tony's face went blank. "I don't understand."

"Isn't that what this quadrant-marriage is about? Forced to pretend you love someone to survive? To be violated night after night, unable to say a word, make a sound, even shed a tear, for fear of death? At least Pot whores get a choice."

I'd become resigned to my fate long ago. But Joe ... how could I forgive killing a man whose only crime was to love me? "I'd rather die than return with you." I spit in his face. "Go to hell."

He let go of my arms and took a step back, face shocked.

Everyone else in the courtroom pretended they didn't see.

Tony took out his handkerchief, wiped his face. "I can't believe I used to love you."

I turned away to lean on the small railing, trying desperately not to cry in front of these people.

He knew how to hurt me, Tony did, more than anyone.

"I ought to kill you right now," Sawbuck growled. He stood close by to my left across the railing. Yet he didn't touch me.

"You're welcome to try." At least thirty officers of the Court stood in the room. "I did what I thought best. It was you and your men who fouled everything up." If they hadn't killed Joe, we'd have been far away. Yes, Tony would've been hurt, but he could've had what was best for everyone.

Sawbuck peered at me. "What the hell are you talking about?"

Doyle Pike strode in. At least eighty, the man nevertheless appeared as perfect as a man of his age might appear: vigorous, well-groomed, immaculately dressed by the finest clothier, silk hat, soft leather briefcase, gleaming walking-stick. He approached me as if entirely at home, confident and unhurried. Tucking his case under one arm, he took my hand. "Come with me, my dear."

The guards escorted us through a side door into a windowless, richly carpeted room with a table of polished oak in its center.

"Leave us," said Mr. Pike. Once the door closed behind them,

Mr. Pike gestured to the table. "Please sit, madam."

So I did, curious as to what he might have to say.

"No one listens," Mr. Pike said. "So you may speak without fear of discovery." He took a pale yellow folder from his briefcase then placed the briefcase under the table. "And no one can force me to betray you, under law older than Merca itself."

I nodded, impressed. But I felt disturbed by today's events. "I did nothing wrong. How can they force me to have this trial?"

"They can't. Change your plea to guilty, and you can go straight to the gallows. It's entirely your choice."

I stared at him, appalled. "But —"

"I'm sure you feel the need to maintain you didn't do this -"

"I didn't!"

"Yes, my dear, everyone says that. And I'm sure that out of all my many thousands of clients over the decades, you're innocent as a newborn babe. But right now, maintaining that isn't helpful."

"You don't believe me?"

"It's even more fundamental: I don't care whether you did it. I'm not here to judge you. My responsibility is to obtain you a fair trial. The only way I can do that is to know the entirety of the matter." He folded his hands atop his folder. "So tell me what happened with the zeppelin. The truth. Or hire another lawyer."

His attitude was infuriating. But I should never have expected him of all people to believe me.

I really needed a drink.

Where to begin? "This goes back much further than the day of the Celebration."

I told him about my private investigation business, and the call to Bryce Fabrics on New Year's Eve, where Mrs. Eleanora Bryce asked me to find her son David.

Mr. Pike didn't seem alarmed, shocked, or even surprised at my running a business. Did he have spies of his own?

"During my investigation, I learned two men were involved in the disappearance: one calling himself Frank Pagliacci, the other fitting the description of Jack Diamond."

Mr. Pike paled. "So this is why you wanted notice of Jack Diamond's whereabouts. What have you become involved in?"

"Master Jack Diamond has targeted me, my father, and the Spadros Family for over a decade." The last time we met, Jack became so enraged at his identical twin Jonathan for sitting with me at the Grand Ball that he attacked him. "These two men run a group called the Red Dog Gang. Mrs. Bryce told me this second man visited her home the week before the kidnapping. I saw the two men place a large bag with a boy in it into their carriage."

Mr. Pike nodded slowly, his face thoughtful.

"I tracked the boy to a factory in Diamond quadrant, yet he's ruined, unable to tell us anything." I sighed, feeling melancholy. "When I went to the factory, Mr. Pagliacci said his goal was to destroy the Spadros Family." Then something else came to mind. "Two boys who went looking for David were found strangled. You might've seen it in the papers."

Mr. Pike raised an eyebrow at that.

"After I retrieved David Bryce, those who could identify these two men began dying. The stable-master, who told me Frank Pagliacci's name. An associate who knew Mr. Pagliacci had his yacht blown up. And Dame Anastasia confessed to being Frank Pagliacci's lover the day she was killed."

Mr. Pike stared at me, mouth open. "Is that so?"

"They've framed me, Mr. Pike. But I didn't do it."

"Can you prove it?"

"Anastasia was my friend! I had no reason to hurt her."

"Is there anything else you can tell me about the day it happened? Anything at all may help."

So I told him about Dame Anastasia's letter, received as I left to go to Market Center with Gardena Diamond and her brothers. I didn't know how else to explain why I was with them but the truth: Gardena was being blackmailed.

At this, Mr. Pike's eyes narrowed, but he said nothing.

Then I told him about the man in brown with the briefcase, and my belief that Frank Pagliacci meant to bomb the zeppelin. "I was desperate to get to the station, but —"

"Wait," Mr. Pike said. "You just learned that Dame Louis had been helping the man who'd not only ruined your friend's son but tormented you and your Family. Why rush to save her?"

"You must promise not to speak of this to anyone."

Mr. Pike nodded.

"It wasn't just Anastasia on there. These men threatened my mother. I'd smuggled her onto that very zeppelin to get her safe."

"Oh, my dear," Mr. Pike said. "I'm so very sorry."

"I got to the station too late, and I was caught there with the others. There was nothing else I could do but to give my name."

"So you were there when it happened."

To this day, I've never forgotten the horrible sound as the Station shattered. The screams of men, women, and children impaled beside me by thick shards of stained glass. The smell of blood, of burning pieces of zeppelin as they fell to the ground.

"Why were you at Clubb Hotel?"

I sighed, watching the zeppelin fall. "Speak with Mrs. Clubb as to how you want to play that. She's taken me under her protection." I focused on him. "But if you want to know the truth, I've left my husband. I don't plan to return."

"I see." He leaned back. "So how will you pay me?"

I stared at the table. "I don't know. But I will. I promise."

"Promises are not good enough. I'm not running a poorhouse."

This reminded me so much of what Mrs. Clubb said a few days earlier that I laughed in spite of myself.

Mr. Pike's face changed, as if he had come to some decision. He took out a form. "Sign here, and we'll get started."

I felt uneasy. "What happens now?"

"Have your things sent to where you're staying. As much as you can get. Everything, if you can." He gave me an evil grin. "We'll sell them." Then he leaned back. "Once you're acquitted, I shall sue the city for false and malicious prosecution. You couldn't possibly have blown up a zeppelin with your mother aboard, and it sounds as if you have several witnesses to back you up."

I signed without reading it. "Why are you helping me?"

"To thwart that sniveling ass Trevisane. I wish I'd seen his face when you named **me** as your counsel." He cackled in delight. "I imagine it about sent him into apoplexy!"

A knock at the door. "The judge requests your presence."

"Come, my dear," Mr. Pike said, "we have much to do."

The Situation

After the arraignment was over, I stood; Jonathan Diamond and Mr. Charles Hart focused on me at once. Today, Jon had no cane with him, which was always a good sign.

Mr. Hart, a portly man of seventy, took my hand in both of his and kissed it. "My dear girl, are you well?"

My head was pounding. I needed a drink. "As well as one might be, given the circumstances." Retrieving my hand took a bit longer than normal. "And you?"

Jon grinned as I offered my hand for him to kiss.

Mr. Hart seemed flustered. "Of course, my dear. I'm perfectly well. I wished to offer my sincerest wishes for your success."

He wished to offer wishes? I had to restrain myself to keep from laughing. "That's kind of you."

"Mr. Hart would like the honor of calling on you," Jon said.

I shrugged. Mr. Hart couldn't be serious. "If you can get into Spadros quadrant unmolested, by all means."

At this, Mr. Hart chuckled. "While I appreciate your concern, I don't believe that to be a problem."

Why? Roy Spadros hated Charles Hart with passion. Would Roy really allow Mr. Hart to come into his quadrant?

The two guards and Mr. Pike stood waiting. The room was otherwise empty. "I'd hate to make these men wait. So if you'll excuse me." I winked at Jon when Mr. Hart wasn't looking.

The guards brought me out to the steps, Mr. Pike following. Tony stood next to Mr. Trevisane, who spoke to a huge crowd of reporters. When the reporters saw us, they descended, notepads and pencils in hand.

Mr. Pike hurried up behind me. "Don't say a word."

I nodded, alarmed at this horde of men rushing towards me.

"Mrs. Spadros! Why haven't you been at Spadros Manor?"

Mr. Pike said, "Mrs. Spadros was in the midst of remodeling her property when beset by these baseless accusations, and will remain there until this matter is settled, to oversee the work."

I smiled, amused at his quick thinking.

"So you're saying the allegations are false?"

"Entirely. One charge has already been dropped! The District Attorney should feel ashamed for wasting the city's funds."

I felt impressed. The man was a master at playing the truth.

"What about reports that Mrs. Spadros tried to flee the city?"

"Nonsense," Mr. Pike said. "Mrs. Clubb hosted Mrs. Spadros at her hotel for a few days. If you'll excuse us —" He led me away; the reporters scattered, scribbling on their notepads as they went.

Tony stepped in front of us. "I must speak with my wife."

"By all means, sir." Mr. Pike bowed, moving a few steps away.

Tony whispered, "I'm sorry for what I said back there."

I shrugged: I wasn't in the least bit sorry for what I said to him.

"You must come home, Jacqui. It's urgent. You don't know what's happened since you left." He seemed to struggle with himself. "Our quadrant is in turmoil. The men look to us for guidance. We can't afford to look divided right now."

"You mean **you** can't afford that." I pointed at his face. The blood spot had spread to the size of a nickel. "What happened?"

"It's none of your concern."

"Don't tell me, then."

"No one leaves the Family, Jacqui. No one. And you can't stay at the apartments, no matter what story you've concocted."

"Why not? I can do what I like with my property."

Tony glanced to one side. A large group of people watched our exchange. His jaw tightened; his tone became laced with sarcasm. "Is it now? Is it really your property?"

"The deed's in my name."

"I paid the taxes. If not for me, you wouldn't have it at all."

"Fine." I grabbed the money Amelia put in my pocket and

threw it in his face. "I've repaid you in full and then some."

Tony made no attempt to bat the coins away or collect the bills as they wafted along, although the bystanders scrambled after them. "I've decided to follow my father's advice in this matter."

I stared at him in shock. Tony had said many times he wanted nothing to do with Roy Spadros. What changed?

"My father may be many things, but he's never betrayed me."

That stung; I turned away. Roy Spadros had lied to Tony about a great many things, including letting Tony think he was his father. But saying that would only make matters worse.

Mr. Pike chuckled, taking my arm as we walked towards the carriage. "You do have a way about you." The tone of his voice reminded me of what he said in his office the first time we met: *where were you when I was thirty?*

I shook my arm from his grasp, revolted. "Fuck you."

He stood silent, face amused, as the Court men escorted me to my carriage.

* * *

Amelia let me inside without a word, not meeting my eye. She moved stiffly as she served luncheon. "That's the last of the food. I suppose you want me to do your shopping."

I felt in my pocket — only a few coins remained. I handed them to her. "See what you can get with this. And get a newspaper."

Once she left, I wandered my apartments. Little remained to show I once had tenants — a bit of trash, a doll under a bed.

I'd get new tenants, better ones. In the meantime, I had to learn to live …

… without Joe.

I leaned against a wall, overcome.

Running through fields in the golden sun, laughing, rolling in the grass together … planning how we'd make the Pot good again.

All that was gone.

A bottle of wine still sat on my dresser. I drank half, then went to the window. Ten yards from each side of my apartment, barricades were set; police manned them.

Grief dropped me to my knees there at the window. I leaned my elbows on the windowsill, my face in my hands.

Joe was dead!

Joe had to be dead. He would have come for me.

By now the whole city knew where I was. Crowds gathered outside, yelling behind the Prison guards, the police. The hay bales and sawhorses didn't stop the curses.

Joe was dead — because of me.

I lay my face on the windowsill. I deserved every curse. I deserved them all.

* * *

A white and silver carriage pulled up to the barricade on my left, flanked by very dark-skinned men on white horses wearing white and silver livery. After some discussion, the sawhorses were moved and the carriage waved through to stop in front of my apartments. A footman a bit darker-skinned than myself came round to open the door.

Out came Jonathan! I wiped my face, grabbed the bottle, and rushed to the door as he came up the walkway. The sun broke through the clouds, his smile bright against his dark, dark skin.

"Come in!" I opened the door wide. The breeze smelled of rain.

Jon looked around. "Where's your maid?"

"She's at the grocery."

He didn't enter. "We'll speak here, then."

I laughed. "If that's how you'd like it." I brandished the bottle. "Would you like some?" Then I giggled at my mistake. "I forgot the glasses! I'll go get —"

Then I remembered he didn't drink.

He glanced at the bottle then said carefully, "No, thank you."

I set the bottle on the small table beside the door and took his hands. "I'm so glad you're here. I hope you're well?"

He gave me a small smile. "I'm well, thank you. And you?"

I shrugged. "As well as I might be, under the circumstances."

"You gave us all quite a fright, Jacqui. If the doctor hadn't said you needed that," he gestured at the bottle as if it might bite him, "to avoid another attack, I'd have you toss it away at once."

"So fierce," I murmured.

His cheeks colored, and he shifted, seeming uncomfortable. "I care for your welfare, that's all."

I gazed up into his eyes and felt quite warm. "I wanted to thank you for retrieving me from the station last week."

Jon smiled fondly. "It's of no consequence. I'm just glad we could get you somewhere safe before any reporters arrived."

I moved towards him. "I'm always safe with you." I touched his cheek, his hair. Jonathan's hair felt as soft as Joe's. "Kiss me."

Jon drew back instantly, hands on my shoulders, elbows locked. "You're drunk."

My eyes stung. "No, I'm not."

Jonathan would never kiss me. Why? Was I not good enough?

A darkened room. It was night; the only light was an oil lamp. We sat on my bed. In the Cathedral. My mother's patron the Masked Man had brought Jonathan Diamond to my room.

I liked Jon at once, but after a glance on meeting, he never looked at me. A sadness lay behind his eyes even then. "If you see someone who looks just like me, it's my brother Jack. He likes to wear white and shave his head, but he looks just like me." Jon smiled fondly to himself.

"Okay."

An awkward silence fell. I hadn't been allowed to practice the things Ma had taught me. Was this my test?

I became excited about this idea. If I passed my test, I would finally get real training to be a whore like all the other girls. I put my hand on Jon's cheek, turned his face towards mine, moved to kiss his lips ...

"Hey!" Jon drew back in alarm. "What the hell? I just got here."

The bitter pain of humiliation stabbed my heart. My eyes burned.

"Can we not be friends? I didn't come here to buy you," Jon said. "I just want to talk to you."

Why was I recalling all these things? First my wedding, then my poor doomed Nina, now this ... what was happening to me?

Jonathan cupped my cheek with one hand, barely touching, hand trembling. "You're not thinking clearly, that much is plain. You're not safe here, Jacqui. You must return home."

I felt annoyed. "Why would I ever want to go back?"

Jon dropped his hand to my shoulder. "It's your home. You have a husband who cares for you." His hands fell to his sides; he glanced away. "It's wrong to live apart from your husband." He focused on me. "I don't know what happened, but —"

"Tony saw me and Joe together." To this day, the look on Tony's face that night is seared into my mind.

But then, at the door with Jonathan, I said, "I've never loved Tony; you know that."

Jon put his hand on my shoulder. "Jacqui —"

"Did Master Rainbow give you my message?"

Jon turned away, facing the street. "He did." Jon stood silent for a moment, then faced me. "When we went to the Kerrs' home, only the maid and her brother were there. He had a shotgun." He glanced away. "I suppose I don't blame them; Tony's men were there earlier. They feared Master Rainbow and I were with them."

"And no sign of Joe."

Jon shook his head, not meeting my eye.

"There's something you're not telling me."

"I don't know anything." Jon's eyes flashed to mine, then away. "But there've been rumors."

"Rumors? What rumors?"

"People claim to have seen him, Jacqui. Since we last met."

"Who claims to have seen him?"

Jon's face changed, as if he came to some decision. "Let me find out what this is about."

I took Jon's hands, relieved. "Thank you." I gazed at the crowd milling around down the street to my right. "I'm sorry. I just want to know what happened to him. If they find his body." Grief flooded through me, but I pushed it aside. "I need to know."

Jon reached into his pocket. A blue-edged zeppelin ticket stub came loose, fluttering away in the breeze as he handed his handkerchief to me. "You honestly believe Tony had him killed?"

I wiped my eyes. "What else could he do? If not him, then his men. Roy. His men." I shrugged. "I'm next. I can feel it. Even though Tony claims Roy said no."

"My gods," Jon leaned his hand high on the door-post, eyes wide. "Roy Spadros forbade his own men to kill you?"

I nodded. The Spadros Family Patriarch had one motivation, it seemed: to torture others. Who did he torture now?

Jon's hand dropped to his side, and he sounded humbled. "I'm grateful beyond words. But I can't fathom what's going on."

"Why was Charles Hart at court today?"

Jon glanced away, shrugging. "He insisted on it."

Ugh, I thought. The man was **old**. And married! It was clear Mr. Hart had developed an unseemly attraction to me, a woman young enough to be his grand-daughter! But to force his way into a closed meeting with a judge? I laughed in spite of myself. "I wonder how much of a bribe he had to pay to get in there."

Jon smiled fondly. "Perhaps not as much as you might think."

I found this amusing. "True. He is a Patriarch, after all."

Yet Jon seemed uncomfortable. "I must be going."

I felt weary, and a sudden loneliness, but I did remember manners. "Thank you for calling on me. And for appearing today in my support. I do appreciate it. Very much."

Jon grinned, and whatever discomfort he had vanished. "It was fiendishly difficult to get here in the first place. Tony allowed me into the quadrant, so thank **him** for it."

I closed the door, leaned on it.

Why would Jon have trouble entering the quadrant, especially if here to see me? He was Keeper of the Court: he should have no trouble going anywhere related to a Court matter. But he came in his own carriage, dressed in street clothes, not in his navy blue uniform and carriage of the Court. Why?

I brought the bottle to my room and took another drink. Maybe I was drunk, as Jonathan said. After everything that had happened, why shouldn't I be?

I heard the side door open and shut. I could tell it was Amelia from the small sounds she made as she moved around the kitchen.

To be honest, at the time I didn't care if it was Jonathan's twin, Jack Diamond, come to torture then kill me for what my father had done to his friend. I almost would have welcomed it.

Joseph Kerr had to be dead.

Why was I still alive?

Amelia came in with a newspaper. She said sarcastically, "You'll eat the way everyone else does. Anything else?"

I felt taken aback. "No. Thank you."

She flung the newspaper at me then stomped off.

She must still be upset about last week, I thought.

Amelia stood slumped against the kitchen wall facing away from me, straightening when I entered.

"I shouldn't have put the gun to you, Amelia. And it was unfair of me to make you give Mr. Anthony my letter." Tony was like a son to her. How his reaction must have hurt!

She didn't turn. "You think I care about what happens to **me**?"

"Well, then, what's wrong?"

She got very still. "You told the boy you'd say good-bye —"

A shock went through me. *Pip!*

"— and you didn't! He just lies in bed weeping." She sounded ready to cry. "Why did you **involve** him?"

She can't even call her own son by his name? "Why do **you** care?"

She turned, quick as a snake, and for an instant I feared she might strike. "You don't understand anything! You act so high above us. But you're just a common Pot rag scrap, whoring about without any decency at all. I have to be here, but that doesn't mean I have to crawl. If you had **any** heart, you'd go to him this minute and beg his forgiveness. But I'd tell him not to give it."

"Well," I said, "at least now I know where we stand."

I went back to my room and shut the door. Amelia's outburst didn't upset me: I deserved it.

Pip Dewey was just ten. His mother had all but abandoned him, and he'd become attached to me. I remembered the peaceful, happy look on his little face when he held my hand against his cheek in the garden. I should at least have left a letter.

I found a piece of paper, a pen, and a bit of ink at the bottom of the bottle in a writing-desk.

Pip —

I'm sorry I didn't say good-bye. I hope you'll forgive me. I was afraid they would stop me from going.

I'm safe and well. I hear you've been sad since I left. I want you to be happy again.

Please write if you want to.

Your Friend,

Mrs. Spadros

I went down the front steps, where a policeman stood guard. "Would you post this for me?"

"Surely, mum, if you have money for the messenger."

What happened to my money?

I rummaged around in my room until I found my handbag with the change I'd set aside for Mrs. Bryce. I gave the policeman his penny and hid the rest well. It might have to last a while: who would give a job to a suspected criminal?

Sitting at my table with a drink, I opened the newspaper.

The *Golden Bridges* was a disreputable tabloid — its byline: "Fuck the fairy tales, get the Real Story." The paper was a day old, and I imagined with Amelia's mood (and the faint smell) that she fished it from a trash-can. But it was unstained and quite readable.

District Attorney Runs For Mayor

Vows To "Clean Up Bridges"

Well, I thought. This explained quite a bit.

> District Attorney Mr. Chase Freezout has made a bid for Mayor of Bridges. According to our Inside Reporter, papers were filed late Friday afternoon.

> This from a speech Mr. Freezout made on the City Hall steps moments after: "So much has befallen our fair city: financial ruin and the destruction of two of Merca's greatest treasures. The bombing of Flight A26 is just one example of the rot which has crept into our quadrants. I vow to clean up Bridges, making it safe and prosperous once more."

> Mr. Freezout will resign as District Attorney should he succeed in his endeavor, but he intends to personally prosecute this current case to its end first. For the Bridges District Attorney to personally prosecute a criminal case is historic.

> Mr. Freezout began his legal career in 1862 and was elected District Attorney in 1879. Although his father Sir Stayman Freezout was forced to cede his

title, lands, and rank after the Coup, the Freezout family still lives on 190th Street, Hart quadrant.

Elections are set for November 4th to fill the post left by the recent death of Mayor Siete Badugi, who has served for the past twelve years. The cause of Mayor Badugi's death is still under investigation.

So Mr. Freezout was an aristocrat, with both the money and the motive to destroy the Families.

But why target me? Did he believe I'd lost the Spadros Family's support? He couldn't possibly have known I'd planned to leave Spadros Manor: I didn't know the timing of it until it happened.

I was missing something here.

I poured another drink and continued reading.

Mad Jack Captured in Spadros Quadrant

Yesterday afternoon, the notorious Master Jack Diamond was captured at a business on 2nd Street.

According to our Inside Reporter, Master Diamond was seen entering one Bryce Fabrics, where he accosted the shopkeeper, a widow. Neighbors, alerted to his presence, removed him from the shop and beat him before Spadros men arrived.

Master Jack was taken to the Spadros-Diamond city bridge where he was released into Diamond Family custody. The Spadros Family plans formal protest.

Although the quadrants are free from overt Family violence, the Spadros and Diamond syndicates have been at war since the Coup. We at the *Golden Bridges* hope that this offense will not throw fuel upon an already tense situation.

"This is unbelievable," I murmured.

Helen Hart Takes to Her Bed:

"Quite Seriously Ill"

Mrs. Helen Hart, wife of Inventor and Hart Family heir Mr. Etienne Hart, has taken to her bed. Doctors have declared Mrs. Hart "quite seriously ill" and "unlikely to survive."

The Harts are not planning funeral arrangements at this time, holding out hope that the lovely Lady of Hart may yet recover.

In the same paper, I found an interview:

Our Inside Reporter Speaks:

The Hart Situation

The *Golden Bridges* now speaks with our Inside Reporter to give you the Real Story.

GB: With the Hart heir over fifty, no sons, and his wife dying, what are the Hart Family's prospects?

IR: Should anything happen to Charles Hart, we predict a battle between his main men.

GB: Indeed, the man is seventy and a prodigious drinker. But could his son Etienne not simply remarry? As ghoulish as it may sound with the wife not yet in her grave, the stability of the city may depend on the answer.

IR: The battle might happen even if he does. A sickly man rarely seen without his mother beside him, Etienne Hart seems most interested in books, not war. He may not be able to hold the quadrant.

Another man was found strangled. The headline brought fear to my throat — had they found Joe's body? But this man was short, blond — not tall and brown-haired like Joe. I sighed in relief, without knowing why. I knew Joe had to be dead, but seeing reports of his death would have made it real.

Amelia set my dinner before me.

"Thank you," I said.

She said nothing.

"I wrote to Pip. You know why I can't go there."

She shook her head.

"Sit down. We need to talk."

Amelia froze. Her lower lip trembled. "Why do you do this?"

"I don't understand."

"I want to hate you! I do hate you! Then you do this."

I remembered the confusion and fear when I asked the staff to sit with me after Tony was attacked. Tony's anger after Tenni — Madame Biltcliffe's shop maid — sat at the table with us. "What does it mean to sit at the table? I just wish to speak with you."

Amelia didn't move for a few seconds, then nodded as if she'd come to some realization. "You don't understand. This — it means nothing to you." She took a deep breath, let it out. "It means nothing." She nodded. "Very well. Then I'll sit."

She was right: I didn't understand. "I don't mean to offend."

Amelia began to laugh. "Your Pot must be much different than people think."

That seemed a fair statement. We were poor, yes, but free, and proud of it. "I've left Mr. Anthony. I won't say why, as it's not entirely my story to tell. But to return to Spadros Manor, even to speak to Pip, would make things more difficult for everyone. Mr. Anthony doesn't understand, which is why he's so distressed."

"He's distressed because he loves you."

I pushed the remorse and grief away. "Him loving me has never been the issue." It only made Tony's problems — and his pain — worse when he learned the truth.

She gritted her teeth, not breathing for a moment.

"There are things I need you to do, yet you mustn't even speak of them to Mr. Dewey. Roy Spadros must not know."

Her head shot up. "I swear, mum, I've told him nothing since I learned he made that deal with Mr. Roy."

Roy Spadros violated Amelia Dewey, which is how little Pip came to be born, and had continued to terrorize her. Her husband only wanted to protect her, yet he did the one thing guaranteed to drive a wedge between them.

Had Roy anticipated this? The man seemed uncanny in his ability to torment others. "I don't care who you report to. But I must know who knows what I do. Mr. Anthony's life may depend on it." I felt like a conniver for playing on her love for Tony, but it was close enough to the truth to be reasonable.

She fell silent for a few seconds. "Mr. Anthony, mum. And his man Sawbuck." She hesitated. "And Mr. Pearson."

I chuckled, shaking my head. "Who reports to Mr. Roy."

Amelia stared at me in horror.

"What did you think all those ledgers in my study were about? My husband caught him at it." I shrugged. "Don't berate Pearson. He has his reasons." The main one being that Roy Spadros held John Pearson's mother as hostage.

Amelia's head drooped. "Yes, mum."

"Go to Spadros Manor, please. Have my things brought here."

"Everything?"

"As much as they'll let you bring."

Amelia peered at me. "So you really don't intend to go back."

"No," I said, "I don't."

* * *

After Amelia left, I ate dinner, opening my last bottle of wine.

Mr. Pike's plan was good. I'd hold an auction to "help the poor." That the poor being helped was me wasn't going to enter into it. But I couldn't run it myself. Who might assist me?

Eleanora Bryce might be willing, if she could find someone to watch David, who still did little more than rock after his kidnapping. Madame Biltcliffe would be ideal but I doubted she'd even speak to me after all that happened. Tenni, perhaps?

Gertie Pike had a baby at home and one on the way. But surely the wife of a law clerk would know how to keep records.

Pouring another glass, I turned out the lights and sat by the window in the darkness, as I had every night so far.

Papers blew past in the wind. A dog barked, off in the distance.

I might have dozed; a knock at the door startled me.

Keenly aware I was in the house alone, I peered out. Two men I didn't recognize stood on my front step. The taller one tipped his hat. "Miz Spadros, we just came by to introduce ourself. I'm Sticks Monarch, this is Eight Howell. We're in charge of this street here."

I gaped at them. "What does that mean?"

Mr. Howell had a deep voice and a big bushy beard. "We come for the packets every month. Your Family fees?"

A laugh burst from me. "Roy sent you, didn't he?"

Mr. Monarch said, "Yes, Miz Spadros, he surely did."

"Well, I'm under house arrest at present."

"Yes, mum," Mr. Howell said. "Every house pays their street number whether you got money or not. You live on 33 1/3 Street. So 33 cents. For the third, you pay an extra penny every Solstice and Equinox. When you get income, we get one out of every ten, pennies or dollars. Put it in an envelope and seal it with your address on the front. We come by the end of the month to collect. Is this a good time? Or should we come when it's light out?"

And it all goes to Roy at the end.

I remembered Madame Biltcliffe's bruises. These two seemed pleasant enough but I had no illusions what might happen should they learn I hid income. "That would probably be better."

"Or ya can come by our place to pay," Mr. Monarch said. "We run the bar on the corner." He pointed up the street to my left. "The Backdoor Saloon. Anything ya want, ya can get there."

Mr. Howell said, "If you need us for anything, mum, just ask. Our street has its own messenger boy. Potholes, someone bothers you," he gestured to the policemen standing by the barricade, "anything at all. That's what you're paying for."

"Very well." There were a few weeks left in May still. Anything might happen. "Can I ask a question?"

"Sure," Mr. Monarch said.

"Roy said you couldn't kill me. But why are you being polite?"

He shrugged. "It's none of my business where ya live, Miz Spadros! Sides, Mr. Roy lets us collect from ya, which's more for us." He glanced quickly over his shoulder. "If our other guys try something, just so's ya know, we're not shooting 'em for ya."

I nodded. "Thanks for letting me know."

The police outside were supposedly there for my protection. But these two just walked right past them and up to my door. If they had evil intent, I'd be dead now.

I closed the door with a laugh. For some reason, I didn't care.

The Law

I stood at the intersection of Shill and Snow in the Pot. The ruined buildings towered over me, clouds scudding dark across the full moon. Bodies lay around me, bloody, their dead eyes staring at mine. Nina, Dame Anastasia, her silly great-nephew Trey, the men from the Party Time factory, that driver-man of Frank Pagliacci's I'd shot — the one who tried to violate me. Marja. Even Daniel lay there.

Beyond them, dozens, hundreds of others lay there, faces turned away. It seemed quite normal for them to lie on the cold gray cobbles.

Air ran towards me from a distance, shouting a warning, pointing beside me. Jonathan's identical twin Jack Diamond stood there, head shaved, dressed in white. He held a knife in his hand and hate in his eyes.

Jack grabbed my arm. "I have you now."

I came awake on the floor beside the chair, heart pounding.

Footsteps ran towards my door, then a loud banging. I got up, found a robe, opened the door.

Three officers stood in the darkness. "Mum, are you well?"

So they hadn't been told about my nightmares. "I'm well. I'm fine. Thank you." I began to close the door.

"Are you certain? We heard a scream."

I felt amused. "Yes, I'm sure. Thank you, constables."

I closed the door and returned to my chair, feeling shaky. I poured the bit left in my bottle into my glass and drank it.

The sky began to lighten. Tony would be waking. Alone.

I pushed remorse aside. Murderers deserved to be alone.

* * *

The doorbell rang at seven.

I went to the door in my robe, bleary-eyed. A group of men stood outside, a horse truck past them. Three more trucks stood behind that one. "Delivery."

"Of what?"

The man checked a clipboard. "A hell of a lot of clothes."

"This way." I had the men start putting the racks in the back rooms. Then I went to the bathing room.

From the first time I'd ever taken a bath when I was twelve, my bath was always drawn for me. The array of levers and knobs were daunting. Turning one did nothing, and I feared spoiling the beautiful brass mechanisms there.

I didn't know how to work the stove either. It didn't look like Ma's stove back home. I couldn't find any wood, nor any place to put it. So I forced a comb through my hair, struggled into a house dress, put a shawl around my shoulders, had some bread and jam, and settled by my tea-table to smoke.

Amelia showed up mid-morning. "You can't even run a bath?"

I felt embarrassed. "Would you show me how?"

So she showed me how to run a bath (you first turned the back knobs to let the water flow). How to use the stove (it ran on electricity from the Magma Steam Generators, just like the lights). Where the cleaning supplies were kept.

We had a cup of tea. This time, Amelia sat without any fuss. "Has no one taught you **anything** useful?"

I was a grown woman of two and twenty! I knew many useful things: how to direct a household of servants; how to watch for rival gangs; how to make deals and lure a mark; how to read and write and figure. I could pick pockets and locks, track a missing person, shoot a gun quite well, and thanks to Josephine Kerr's instruction, fight with a knife. I'd also seen people do things I thought I might imitate, such as putting on makeup (Amelia always did mine for me) and driving a carriage. "I suppose I need to know new things here."

Amelia chuckled. "That you might."

The rooms full of clothing were fine, but I needed more basic items. "Amelia, can you fetch my morning tea when you return?"

"Of course, mum."

She seemed unaware of my morning tea's true purpose: to ensure no heir came to Spadros Manor though my womb.

I had no plot against Tony; bearing children held no appeal. As long as I was captive, a child would only make life more difficult.

I would never consent to lie with Tony after what he surely had done to Joseph Kerr. Yet my encounter with the driver the week prior reminded me of the dangers here. At any moment, a man might force himself upon me, and I was very lucky the last time.

Amelia said, "Mum, why did you bring all your things here?"

So I told her of Mr. Pike's plan: to sell my things at auction. I told her the auction was to benefit the poor. "I've never felt comfortable with this, Amelia. When I was a child, I learned that sufficient clothing was all a person really needed. This," I waved at the racks standing in the hallway, and realized my truth. "It borders on obscene, when people freeze in the winter."

Amelia straightened, and her countenance changed. I think for the first time, she respected me. "I've never heard you speak so."

"I suppose what you said yesterday was true. I **am** from the Pot, and marked by it forever. I can't help my people, but if I help yours, perhaps I can spur them on to some small kindness."

At this I felt a deep sadness. We lived in the same city, under the same dome. Why were we hated so?

Amelia swallowed. "Then I will help you. What do you need?"

I gave her the list of who might be willing to help. I couldn't send mail except through the policemen outside, and who knew whether they opened it? But Amelia could contact many people without being noticed. "I must keep back our Fees. But I'll also reserve 1% of my sales to be split between those who help."

She seemed taken aback. "You wish to **pay** me?"

"You're doing work which Spadros Manor neither cares for nor has endorsed. Surely you should be compensated for your time."

Her eyes widened. "I've never ... if that's what you wish, mum, I know my mother would appreciate a new coat for Yuletide."

I smiled at her. "If all goes well, she'll have roast ham too."

Amelia's eyes reddened. "Please forgive my harsh words,

mum. I was angry and spoke foolishly."

I took a deep breath. Perhaps I could help some of the poor in truth. "Here's what we'll do, once we learn who'll aid us ..."

We needed somewhere to hold the auction, an auctioneer, and a banker. Anywhere I went would swarm with police, so security might not be an issue ...

Amelia said, "Why not hold it here? Then we wouldn't have to pay to have this moved again."

Would the Court allow it? This was my building, after all. "Let me think on it." Perhaps Mr. Monarch would have some ideas.

The doorbell rang. Amelia rushed to answer it. She returned with fear in her eyes. "Master Ten Hogan to see you, mum."

I went to the door, dreading another meeting with him.

But Sawbuck stood in the open doorway, perplexed. "What did you mean, **we** fouled it up?"

I snorted. "Do you think I have no sense whatsoever?"

His gaze flickered to Amelia, who stood behind me.

Her demeanor towards him turned fierce. "You'll not harm her, sir, or you'll answer to me."

Amusement crossed his face. He patted the holster hanging from his belt. "Mrs. Dewey, if I wanted to kill her, she'd be dead."

We sat in the kitchen with tea. I didn't really want tea, but in Bridges all discussions seemed to require it. "Amelia, I must ask you not to listen at the door. It's safer if you don't overhear us."

She paled. "Yes, mum, of course, mum."

If Tony ordered Joe killed, Sawbuck would know. He might have even done it himself. But would he come here if he had?

I took a sip of tea to reassure Sawbuck, who despite his words had a wariness to him. Yet I felt much the same. No one was more devoted to Tony than Sawbuck. Would Sawbuck reveal the truth about Joe if Tony told him not to?

I decided to answer Sawbuck's question, then see where it led. "How much do you know?"

He glanced away. "Mr. Anthony told me everything. About Miss Diamond and," his eyes flickered to the door, "the boy. About your ... wedding. Damn." He bit his lip, not speaking for several seconds. "About your friend whose brother went missing." He rested his elbows on the table, not meeting my eye. "I don't know whether to be more angry at Mr. Roy for doing this or at you for telling him about it."

Him being Tony. "He had to know the truth. No one else was ever going to tell him. I know it hurt —"

"You know it hurt!" Sawbuck sounded outraged. "You know it **hurt**?" His voice dropped to an angry whisper. "You told him everything he based his whole life on was a **lie**! That you **loved** him, that you stood **by** him, that you —" At this, he faltered. "And you told him in a letter from a servant, after letting him see you in an embrace with that scoundrel. I don't think he'll ever recover."

"What happened to his face? He —"

Sawbuck put his face in his hands. He sounded in agony. "Why did you let him go to the police about Marja?"

This change of subject puzzled me. "It was his idea."

He peered at me. "You truly don't understand."

I felt bewildered. "He said he might get them to help!"

Sawbuck laughed bitterly. "The Four Families have one law: handle your own affairs. Breaking that law means death."

"What does that mean?"

He put his arms on the table. "You settle matters yourself."

I frowned. "You mean **he** should've pursued Marja's killers?"

Sawbuck nodded, staring at the table. "His men have been in turmoil from the night you left. Mr. Roy forbidding them to kill you only agitated them further. When they learned Mr. Anthony went to the police …" he rested his chin on his arms with a weary sigh, "some of his men turned on us."

Tony was the Spadros heir. Sawbuck, Tony's right hand man. Tony's own men … Roy's men … **turned** on them? "Surely Tony knew this law. Why would he —?"

Sawbuck looked up at me and I knew.

I put my hands to my mouth in horror. Tony knew I found him lacking! He was desperate to make me value him. Love him.

My gods, Tony … did you love me that much?

When Sawbuck spoke next, he sounded bitter. "So what was this masterful plan you concocted?"

Now I began to wonder if I'd done the right thing.

I said, "My husband loves Gardena Diamond. He's in love with her." Why did it take me three years to see it? "I'm —" for a moment, I faltered. Joe was dead. "I **was** … in love with Joseph Kerr. I thought if I disappeared, Tony could search for me. Get the whole damn city searching for me. There would be no scandal. No one would know. Then after a year or two, he could declare me dead. He'd be free to marry her, as everyone intended."

My letter was so clear. Why didn't Tony understand?

"But you killed Joe before he could get to me," at this, I felt despondent, "and now it's all just a huge fucking mess."

The front bell rang, and I heard Amelia answer it.

Sawbuck said, "I didn't kill Joseph Kerr."

Can he not at least give me the courtesy of the truth? "Don't play games with me, Ten, I won't have it!"

"Mrs. Spadros, I went to his house as soon as we found you missing. We tore the place apart. He's not there. He's not at his usual places. The house is empty. His grandfather and sister are gone." He let out a bitter laugh. "The Harts were frantic to stop a war. Right now, they scour their quadrant for him."

Josie and her grandfather — gone? Their house empty? But Joe said they planned to stay in Bridges. "This makes no sense."

Sawbuck sounded weary. "Sure it does, Mrs. Spadros. You got played." He shook his head, shoulders slumped. "You both did."

"What?"

"You're not the first woman he's lured from her husband."

"Nonsense! Joseph Kerr and I promised ourselves to each other six years ago. It's simple, now that I consider it. Josie knew we planned to leave. She moved her grandfather so he wouldn't be forced to tell you where we went."

"Gods," Sawbuck said as he rose. "They played you right proper. Why, I don't know, but I intend to find out."

The Box

I went to my room with a sigh. Sawbuck obviously hated the Kerrs as much as everyone else in the city did, and was ready to believe any sort of lie about them.

If Joseph Kerr were alive and all these people searched for him, he would've been caught already!

An opened crate sat on my dresser. And what a welcome sight it was! Six bottles from the Clubb Gardens Winery.

A note lay inside:

> The doctor says you must not run out of drink, or you will fall ill again. This is a token of our goodwill and desire to be of assistance.

Alexander and Regina Clubb

The Clubbs had no true regard for my health! They just wished me to stop telling Gardena Diamond not to see their son Lance!

They couldn't have me killed after I'd warned Gardena of their plans: Gardena might be naïve, but she wasn't stupid. So they'd promised to support me during the trial if I stayed out of the way.

Regina Clubb asked me to speak no word against Gardena and Lance's courtship, but I'd be damned if I spoke a word for it.

Amelia came up. "Is there anything else I can get you, mum?"

"Bring the bourbon. I'm the only one who drinks it anyway."

Amelia stared at me. "The bourbon?"

"Yes, the bourbon. From Spadros Manor. All of it. As much as they'll let you bring." I snorted to myself. "I'm planning a party."

She obviously didn't understand me. "Yes, mum."

"Did they send any writing-paper?"

Amelia gave three tiny quick nods, her face a frozen mask.

"Bring it, then. We have work to do."

When Amelia brought in the writing-box Tony gave me for our anniversary, I thought I might die from the poignant grief which attacked. Amelia set the box down and made haste for the door, closing it behind her.

Tony? Why would you send this to me?

He knew.

Of course. I should have expected him to know. Amelia had to go to Tony for permission to have my things sent in the first place.

Tony knew how to hurt me, more than anyone.

Inside the box were three things I didn't expect: my moonstone necklace, our wedding ring, and a note.

Two I'd returned to him with the letter I sent with Amelia when I left Spadros Manor. The third read:

Jacqui —

I'm no fool.

You have no money. You'll never be received in society so long as you live there. So you could only want your finery to pay whatever Pike is charging for this debacle.

The man only wants money. He does you no favors, nor will he help you once the hope of money is gone.

Each of these things you've taken from my home was given from my sincere and earnest regard. Yet now that I've seen who you are, I'm glad to let them go.

I've made many difficult decisions these past few days, but on this I refuse to yield: neither my son nor Miss Diamond is to be exposed to scandal. Any attempt to file for divorce, and I will revoke my father's protection.

I won't force you to return, but neither will I allow you to leave the city with that scoundrel. I would rather die.

Why would Tony write as if Joe were still alive?

Could he **not** know Joe was dead?

Tony had lied about so much: why he married me, his love for Gardena Diamond, the son they had together. But he couldn't stand before me, look me in the eye, and say he didn't kill Joe. So he sent this letter, then had Sawbuck come here.

Gardena, of all people, had it right: Tony **was** a coward.

I shook my head, remembering the night I thought Tony worthy of respect. How foolish I was to ever believe that of him.

* * *

After luncheon, I sat in my room drinking, the curtains closed. The bell rang. After a moment, Amelia knocked. "Master Jonathan Diamond to see you, mum. I've seated him in the parlor."

"Thank you, Amelia, I'll be out in a moment."

"I'll be in back sorting your things, if it please you."

"That's fine. I'll call if we need something."

"Very good, mum."

Jonathan came to visit often, true, but every day? I wondered what this was about. I drained my glass and went to the door.

The drapes stood open in the parlor, which like at Spadros Manor faced the street. Jonathan sat with the afternoon sun behind him, his hair a glowing storm-cloud as he smiled up at me.

I had that fluttery flustered feeling again, like the day he visited before I went to rescue David Bryce ....

I realized I was just standing there. Feeling foolish, I sat beside him. "How are you?"

He gave me a bemused smile. "I'm well. And you?"

"I'm feeling quite well, thank you."

He pointed across the way to the room beside mine. The room was packed with clothing. "You've brought your things here?"

"I have." I leaned my head on my hand facing him, elbow on my knee. "Has anyone ever told you how beautiful you are?"

Jon chuckled. "So you **won't** tell me why."

I let out a short laugh. "Mr. Pike wants me to auction it all. To pay him. The man does love his money."

Jon leaned back with a grin. "So I hear." He turned toward me so his knee was on the sofa between us, his arm on the sofa's back. "Will you need help?"

"Why, if you'd like to help, I'm sure we can find work for

you." I twirled a lock of hair. "I like it when you're around."

He turned away, moving to sit straight on the sofa. Yet his cheeks colored. "You flatter me."

I took his hand. "Do you wish things happened differently?"

Jonathan's thumb stroked my finger. "What do you mean?"

"That I'd never been sold.

Jon froze. "Your life has been very hard."

"Jon, look at me."

He hesitated, then his eyes became moist. "Jacqui —"

"What's wrong?"

He reached up to smooth my hair. "Why would you ask this? Of course I wish you'd never been sold. It benefits no one," his eyes dropped, "except perhaps Roy Spadros." He gazed at me again. "All I've ever wanted was for you to be happy!"

Moved, I reached over to touch the side of his face. The sight of his skin against mine was so beautiful it took my breath away. "All I want is for you to be happy, too." Something in his eyes drew me towards him, and his face came close to mine.

The next instant, he raised his hand to my lips. "No. This is wrong." He jerked away, rose. "I — oh, gods, I can't do this, Jacqui." His hands balled into fists as he stood facing away. "I won't do this. Not this. You have a **husband**." It sounded as if he spoke through gritted teeth. "Tony has trusted me as a brother. I will **not** — be this kind of man!" He paused for a long moment, breathing heavily. "I **refuse** to betray him."

I felt chagrined. "I'm sorry, Jon. I —" *Oh, gods. Have I lost him?* "You said it before. You wish us to remain as friends."

Jon went perfectly still. "Yes," he said finally. "You've both been hurt enough." He went to the door and was gone.

I wanted to run after him, to cry out, "I'm sorry, I'm sorry, I just wanted someone to hold me," but it was too late. I'd made a fool of myself. Jon had made his feelings clear long ago, and now it seemed I'd hurt him, on top of everyone else.

The Bourbon

After drinking much of the night, the next day I felt terrible. But it wasn't just the queasy pounding headache. I felt out of control. I should never have behaved as I did towards Jon.

Something was wrong with me.

Today will be different, I vowed. I'll have this one drink, just to feel better, but no more.

I drew my own bath, washed and combed my hair, and tried braiding it. Ma taught me to braid, of course, long ago, but it had been years since I'd done it myself. I hadn't so much as tied my own shoes in six years. It seemed unbelievable, yet sad.

I was lighting the stove when Amelia hurried over. "Watch your shawl, mum. I've seen girls light themselves afire before."

"Oh," I said, suddenly fearful. "Thank you."

I let her scramble some eggs for us. We had eggs back home, but she seemed to want to do it.

Should I ask? "How is Mr. Anthony faring?"

Amelia seemed intent on cooking. "Much the same." She shrugged, giving me a quick glance. "But at least he's eating."

Grief, anger, fear, and worry all mixed together. "Eating?"

The sound of stirring stopped, and she clicked the stove off. "He didn't eat for days after you left."

I squeezed my eyes shut, clutching the sides of my dress. Tony never would eat when upset.

I must not take pity on him.

Too many had died to get me away from the Spadros Family. I couldn't go back. "Is his mother with him?"

"She visits daily, for several hours, and his manservant ... or his footmen ... or Master Hogan ... are by his side always." The scraping resumed, and she moved to the table. "Your food, mum."

Tea and plates were set out, and she went to a drawer to fetch silverware. I sat, no longer hungry, but I ate anyway.

* * *

Later that morning, the bourbon arrived! I had a nice long drink to celebrate — surely that wouldn't hurt — then placed the eight bottles next to the four bottles of wine still left.

Jonathan didn't return the rest of the week. But I didn't blame him. I imagined he felt the way I'd felt with Mr. Hart's advances.

I'd ruined everything, and it was my fault.

I sat in my room when I wasn't in bed crying. I missed Joseph Kerr terribly. I missed Jonathan Diamond almost as much.

If someone had asked if I missed Tony, I would have denied it. But I know I did. The police stopped knocking after the third night's screaming, giving me strange looks thereafter.

I didn't blame them either. During all those years with Tony, I must have sounded a madwoman, but he never once berated me for my nightmares.

Once Amelia left each night, I walked the halls for hours, alone. One night, tornado sirens went off, but I ignored them.

How could I have been so foolish, so selfish, so stupid? Why did I put Joe into such danger? How could I ever once have thought my plan would end in anything but Joseph Kerr's death?

I should have been stronger. I should have refused him. We would have lived in misery, but he would be alive!

Why hadn't Roy killed me? Did Roy know of my torment, intend for me to suffer here? That must be it, I decided. Roy Spadros only ever wanted others to suffer. He thrived on it.

The only thing I could focus on was giving water to my poor injured bird, which I did every time I saw it.

What else did I have to live for?

I drank wine for breakfast, and bourbon the rest of the day.

"The eggs have gone bad," Amelia said. "Why didn't you eat?"

"Not hungry." Even I could tell I slurred my words.

Amelia took hold of my arms. "You have to stop this drinking.

You'll make yourself sick. And you're not eating nearly enough."

I felt bitter. "Why do **you** care?"

"Come on," Amelia said, her voice kind. "It's past luncheon, and you're still in your nightgown. Let's get you in your bath."

Later, Jonathan Diamond came to call. I knew I was drunk, so I determined to act as proper as any quadrant-lady. I deliberately sat across the low coffee table from him as Amelia served us tea.

Again, he'd arrived in his white and silver carriage, dressed for the street like any other gentleman. Which puzzled me.

"I hope you're well, Master Diamond. How may I assist you?"

He smiled. "Is it too strange for me to visit my dearest friend?"

Friend.

With the word came the sharp bitter pain of regret.

I blinked away the memory, took a deep breath. "Of course not." What could I say to him? "But I did wonder why you had to ask permission to come here. Aren't you Keeper of the Court?"

Jon glanced away, crossing one leg over his knee. "I removed myself from your case. My brother Cesare will take my place."

Cesare Diamond. A man who hated me with passion simply because I was born in the Pot would oversee my future.

Jon continued, "Everyone knows of our friendship. And so," he let out a breath, "whilst I still act as Keeper of the Court, I may not do so with you." He swallowed, still looking away. "I approve." He leaned forward with a fake smile, not meeting my eye. "It refutes the rumor that you're being shown some favoritism."

"Favoritism?"

"Rumors abound, the sort depending on who speaks. Allowing you to live, allowing you to remain here rather than the Prison. Many feel this trial's a sham, that the judge is bought, that you'll be set free no matter what the courts find." He gave me a quick glance. "Because you're with a Family. People are very angry."

I was a "Pot rag" — what else could I expect?

We sat in silence as the birds chirped outside. My little bird still lived, though it seemed weaker every day. I tried to feed it, but the morsels only lay in its mouth.

I desperately hoped my bird would recover. *I only wanted you to be free.* But a cat had clawed it, and now it lay dying.

I almost got up to get a drink, stopping myself only just in time. "Any news of Joe? Have they found him?"

Jonathan slumped forward, his forehead in his hands, his elbows resting on his knees. "Jacqui … "

His demeanor surprised me. "Oh, gods, did they find his body? What did they do to him?"

Jon shook his head, which still lay in his hands. "I fear to tell you. I fear …"

"What?"

"You won't like it."

I peered at him, unable to make sense of what he was saying. "I beg you. Please tell me what you know. I — I don't think I can bear not to know!" I felt like crying. "Joseph Kerr meant everything to me. I must know what happened. Who did this. Where he lies."

Jon raised his head, and I'd never seen such an expression on his face. Concern, and yet dread. I could see the gears turn as he decided how much to tell me.

It's bad. "What did they do to him? Did they —"

"He's alive, Jacqui."

"What?"

"He was seen yesterday at a pool hall in the Hart slums."

I frowned, confused. "Are you sure it was him?"

Jon glanced away. "Several swore they knew him. The others all said the same thing: brown hair, tall, light brown skin, green eyes, very good looking. He arrived with a red-haired woman. The woman said he hired her to … um." At that, Jonathan blushed. "This was **very** close to the Pot."

A laugh burst from me. "That's your evidence? The word of ruffians? There must be fifty men in Hart alone who fit that description."

"There's more." Jon hesitated several seconds. "This was told to me in confidence, Jacqui. You must repeat it to no one."

"Go on."

"Being Keeper of the Court means you learn of things others might never know."

I relaxed. "Go on." It was obvious there were rumors, but they were only that. Would they ever find Joe's body?

"There are five cases brought before the Court by the families of five women — from all four quadrants — who make claim against Master Joseph Kerr of Hart quadrant."

"For what reason?"

Jon looked away. "Seduction with the promise of marriage, with a resulting child. The youngest was fifteen."

I stared at him in horror.

"Two of the children have been born, and Jacqui, they look like him." He grimaced, glanced away. "The fifteen-year-old took her own life — the child still inside her — in terror of being sent to the Pot."

I shook my head. This made no sense.

Then rage filled me. "Get out."

Jonathan rose. "If that's what you want." He went to the door, rested his hand upon it. "If Joseph Kerr is dead, why would Tony be searching for him?"

I hurried to him. "He's searching for Joe?"

"Tony staked a $10,000 reward for Joseph Kerr to be brought to him alive. Why do you think his 'friends' tried to capture him?"

I stared at Jon's back, astonished. *Ten thousand dollars?* A man's own mother would turn him in for that amount.

Jon faced me, but his demeanor was sober, almost sad. "Not only that, Joseph Kerr owes a great deal of money; three loan sharks and six gambling halls that I know of have sent men after him. Charles Hart ordered Mr. Polansky Kerr and Miss Josephine seized. Alexander Clubb left instructions that anyone fitting their descriptions in any way be detained at the zeppelin station. Flights are being delayed right and left on just this order. Why would these men go to such lengths if Joe were dead?"

It was inconceivable. "Tony sent you here."

"What? No, Jacqui, I —"

"Tony sent you and Ten here with these elaborate lies so I'd think Joe cared nothing for me and I'd return to be caged like an animal. The idea that Joe would **ever** abandon me! You lied about Roland and I forgave you for it, but this time ...." I shook my head, outraged. "You've gone too far. This is a lie I can never forgive." I grabbed the door handle, yanked it open. "Get out."

Jon looked stricken. "Jacqui, I swear I'm not lying."

"Get out!"

The guards ten yards away turned to stare.

"If that's what you want, Jacqui. But I didn't lie."

I slammed the front door. A picture fell, its glass shattering across the hall. I went to my room.

Amelia gasped, rushing in. "Mum, are you well?"

"Fetch me the letter-box."

"Yes, mum."

I wrote:

> You could never allow me to be free, is that it? You hate the idea of me leaving so much that first you murder then you slander the only man I've ever loved just to trap me again. I won't have it. I'll die before I return to you.

I put it with Amelia to post to Tony. As she left, she said, "Anything else, mum?"

"No, Amelia."

"I'll get some groceries then."

I poured another bourbon.

But something in the way Jon spoke nagged at me.

I thought back to when he lied on Queen's Night after the dinner: he told me Roland was his brother Cesare's son. I'd been focused on Tony and Gardena, yet even then I knew something wasn't right. But just now …

I stood, pacing, the curtains fluttering in the spring breeze, and the air was strangely silent.

Oh, gods.

Still alive?

It had to be some lie. Tony lied about Gardena, he lied about Roland, he probably even lied about it being so dangerous that I had to be caged everywhere I went.

My mind flashed to the times I barely escaped violation by a scoundrel. Vig was there the first time, and I had my pistol the second. Tony simply couldn't conceive that I could handle myself.

Why would Tony concoct such a lie? Why would Jon spread it?

I sat, drained my glass, poured more bourbon.

Lit a cigarette, hands shaking.

Jon couldn't lie like this, bold-faced, without any shame or guile. I **knew** when Jon lied, because it was so rare.

Jonathan Diamond believed Joseph Kerr to be alive.

But it was impossible. How could Joe be alive? What would possibly make him not come to me?

Joe would have tried anything to get to me. He would have sent someone, if only to learn if I was well. When he learned I'd been ill, put under house arrest … he would have been frantic.

I paced the room. There must be some reason he couldn't come to me. Maybe he feared Tony would harm me if he did. Maybe he feared the men who sought him had spies here, or at the hotel when I was there. Perhaps they chased him off.

But to not even send a message …

No. Joe would never abandon me like that.

Joe could be lying in a ditch somewhere. He could've been waylaid. He could've been killed by one of these men …

Three loan sharks … and six gambling halls …

Joseph Kerr owes a great deal of money.

I sat heavily. **Jon** thought it was a great deal of money.

Jonathan Diamond had access to as much money as Tony did.

How could Joseph Kerr owe so much money?

His sister Josie had spoken of their grandfather's desire not to take money from the Hart syndicate, and they'd suffered for it. Their poverty was obvious. Joe said they couldn't even afford to feed the horse we'd loaned them.

I could understand Joe taking out loans. I could perhaps understand going to a loan shark if their credit was very poor. They were Kerrs, after all, the last descendants of that old, hated monarchy. Perhaps they weren't deemed worthy of proper rates.

But why would Joe gamble?

How could he get himself into **that** much debt?

The side door opened and shut.

Joe asked if I had any money … any money at all …

Dread gnawed at me. *I gave him all the money I had in the world so he could get our tickets ...*

The night we left, Joe showed me the tickets. Three tickets, edged in red. One for him, one for me, one for my Ma.

I didn't get a good look at them, but they were real. I saw them.

I rose, frantic. "Amelia!"

She came running in. "Yes, mum?"

"Do you know anything about the zeppelin?"

"Like what?"

"When you get your tickets. What do the colors mean?"

She let out a relieved laugh. "Well, mum, I've never bought them. But the colors are for the year. That's why everyone goes on holiday during Yuletide. You buy them whenever you like. But the outgoing ones are only good until midnight, New Year's Eve."

"So what's this year's color?"

"Blue, I think."

"It can't be ..." Joe's tickets were red.

The stubs on the station floor two weeks ago — edged in blue.

The ticket stub fluttering away from Jon's pocket — edged in blue.

Had Jon been out of the city and back again since he brought me to Clubb Hotel? Where did he go?

"Mum? What's wrong?"

"Blue? Are you certain?"

"No, mum, I've never bought one. If it's important, I can ask."

"What color were they last year?"

She chuckled. "That I remember. A dark yellow. My uncle's grandson works at the ticket factory. Last year at Yuletide he said they looked like —" she blushed, hiding her mouth with her hands.

"Like what?"

"Like they was dipped in piss. Forgive me, mum, I —"

I waved her off. "I've heard the word before."

"Yes, mum." She rushed out, closing the door behind her.

Blue this year.

Ticket stubs edged in blue littered the zeppelin station floor ...

A ticket stub edged in blue fluttered away in the wind ...

They were **yellow** last year?

How long had Joseph Kerr held those red-edged tickets? Why would he trick me this way?

"I trust Ten," Tony said, "and I trust you."

I collapsed into a chair and began to weep.

I left Tony … dear sweet Tony who trusted me. Who loved me. Who stood up to Roy Spadros for me. Who gave up Gardena and Roland for me.

And then the only man I had ever truly loved took all the money I had and left me!

Left me to face Tony. To sit at the zeppelin station, humiliated and alone. To become Regina Clubb's pawn because I had no other option. To the mercy of Frank Pagliacci, Jack Diamond, and Roy Spadros. To face public shame, and at the end, the gallows.

Joe knew what would happen if I remained in Bridges.

And he left me anyway.

I cried tears of shame, of fury, of anguish and hate. I threw my glass at Amelia when she asked what happened, and wept at the mark on the door, the shattered ruin, the wasted drink.

I wept as I brought another bottle to the table, and as I wrote to everyone, asking their forgiveness.

Ma never came to check on me, not even when I was sick. I remembered her disdain the night she sent me away.

Was she glad to be rid of me?

I set the letters out on the table in the hall. "Amelia," I called out. "Send these at once."

"Yes, mum." Amelia peered around the corner from the end of the hall. "Then I'm going to see my daughter, she's unwell."

Amelia was probably glad to be away from me too. "You do that." I closed the door to my room, locked it.

Then I saw my little bird, its body torn by that wretched cat.

My bird lay unmoving … dead.

"No!"

I clung to the cage in anguish, weeping. My little bird!

My little bird.

"Oh, gods," I wept. "Finally you're free."

I would never be free. Tony would never release me. Despite Mr. Pike's words, no one would believe me innocent. I'd have to betray everyone to get out of the city. And Joe … how could I ever be free of this torment, knowing the man I gave everything to took my love and crushed it beneath his feet?

Five women, Joe? And one of them fifteen?

I searched for a glass, my house shoes crunching as I went. I returned to my table, opened a bottle and drank straight from it. I'd never done so since I first drank vodka, the night Air died.

Air. Gods, Air, why did you ever care for someone like me?

He was as big a fool as I was. He made the mistake of loving me. I killed him. No matter what his mother said, I killed him.

I loved the way the liquor burned through me, the way it did those few moments me and Air were happy together. Perhaps it was a sign. Maybe I would see Air again before it was all over.

I lay my pistol on the table in front of me. I put my dagger next to it. The curtains blew in the breeze, and the air was warm. It was a good day. I couldn't have picked one better.

The bottle beside me was empty, so I got up, opened another one. After some time, I squinted at the bottles on the table. How did two empty bottles get there? I needed more to drink.

A full bottle sat on the sideboard across the room, so I got up to get it. But my foot slipped out from under me. The room moved, and I felt sick. I thought I might be falling.

In fact, I was sure of it, but I didn't really care anymore.

The Horror

Frantic voices. Angry words which made no sense. Sobbing. Screams. Laughter.

But instead of the woman from the hotel — Mrs. Clubb? — this was a deep, rich laugh from a large man.

At Clubb Hotel, I'd feared I was mad. Now I knew I was.

He laughed in triumph as I flew through a storm-cloud, thunderbolts crashing around me. And I knew — I just knew — that he didn't just mock me. He pursued me!

I could hardly breathe for fear of the man pursuing. He laughed as he chased me through the green-gray storm, a massive wall approaching to cut me with knives of silver.

But I flew too fast, too high, and I began to fall from a terrible height. And the laughter came closer … and closer … behind …!

A strange room, my heart pounding in a shaking sweat. The room golden, hot, the sound of fire blazing from behind. Flames shot forward from each side.

Someone terrible was after me.

Yet I couldn't move. I couldn't move!

Jack Diamond, head shaved and dressed all in white, emerged into the fiery light. Something glinted in his hand.

I stared at Jack in horror. I'd left the window open. Somehow he'd gotten in my room, taken me here!

But how? Where was I? What would he do to me?

He moved forward. "Oh, good, you're awake."

Terrified as I'd never been, I screamed, pushing myself into the cushions behind me.

Jack's face filled with alarm. "Oh, gods."

But it wasn't Jack's deep, deep voice. "Jacqui, it's me." He didn't sound like Jack Diamond at all.

Jack pulled the skin off of his head, and the coiled black hair underneath was thick and wild.

I stared, aghast. How did Jack pull the skin off of his head?

Two old people tottered in. Jack said, "Turn on the lights."

A dark-skinned man with black hair wore a khaki shirt and pants. He held a dark brown finely-knitted hat in one hand and a water glass in the other. He put the glass on the side table and sat on the bed beside me. "Jacqui, it's me. It's just me. You're safe." He clasped my hand. "I will **never** let anyone harm you."

I clutched his hand, sobbing in relief. "Jon? Oh, Jon, I was so frightened. I thought you were Jack here to kill me."

Jonathan Diamond sat holding my hands, face sad.

Suddenly, I realized how deeply this must hurt him. "I'm sorry. But I … I couldn't move, and —"

He gave a dejected smile. "And I look like him."

"Yes. Well, no, not now that I see you properly … you look like **you**. Why can't I move?"

Trees rustled behind me outside. The breeze floated the sheer white curtains beside me. Shadows lengthened in the setting sun.

"You're tied to the bed. But now you've returned to us," Jon's eyes reddened, his hand tightening on mine, "maybe now we can untie you." He and the old woman beside him removed the sheets which bound me to the narrow bed. Then he sat beside me again.

I smiled at Jon, feeling safe, content. Then I felt confused. "Where am I?"

"You're in a cottage in the Spadros countryside. The doctor will be glad to hear you've awakened."

"What happened?"

An instant of grief crossed his face. "I found you on the floor." He seemed haunted by the memory. "Amelia had left you alone. When she returned, she cleaned you up. I brought you here to get well." He spoke as if leaving out a great deal.

I'd sent Amelia to fetch bourbon … or was her daughter ill?

I tried to sit up and the room turned gray. Jonathan stood over me. "Don't try to rise, my love, please, just rest." His hand felt cool on my forehead, and I closed my eyes.

I dreamed Jonathan wept. I drank watery alcohol. I dreamed Tony said, "I love you," and fear gripped me. Would he make me go back? Jon kissed my hand: I felt safe, content.

I opened my eyes and it was dark.

I lay propped up, with pillows behind me. Jon sat asleep in a chair beside me. He had different clothes on.

What day was it?

Jon came awake with a start and grasped my hand, eyes bloodshot and alarmed. "What is it? Are you well?"

"I think so, but I haven't tried to move since that last time."

Jon smiled to himself. "We've had difficulty keeping you in bed." He checked his pocket-watch. "Time for your draught." He went to the dresser, opening a notebook. He lit a small lamp. I saw him pour water from a pitcher, then heard him pour again, then count under his breath. He poured liquid once more, then brought me a glass of something darkly opaque. "Drink it down."

It tasted like almost completely watered-down bourbon mixed with herbs. It was fairly disgusting, but I drank it all, handing the glass back to him. "What's this about?"

He sat the glass on the nightstand. "You poisoned yourself with bourbon. The only way to bring you back to health without causing epileptic fits is to wean you off alcohol altogether. It'll take another week or so. But you must never drink again. Another poisoning would surely kill you."

Never drink again. I didn't know what to say. Of course, I'd often considered cutting back some, but ....

He sat beside me. "It will be the most difficult task you've had to face, but you're stronger than you think." Jon's face was resolute. "I'll help you, for as long as I can."

Grief flooded over me. *What do I have to live for?*

For a long time I couldn't speak for sobbing, then I turned away. "Why bother?" What I'd done to Tony. My little bird. Everyone. "I don't deserve to live."

I felt Jon's hand warm on my shoulder. "You do deserve to live! You have a husband who loves you, Jacqui. Even now. You have … a maid who awaits your return. You have … friends who care about you." He took a deep breath. "Who **love** you."

Most of my friends are dead. Or have betrayed me.

But then I remembered what Mrs. Clubb said, about how I was wrong to say I had no friends and no future.

I didn't wish to believe it.

Yet here Jonathan sat. The doctor visited. These servants must have cared for me. "I'm sorry to be so much trouble."

Jon patted my shoulder, and I could tell from his voice that he smiled. "You would have to do much, much worse to cause me trouble." I heard him take a deep breath; his voice trembled. "I would do anything for you, Jacqui. Anything. Even unto death."

I closed my eyes and cried as he smoothed my hair.

When I awoke, I was no longer tied.

Tony stood in the doorway, deep sadness in his eyes. Then he knelt beside my bed near where my hips lay and took my hand.

I bit my lip, trying not to cry. What could I possibly say to him?

His bandage was gone; a red scar lay on his right cheek. "I've had a long time to think about what you wrote —"

Oh, gods, I thought. The letters —

"— and what I wanted to say —" he hesitated, tightened his grasp on my hand, gazed down at it, "— is that even though your vows to me were forced, mine to you never were. I've been angry. I've said things I regret. But even though perhaps we can't live together — now — I never wanted you to **die**!" He brought my hand to his lips, then to his unhurt cheek, and it reminded me of Pip that day in the garden. "My father told me once that to take your life is a grave error, because whether your cards are good or bad, it's your duty to play them to the end. If your life is bad, you only give them to some innocent to endure in your stead."

Why would Tony mention suicide? "Ten told me everything. I don't want you to die for trying to please me!"

He said nothing, yet his grip on my hand tightened.

I couldn't let myself feel for this man. Too much had happened. "I've said things I regret as well."

He gazed into my eyes. "I don't want you to suffer, Jacqui. I've only ever wanted you to be happy." But he said it as if he despaired of ever being so himself.

I couldn't let myself pity him, or I might agree to go back.

Tony sounded lost. "Were you **never** happy?"

I shrugged, not meeting his eye. Telling him how much torment I'd been in all these years would crush him. Relating a happy moment would only give him false hope.

"I need you, Jacqui. I need you. I can't do this without you."

"Do what?"

"Find this Red Dog Gang. Regain control of our quadrant. Show my men I'm capable of leading them!" He rested his forehead on the bed's edge, gripping my hand as if drowning. "I dread the man who directs this horror! I hear the ticking of his merciless mind, feel the rumbling of his terrible machine of war. Like fog, he covers everything, lies behind every window, yet offers no place to hide. His only wish is to crush us!" He raised his head, rested his other arm on the bed. His eyes pleaded with me. "Please come home! I can't protect you otherwise. I **need** you to be safe. I'd die if they harmed you."

I turned my face away, and he released my hand. It pounded, tingled, ached. I focused on the sensations for a long time, examining their pain in every detail.

They were important.

They were a reminder.

Tony thought he loved me, but his fierce grasp on my life hurt.

The Boy

A far off door opened, and footsteps came down the hall.

Tony looked over his shoulder at the doorway; there stood Gardena and the little boy I'd seen months ago on Market Center.

Gardena said, "Say hello to your daddy."

Gardena had Jonathan's dark skin and eyes; as Jonathan came to stand behind his sister, their eyes were both rimmed in red.

Roland Anthony Spadros, a boy of four, held wildflowers, and peered at Tony, hesitant. Then he looked to his mother.

Tony appeared completely astonished. He didn't rise; he turned round to face the boy, his voice full of emotion. "What a fine boy you are! Oh, my dear, dear son," he said, "come to me."

The boy ran to him, black ringlet curls bouncing. The happiness in Roland's face as he hugged his father for the first time made everything worth it.

Tony said, "Are those flowers for me?"

Roland said quite seriously, "No, sir." He presented them instead to me. "I'm sorry you're not feeling well."

I smiled at him, taking the flowers. "I'm feeling much better. Your uncle Jon has taken very good care of me."

"Mama said you're my Mama too." He seemed confused.

"You may call me Jacqui."

At that, he made the most adorable little bow. "Thank you, Miss Jacqui." He ran back to Gardena, hiding his face in her skirts.

She knelt before him. "Would you like to go outside with your Daddy and Uncle Jon? I hear there are animals, like at home."

His face made an "oh" as he jumped up and down in delight.

"Take hold of Uncle Jon's hand, please," she said, rising.

Roland grabbed Jon's hand; Jon smiled back at me as he let himself be dragged away.

Tony went to Gardena. "Thank you." Then he went round the corner and was gone.

Gardena stood in the doorway staring blankly for a moment, then wiped her eyes. "Oh, Jacqui, what have you done?"

"Come sit with me, Dena."

She pulled a chair close and sat, not looking at me. "I'm so sorry. For everything. Most of all, how you learned of it."

I let out a sigh, feeling discouraged. "You were afraid. He was afraid." I couldn't say what I most wanted to, that I tried to disappear so that they could be a family. "I don't blame you any longer. I'm just glad my husband can see his son."

Gardena gave a small smile as she gazed at my bed-sheets. "It was Jon's doing. He told my father everything. Gods, Jacqui, I never knew what it's been like for you all this time."

This surprised me. "Jon never told you?"

"Not a word."

"I told my husband the truth. But I don't know what I should have done anymore."

Gardena snorted. "Anthony was furious at first, because Jon knew everything yet never told him. Yet Jon's only wish has been to offer support to you both."

"Remember when you acted so silly in my garden? You said we'd have a sleep-over, do each other's hair, tell each other' secrets." I regretted not taking her seriously. "Were you trying to tell me of Roland, even then?"

Gardena shrugged, head down.

She hadn't yet once looked at me. "Dena, what's wrong?"

Her eyes reddened. "I've done you such a great injustice. I was a stupid frightened girl trying to be a woman, whilst knowing nothing about what that meant. And I knew what I did was wrong." She glanced at me, then away. "I knew Anthony wasn't yet of age. I knew he'd never been with a woman. I knew you two were betrothed. I knew I exposed him to terrible danger, from both his father and mine." She shook her head, her voice breaking. "Yet I did it anyway, for my own selfish gain."

I shrugged. He was seventeen, old enough to refuse. She was only nineteen, and we'd never met. "And now you have a son."

She smiled fondly at my bed-covers. "Yes. He's the joy of my life." Her smile faded. "But I've given him no future." She let out a sigh. "At best, he's a Spadros bastard in Diamond quadrant. At worst, he's the son," she said bitterly, "of a whore —"

"Dena —"

"— who should by rights be in the Pot. What kind of life can he ever have?"

"Gardena, look at me."

She turned red eyes to mine.

"You are not a whore." I smiled, remembering the brash young women I admired so as a child. "Back home, that would be a mark of honor."

Gardena's eyes widened, horrified. "Really?"

I chuckled. "Really. And you have many options open to you." I recalled the things Mrs. Clubb thought I was jealous of Gardena for. "You're young, beautiful —"

Gardena blushed.

"— able to bear sons, healthy, and from a good Family. Why should you not marry who you choose?"

I wanted her to choose Tony. But I couldn't say that. Not if I wanted to keep my bargain with the Clubbs. At this point, I needed every break I could get if I were to escape the gallows.

"No one will have me. My father has worked tirelessly on my behalf for years. Every man he approaches balks at the thought of marrying a 'spoilt woman,' taking on the care and responsibility of another man's child. Everyone except Lance … and I … Jacqui, after what you said to me back at our luncheon —"

"Your son is an heir to Spadros and Diamond. All Lance needs to do is make Roland love him, and the Clubbs have three quadrants. The Harts could do nothing."

"— I just don't know."

"My husband loves you desperately. I intended —"

"No, Jacqui! No! This is horrible! How could I bear it, knowing you tried to die so I might have your husband? It's not worth it."

"That's not what I meant."

Her head drooped. Tears ran down her cheeks, dropped to the bed. "Then what did you mean?"

"You know what happened. I left him."

"You left him … so he could marry me? That makes no sense!"

"I — I loved someone else."

"Oh. Jon never told me **that**."

"But …" Grief came crushing down upon me. But I would not cry, not now. "Things don't always work out the way you expect."

She sat silent for several seconds. "I'm sorry."

We sat there as the birds chirped outside, deep sadness filling my heart at the sound. My poor little bird.

"Jacqui, what should I do about Lance?"

I felt numb. "What do you **want** to do about Lance?"

"I don't know. If his parents are scheming to take Roland from me, if Lance only wants me for my son's claim on Spadros Manor, then I won't have anything to do with him."

She left the unsaid dangling. *But if he truly loves me …*

Lance might truly love her. I didn't know. Gardena was almost 25, a spinster with a bastard son. Any moment, her situation might be revealed, putting them both in terrible danger. This could be her last chance at marriage and a secure future.

But if she married Lance, Tony might never see his son again. Little Roland, the potential heir to Spadros, Diamond, **and** Clubb, could become a pawn in some future Family struggle. Or be in danger from someone in the Clubb syndicate's succession. Or even from Lance's own men.

Why had Joe abandoned me? Tony and Gardena might be together now, naturally drawn closer in their search for me. There had to be some reason, something where this made sense.

I'd placed every hope in Joseph Kerr, and he'd failed me.

"Jacqui, what's wrong?"

I shook my head, despondent. "All I ever wanted … I just want to make sure Roland is in my husband's life! It gives him such pain to parted from his child." *And from you*, I wanted to say. But I couldn't say that. "I only fear that …"

"That Lance may not honor him as Roland's true-born father."

I nodded, unable to speak.

Gardena nodded slowly. "Then I will insist on it."

But once married, would Lance have any reason to honor that?

"Roland keeps asking for Lance, Jacqui. Asking why we can't visit. I don't know what to tell him."

I felt afraid for Tony. And for little Roland. "It's your choice, Dena. Only you can trust whether he'll remain true to his word."

Gardena left, returning twenty minutes later to say goodbye.

Tony never returned. I lay listening to doors open and shut, to murmured conversation, the sounds of a carriage. Two carriages.

Then Jonathan appeared in the doorway.

"You have hay on your knee," I said.

Jon chuckled, brushing off his trousers. "I hope you're well?"

I considered the matter. "I am." Emotion swelled at the memory of Roland's little face. "I'm glad Tony got to see him."

Jon nodded rapidly, lips pursed, not looking at me.

"Is something wrong? Come sit with me."

Jonathan sat where Gardena had, eyes downcast. He took a deep breath. "I have to believe all will be well in that regard."

"Why did you bring them here? I fear Roy may learn of it."

Jon snorted, a small smile on his face. "He already knows."

"How did he find out? I never told anyone, I swear —"

Jon took my hand. "Tony told Roy himself."

"What? Why?"

"Tony told me he needed to start behaving like a man."

This took me aback. "Really."

Jon nodded, eyes unfocused. "Tony went to Roy and confessed it all." Jon turned to me in disbelief. "He said Roy embraced him, wept at the news. Roy said he was proud of him."

I never expected this. "This is incredible." We sat in stunned silence. "Does Tony not fear for his son's life?"

"He does. But he feared it'd be much worse should the news emerge some other way." Jon peered at his hands. "Yet this is far from over. What Tony did infuriated my father."

"Oh? Why?"

"Tony never asked leave to speak of it! If Roy had reacted with anger, tried to seize Roland, harm my sister —" Jon shook his head. "Our border guards were unprepared. Tony should've included us in the decision. Or at least given us notice."

"What will your father do?"

"What can he do?" Jon sat silent a moment, then chuckled. "If I hadn't pointed out that keeping the Spadros heir from his son could cause the very war he feared, we might not be having this discussion."

That eased my mind on another matter. Would Lance Clubb risk war to keep Tony from Roland? Unlikely. But the thought of Roland growing up with Mrs. Clubb gave me pause. For years, the boy had lived apart from his father. She could speak any sort of lie in his ear, turning his fragile love for Tony into disdain. I gripped Jon's hand. "Don't let Roland become a Clubb discard."

Jon nodded slowly, face thoughtful. "We've had many such discussions, before my father ever agreed to the courtship."

"But these discussions must include Roland's father! If the Clubbs know harming Roland turns half the city against them —"

Jon placed his hand on mine. "Tony has no firmer advocate in Diamond Manor." Then he chuckled. "I'm sure my father rues the day he had **me** of all his sons appointed Keeper of the Court." He gave me a wry grin. "You learn much listening to these trials."

I felt relieved. "What's it like? Being Keeper of the Court."

He shrugged. "Much paperwork and boredom. A few exciting moments when the lawyers spar with each other. Much of it is sad." He straightened, let out a breath. "But it's a noble office, one few younger sons of great houses get opportunity for. It suits me."

"I'm glad it does. Who acts in your place now?"

Jon grinned. "I'm sure my father coerced someone into duty."

"You don't know?"

"I don't even care. I told him I wouldn't leave here until you were well, end of story."

"My word," I said. "I'm surprised you defied him so."

"It's of no consequence," said Jon. "Until you're well, the rest of Bridges can go hang."

The Grief

The next day, I was able to rise from bed, sit in a chair. The servants aided me, yet they never spoke, even when I spoke to them. In the reflection, my eyes were strange: a faint yellow where white should be. And a tender red scar lay on my left temple. I recalled drinking, the broken glass on the floor, falling.

Jonathan said I looked much better, and the way he said it made me afraid. How ill had I **been**?

Jon and I took tea on the terrace outside the front door. The cottage lay in a valley surrounded by pines, an arbor of black roses stretching along one wall. Beyond to our right lay a wide path through the trees. Cows lowed softly from beyond view.

The day was lovely. The elderly servants poured tea, brought fruit and cakes, then retreated. It wasn't until Jon pointed it out in hushed whispers that I noticed none of them had thumbs.

Jon's face was filled with horror. "They have no tongues, either. What happened here?"

My mind seemed slow, confused. "I don't know."

"Spadros men come weekly with food already prepared, wine and beer. They place it on this table, then leave immediately." Jon let out a breath. "These people are being kept alive for a reason."

This stank of Roy Spadros. "Have you asked about it?"

Jon gave a sudden bitter laugh. "Would Spadros men tell a Diamond? But I don't believe they know. They have orders and they follow them. I've seen men on the hills, rifles pointed at the delivery men. I'd bet the men on the hills know even less."

I peered at the hills, uneasy.

"Soon, you'll be well enough to leave this place," Jon said.

Then he shuddered. "I hope never to return."

"Have you been treated well?"

"Yes," Jon said. "And the doctor comes every few days to examine you. The last time, he examined everyone." He chuckled, amused. "I don't think he approves of my being here, but fortunately it's not up to him."

I smiled. "I will tell him you've been nothing but a gentleman."

* * *

I remained at the cottage until the water I drank had no bourbon in it. I also took what the doctor called "liver tonics," which seemed to help. My hands still shook at times. But gradually my mind cleared, and if I smoked I felt better.

Jon suggested I begin a journal. We spent afternoons in the garden. In the evening he read to me in the parlor. Yet I felt he kept a certain distance from me. He took long walks alone. He sat for hours gazing at the hills, seldom answering when I spoke.

From his behavior, it seemed something was terribly wrong. I felt somehow that whatever was wrong must be because of me, because he never spoke of it, even when I asked.

At first, I felt so alone. And I wept when a bird chirped, or an evil memory intruded. Yet the gentle warmth of the sun, the scent of the black roses covering the arbor on the terrace, even the view of the hills soothed me. I think they helped me heal.

And I slowly realized — feeling more than a bit foolish once I did — that of course he wasn't free to share every burden with me. Jon was Keeper of the Court. Not only that, he was a Diamond, and held secrets we might never be able to speak of.

This thought sobered me. Jon had been so devoted during my sickness, even whilst carrying his griefs. I hoped the day might come when I might be able to help him in some small way as well.

* * *

Dr. Salmon came to visit twice a week. The last time he visited, he examined me most thoroughly, one of the old women standing beside him. "You seem remarkably well, all things considered. I thought at one point we might lose you."

This took me aback. "Was it really so bad?"

"Yes." He placed a lined hand upon mine. "I'm sure Master Diamond has told you that you must never drink alcohol again."

"Yes, he told me. He's been the best, the kindest caretaker one might ever have."

He patted my hand, his ancient eyes moist. "You're a very, very lucky young woman." His lips tightened into a thin smile. "We'll have to be most careful if you should come with child, but you should still be able to bear a healthy heir."

I snorted. "I'm not going back to Spadros Manor."

"What if you fall ill again?"

"My maid is with me. Police stand guard. My husband won't force me to return, so I fail to see why it's any of your concern."

"I care about your well-being, whether you do or not." He turned away. "Very well. I'll call on you in a few days."

"How do you know where I live?"

He frowned. "Why, Master Diamond and I brought you here."

That made sense.

But I still worried. "Something very odd happened this year."

This drew his attention. "Tell me more."

"I've remembered things I didn't before. It would seem obvious for me to remember them, and I feel as if I should have remembered them, but I didn't. Then the memory came suddenly, without reason and with great force. From a smell, or a word."

He nodded slowly. "Memory is a delicate thing. Were the memories painful ones?"

I felt suddenly unable to speak.

"Sometimes — if the memory is very painful — the mind doesn't want to remember. The memory is hidden, if you will, until it's needed." He gave me a gentle smile. "It's all quite natural, and there's no need to fret about it."

"Will there be more?"

"If you have more, there may be more." A puzzled look spread over his face. "You're quite young. Usually people are in their thirties — or older — before this sort of thing happens. If it does."

"Well, thank you. It's good to know." I let out a laugh, relief sweeping over me. "More than once, I've feared I might be mad."

He smiled at that. "You had a bad time at the hotel, but that was due to drink. Or rather the sudden **lack** of drink after long overindulgence. Now that we've gotten you clear of it, I think you're recovering nicely."

* * *

A Spadros "plain" carriage — dark brown without markings, so it resembled a taxi — took me and Jonathan Diamond back towards the city. We sat across from each other during the long trip, but diagonally, gazing out of the windows beside us.

I'd felt ashamed to speak of my missteps up to then, but I didn't want to part without resolving the matter. "I'm sorry for what happened that day in my parlor."

He continued to gaze out of the window. "Think nothing of it."

"You must not berate yourself. It was wrong for me to put you in that position." Wildflowers bloomed along the road, but the summer's light seemed dim. "The fault was entirely mine."

He nodded, not looking at me.

"And I do wish very much to be friends." I turned to him, my heart full. "I need you. I — I need someone to talk to. I need a friend. At present, I have very few. Well, to be honest, without you I have none. When I return, I'll once again be alone, and I ..." at this point, I felt as if I rambled, so I straightened, collecting my thoughts. "I don't want you to fear to visit."

He gave his first real smile in days. "Then I'll be sure to visit."

At this, I felt much relieved.

Jon leaned forward, his elbows on his knees. "I worry for you."

This surprised me. "Why? The doctor says I'm fine."

He turned his head to peer out of the window. "How do you feel about what Master Kerr has done?"

"I don't **know** that he's done anything."

Jonathan crossed his legs, leaning away, resting his elbow on the window's edge.

"You believe Joe to be a cad? A scoundrel?"

Jonathan gazed out of the window. "It doesn't matter what I believe. But your marriage is harmed, perhaps forever. Whether dead or alive, a man you love didn't stand for you. Fight for you. Protect you. Instead, he went out of the window when your husband appeared in anger, leaving you to face the consequences alone." For a moment, his jaw tightened. "His sister — a woman you've known since birth — has disappeared. Your own men have betrayed you. And you're accused of Dame Anastasia's murder." He uncrossed his legs to face me, elbows on his knees. "This on top of all the death and torment in your life. You've lost **so** much." He put his hands together, resting his forehead upon them. "Please, Jacqui — let yourself grieve."

My eyes stung, but I shook myself, straightened, and my vision was clear. "I've cried many times, Jon. Just because I don't care to do so in front of you —"

"You used to." Jon gazed out of the window. "You said you needed a friend to talk to. I hope I'm here when that time comes."

I recalled his zeppelin ticket flying away. "Do you plan a trip?"

A wistful smile. "How many men understand their future?"

For this I had no answer, even if I'd known what he meant.

The News

I peered at Jon as the carriage continued towards my apartments. I'd been at the cottage three weeks. What happened while I was gone? Jon had said nothing about current events, and no newspapers arrived at the cottage. I'd surely missed my court dates, and I dreaded what Molly and Mr. Pike would have to say.

As we came closer to the city I began to feel afraid. What if Tony had me locked in the carriage as he did before, forced me to return to Spadros Manor after all? I'd never be allowed to escape!

Dread gnawed at me as we approached the outer road. But the carriage sped past 192nd Street, and I felt a huge sense of relief.

We stopped in front of my apartments behind Jonathan's carriage, which had returned for him. Once we had alighted, I said to Jon, "Thank you for everything."

"Rest well." Jon tipped his hat, and climbed into his carriage.

I expected Amelia to answer the door, but instead Blitz did!

I drawled, "Blitz Spadros. Whatever are **you** doing here?"

He chuckled, and the look in his eye told me he remembered the night in the back of Vig's saloon when I asked that very thing. Opening the door wide, he turned into the hall. "She's back!"

I was pleased to see Blitz, although puzzled at him being here. Blitz was Tony's distant cousin and our night footman. He claimed he never needed much sleep; perhaps he brought news.

I couldn't imagine any news from Tony being very pleasant.

Amelia emerged from a back room; Mary Pearson followed. Mary was twenty and pretty, with straight light brown hair which in some lights looked blonde. She was a maid at Spadros Manor, and the butler's daughter.

"Mary! This is a pleasant surprise."

Blitz was grinning, which always reminded me of Tony.

I said to Mary, "I hope your parents are well?"

Mary seemed surprised. "They are, mum, thank you."

Blitz put his arm around Mary. "May I present Mrs. Spadros."

"Wait," I said. "You got married?"

Blitz said, "We're your staff."

"How wonderful!" I always liked Blitz, and Mary too. "I never even knew you fancied each other!"

Mary blushed, relaxing into his side, and it was so sweet and charming that it warmed my heart.

Amelia said, "You've had a long, tiring ride. Would you like some tea?" So we sat in our parlor as Amelia brought in the tea-tray. "Before I forget, mum. You have a meeting with Mr. Pike on Tuesday at half past ten. The Court carriage will take you."

"Thank you, Amelia."

She wouldn't sit with us. "You have need to speak with your housekeeper and butler, mum, and I have much to do."

Once Amelia left, I said, "However did you come to be here?"

Mary looked to Blitz, who put his cup down, hesitating a long moment. "I've always supported and I dare say loved my cousin. But the night Mr. Anthony struck me for doing my best to follow his instruction, I knew we needed to leave. Your illness gave us the perfect opportunity." He grinned at Mary. "We'd been wanting to marry for some time. Her father gave permission, and I don't think Mr. Anthony much cared one way or the other."

"So did you marry at Spadros Manor?"

Blitz let out a short laugh. "Hardly. They were still patching all the holes inside." He glanced at me. "You know —"

Tony's men attacked him **inside** Spadros Manor? I took a deep breath, feeling shaky. "So where did you marry, then?"

"Vig's place."

"Vig's? How is he?" Vígharður Vikenti and I had been friends for years, and he owned a saloon not actually that far away.

"Much better," Blitz said. "We helped him clean up the place.

With Natalia doing the cooking, it's about back to normal."

Natalia was — as she said it — "of the Romani," a bit older than I was. She wasn't one of Vig's "working girls" in back — I think she was a dancer. But she and Vig always seemed at odds; I never expected her to stay long. "Natalia's — cooking?"

Blitz laughed. "She's a better cook than his mother."

Grief struck hard. Roy's men destroyed Vig's saloon — where he lived with his mother — as punishment for Vig refusing to inform on me to Roy. That night, his mother's heart gave way.

It was all too much. "She helped me when no one else would." I wiped my eyes, raising my teacup. "To Vig's mother."

"To Vig's mother," Blitz said. "May she receive better cards next time." I don't suppose Mary knew Vig's mother, but she toasted her just the same.

I put down my teacup. "I thought Natalia would've left."

"She tried," Blitz said, "but between the Travelers' Federation searching everything and the Clubbs searching everything, it's hard for her people to travel as they want to."

I stared at him, not understanding.

"They smuggle themselves in the cargo."

"How very clever," I said.

Lance Clubb was going to smuggle my Ma out, before the zeppelin exploded. Why didn't I think of doing that? I could have been out of the city long ago.

But I wouldn't have gone without Joe, and it seemed that Joe wouldn't have gone with me in any case. I didn't want to think about that, really, or I'd end up crying. "What must we discuss?"

Mary smiled. "It's so small here there's not nearly much to do."

I said to Blitz, "Did Amelia tell you of the auction?"

"She did." Blitz gave me a grin which said he knew exactly what I was up to. "We have a date: June 14th. It's all set up."

"Notify Mr. Blackberry of the *Bridges Daily*."

"Will do."

"I've seen no news," I said. "What's happened in Bridges?"

"Oh, mum," said Mary. "You have no idea."

Not only had a group of Spadros men turned on Tony, even

more refused to follow Roy anymore. "They're calling themselves the Ten of Spades," Blitz said, "and they vow to kill you."

"Really." For some reason, this didn't surprise me.

"Well, not really. But if they had you in their sights they wouldn't hesitate. They hate Roy, despise Mr. Anthony, and feel the Family's left the old ways. They want new leadership —"

"In other words, them."

Blitz laughed.

Sawbuck and his men had been in firefights with these rogues — who numbered much more than ten — several times in the past month. "They're trying to show they aren't afraid of us," Blitz said. "Looks like Mary and I got out of the way just in time."

"Do you think they'll come here?"

"With all those police outside? I doubt it. But once the trial's over … ?" He let it trail off with a shrug.

"Well, let's worry about that later." With my luck, I'd be hung before the rogues caught up to me.

"It'll turn out, mum," Mary said. "I know you didn't do it."

Mary brought out a box full of old newspapers and began reading to me. A steam pipe exploded in an abandoned home on West 6th in Spadros. Several homes were destroyed and a dozen killed. The power went down in Clubb for a whole hour at sunset, leaving several square miles in the dark at dinnertime.

People were angry at the Inventors' Board for not maintaining the pipes and wires. "What do we pay them for," one editorial said, "when they aren't doing their jobs?"

The Inventors I'd met so far had an intense interest in the Magma Steam Generators. Inventor Maxim Call would probably say, "if the generators don't work, you won't need the pipes."

Yet the Inventors directed the Apprentices, craftsmen, tinkerers, and assistants who did the real work. Had their minds become so fixed upon discovering how to repair the Generators that they'd lost focus? "Blitz, send word to Inventor Call. I'd like to speak with him."

"Be happy to."

The Clubbs — true to their word — had sponsored several editorials asking why the District Attorney persecuted a woman on such flimsy evidence. "Who analyzed the handwriting on these documents? Can we trust him any more than we trusted the so-called 'Doctor' who certified those 'miracle gems'?"

"Oh, that's a good one," I said.

The *Golden Bridges* held a great deal of speculation as to why the trial hadn't begun. Rumors I'd fled the city, rumors that they'd secretly hung me without a trial. A group marched on City Hall in protest of the latter, to be met by Bridgers, protesting that crime families should be running the city at all.

"Was Jack really captured in the quadrant?" I never dared to ask Jon about it.

Blitz chuckled, a wry grin on his face. "I was with Sawbuck when he learned the scoundrel wished to enter. We let Master Diamond in, then followed to lay in wait. I felt surprised by how fast the neighbors converged."

"I warned them about him. Was he badly hurt?"

"Nah," Blitz said. "Just fists and boots. We took him before they went for bricks and pipes."

I almost felt sorry for the man. Clearly Jack was mad to enter the quadrant again, especially after Tony threatened formal protest for his harassment of our merchants the first time.

Blitz said, "His father was not at all happy, I'll say that."

Mary laughed, as did Amelia, who had come for the plates.

I said, "I know the woman who owns the shop. Do you think they'll let me go to her? She must have been terrified."

"Not a chance," Blitz said. "But they might let her come here."

"Look into it."

Blitz said, "What do you want to do for Midsummer?"

I felt melancholy. That was a holiday, but it was also Tony's 23rd birthday. I doubted this Midsummer would be very happy for anyone. "Whatever you want is fine."

Blitz sobered, no doubt realizing the same. "My apologies."

I rose. "Thank you. All of you. For everything."

I returned to my room and lit a cigarette. I sat at my tea-table smoking, desperately craving a drink. I always drank sitting here.

Amelia sat in the kitchen polishing the silver, springing to her feet to curtsy when I entered. I got a glass of water, returned to my room, and sipped the water, wishing it were wine. The thought of drinking bourbon made me more than a little ill.

A few moments later, Amelia came in with a tray holding a water carafe, some empty glasses, and another glass filled with tan liquid. "Your tonic, mum. The doctor said once a day."

It was bitter, which seemed fitting. I'd ruined my poor liver as badly as I had my life. "For how long, once a day?"

"I don't know, mum, you'll have to ask him."

After luncheon, Amelia gave me a tour of my apartments. Amelia and Mary had straightened my rooms, then cleaned and organized everything. "The auctioneer and banker are hired," Amelia said. "We have furniture, awnings, a tent, and workers. It took some time to find ones who didn't want money up front."

The ball dresses hung in one room, the street dresses in another. Amelia and I stood in front of rows of walking dresses.

Gods, I thought, how is it I have so many things?

I had Amelia save aside four outfits for court, three dresses to wear inside, and my brown widow's outfit I only wore on cases. I could only hope that someday, if I survived this, I might work cases again.

"The Spadros men said they'd build a place for the uppers to sit," Amelia said, "and secure food carts for the crowds."

"What about those who live here?"

"Mary went round already and told them of it. All on this block get to see your things for free, before the crowds do. Mr. Monarch thought that'd make them feel better about all that's gone on."

It sounded good. But I wondered if it would be enough.

In the large room upstairs, the lighter items such as hats and jewels lay displayed on tables and shelving. Everything had been tagged, categorized, and put in the order the auctioneer wanted it. I felt impressed. "You've done very well."

Amelia smiled. "Mary's been a big help, mum. She's done a lot of this when Mr. Blitz sleeps during the day." She giggled. "Never thought we'd have two lovebirds here."

I chuckled. "It **is** amusing."

"Oh, mum, that reminds me. Do you want to sell the cage?"

I stood considering for a long moment, then nodded.

"Very well, mum. I'll have Mr. Blitz move it up here."

Then she pointed at the jewelry. "A Mr. Roman contacted me when he heard of the auction, asking for 'the honor of evaluating the gems.'" She grinned knowingly. "He said it just like that. I don't think he wanted anyone to devalue the things he'd made."

"So they'll let us hold the auction here?"

"I spoke with Mr. Roy's men." She peered at her hands.

My Family fees for May. "Who paid them? I must reimburse."

She didn't look at me. "There's no need for that."

"Nonsense." I strode down to my room, returned, thrust the thirty-three cents into her hand. "In this home, you're no servant to be exploited for my benefit." At Spadros Manor, they would've taken the money without considering how it impoverished her. "You're a free woman. You deserve to be treated as such."

Where did she get the money in the first place? "You're paid for informing on me, aren't you?"

Her head drooped. "Yes, mum."

"Take every cent. Maybe we can find some benefit in all this."

"Mum," Amelia said soberly. "Something you'll want to see."

She took me out front and to the right, to the small patch of ground beside the stair. Hoots and whistles rose from the barricades as we emerged. A flat gray stone the size of a dinner plate lay on the ground. "We put your bird here."

I crouched down, heart clenching, to lay one hand upon the smooth cool surface, the other upon the rough wall before me.

I only wanted you to be free.

I struggled to hold back the tears, unwilling to cry in front of those men. "Thank you, Amelia."

Amelia turned to face the street.

How I wished I'd never let my bird go the night I left! If not for that, it might be alive and happy still.

Was leaving Spadros Manor a mistake?

No. I was no tame bird, born to live my life in a cage.

If only there had been some other way.

The Father

I went to bed early, tired by the long day, and slept late. I had no schedule, no one to call on, and I liked it. Looking back, I think my body was still healing from what I'd done to myself.

The noise outside my window rose and fell all day as people moved around behind the barricades. It was almost tea-time when the noise rose significantly. At first I saw nothing, but then several sorrel horses appeared, ridden by men in red and silver livery, followed by Charles Hart's red and silver carriage.

Dismayed, I rushed to the parlor. "Blitz! Mary! Amelia! Come here this instant!"

Amelia came out of the kitchen. "Mum, what's wrong?"

"Mr. Charles Hart is here."

She dashed towards Blitz and Mary's rooms. A few minutes later, Blitz hurried up, putting his jacket on as the doorbell rang. I glanced back to see Mary duck into the back entry to the kitchen, her hair flowing about her shoulders.

"Blitz," I whispered, pointing at his fly.

His face turned horrified, then crimson as he zipped.

The doorbell rang.

Blitz took a deep breath, let it out, then opened the door as if he did this all the time. "Good evening, sir. Welcome."

Mr. Charles Hart was accompanied by several men who resembled him in some way, although much younger. Many came in past him to scrutinize the quarters.

Mr. Hart took off his top hat and handed it to one of his men. Then he moved a step inside, perhaps unwilling to stand in plain view of the street. When his men returned, nodding, he said, "I hope it wasn't too rude of me to visit for tea."

"Of course not, sir," I said. "Please come in."

Mr. Hart sat on the parlor sofa. Blitz stood by, as Pearson had so many times back at Spadros Manor. Amelia brought tea. Mary (her hair in a proper bun now) brought sandwiches and small cakes, then all three of my "servants" retreated.

Mr. Hart's men vanished to various corners of the house, presumably watching out of the windows for attackers.

It was what I'd be doing. In light of Roy's hatred for the man, I fully expected a bomb to be tossed in the window the entire time.

We sat eating and drinking in silence, then I ventured, "To what do I owe this tremendous honor?"

Mr. Hart gave me a gentle smile, so unlike his fearsome reputation. "I wished to see you."

"I'm astonished to see you here." A black-haired man dressed in street clothes walked past, his eyes very much like Mr. Hart's. A cousin? "You're a Patriarch, the father of an Inventor." I felt awed, yet uneasy. "Who am I, sir, that you should risk your life and the lives of these men simply to have tea with me? I don't deserve such honor. Nor do I want such responsibility."

He shrugged. "Perhaps things are changing. In any case, the responsibility's all mine. Perhaps I'm a fool: I put you in as much danger as any of us." He set his cup and plate down, gazing into my eyes, and spoke earnestly. "But I had to see you, Jacqui."

For a stranger to address me by my first name was the height of familiarity. I shrank back, disturbed. "Mr. Hart —"

He shook his head. "I don't know what Roy Spadros told you, but I've never meant you harm." Both his eyes and voice held an intimate passion I didn't expect. "I've held you in nothing but the most tender regard from moment I first lay eyes upon you. I —"

"Sir. Please. Stop." I rose, yet he sat, although he should have by rights risen the moment I did. Agitated, I began to pace. "Yes, I've left my husband's home, for reasons I won't share with you. But I'm a married woman, sir. You're a married man. A father. A grandfather! It's not only unseemly, but ..." I recalled Jon's words, "a betrayal of my husband, who you called friend and brought under your roof, for you to speak to me so." Since he didn't have the courtesy to rise, I returned to my seat. "I'm grateful for your regard, sir, I truly am, but I will not become your mistress."

Mr. Hart gaped at me. "What has Roy Spadros **done** to you?" He turned away; when he glanced at me again, his eyes were red. "Now I understand why he's allowed our meeting today." He shook his head slowly, his downcast face stunned, disbelieving. Then he faced me, voice full of emotion. "I deeply apologize, Mrs. Spadros. I was wrong to speak so, or to cause you discomfort, particularly at such a time. Please forget I said anything." He rose, not looking at me. "Forget I ever came here." He took a few steps away, calling to his men in a language I didn't understand.

Compassion swept over me. *He must feel humiliated.* I put a hand on Mr. Hart's arm. "It wouldn't offend me to be your friend. If that be acceptable."

But at that, he smiled, and it was a real smile. "It would be an honor, madam." He kissed my hand quickly, as a gentleman should with a woman married. "Thank you for your hospitality."

The man had more depth to him than I'd thought.

Blitz came out of the kitchen to stand beside me as the carriage moved away. "What did he want?"

What **did** he want? I had the feeling when we spoke that our words somehow missed each other. "I thought I knew, but now, I'm not entirely sure."

The four of us brought the plates to the kitchen.

I said, "What language did Mr. Hart speak to his men?"

"Mandarin," Blitz said. "It's the language of his people."

I nodded. Like Tony's people spoke Italian. "This Mandarin sounds like nothing I've ever heard before."

"Fiendishly difficult," Blitz said. "In fifty years marriage, not even his wife has mastered it. We've tried to learn it over the years, to infiltrate, you know, but only a few have had the knack."

I laughed. "Is that all you men want? To best each other?"

Mary and Amelia smiled to themselves.

Blitz gave me a flippant grin. "What else is there?" But then he sobered. "Of course not. But we live in Bridges, Mrs. Spadros. If you don't gain territory, you lose it. If you're not careful, you'll die full of lead in an alley. This is no game."

I returned to my tea-table by the window, puzzled. I'd thought Mrs. Hart would know her own husband's language. "Blitz?"

He opened the door. "You need something?"

"Come sit with me."

He chuckled, taking a few steps in, yet left the door open. "Amelia told me about your Pot ways. You want me to sit, in full view of the street? You'll be the scandal of the quadrant."

"Stop this nonsense and sit down," I said. "Pull the drapes if it makes you feel better. What does it mean to sit at the table anyway? Pearson and Jane used to sit with me without such fuss."

"Mr. Pearson told me you insisted on it for so long they feared causing offense by continuing to refuse." Blitz didn't pull the drapes; instead, he pulled his chair out a foot from the table then sat. "Generally, servants don't sit at table with their betters."

At this, I felt sad. "Yet you're Tony's cousin!"

Blitz grinned, leaning his chair back. "A distant one, with many an ancestor from 'under the table.'" He rocked on the chair's back two legs. "The great and powerful Vincenzo Spadros was my forebear. He never married, yet the man loved women both high and low. Mr. Anthony has distant cousins to spare."

"How did they manage not to be sent to the Pot?"

Blitz let out a short laugh. "No one cares who fathered a slum boy, Mrs. Spadros. When the rule-marms come by, you can always find someone to take credit."

Just so. "What do you know of Mrs. Judith Hart?"

Blitz stopped his rocking. "Ah. Now that's one to keep an eye on. What would you like to know?"

"You said she doesn't speak Mr. Hart's tongue. It seemed odd." About as odd as Tony never even trying to teach me Italian, although I thought I understood that. I was from the Pot, never to be trusted with the Spadros Family's real secrets. Yet Judith Hart didn't look like any of the Families, other than the red in her silver hair. "What Family is she from?"

Blitz shook his head. "She wasn't in a Family. She was born on Market Center. The Bridgers' Grand Master is her father."

"The Bridgers' Grand Master? Her **father**?" This was an entire surprise. "The man must be ancient."

Blitz nodded. "Nigh close to a hundred, and as fiery as ever."

I recalled what Doyle Pike's granddaughter-in-law Gertie said:

"Ugly women are doomed to live at home as a burden to their fathers, or sent off to try to join the Dealers. But in the Bridgers, it's the pretty girls have the most trouble. All the men want them, yet none are allowed to pay them court. Most pretty ones run off."

Even at seventy, Judith Hart was still handsome. As a young woman she was probably quite pretty. "What else do you know about her?"

Blitz shrugged. "Only the obvious."

I frowned. "What?"

"One child in fifty years' marriage. And in public, they barely tolerate each other." He glanced away. "The rumors are Mr. Charles Hart has a great deal in common with my forebear, if you take my meaning."

Ah. A philanderer.

Though Mrs. Judith Hart refused to acknowledge my existence, for an instant I pitied her. She must be well aware of Mr. Hart's feelings for me, the latest in a long line of women.

"So young Judith left the Bridgers with young Charles, and when she was found with child ...." I smiled to myself. "A young man might find it difficult to risk the Bridgers' Grand Master's wrath, whether he was in love with said young woman or not."

Blitz grinned. "That was what, ten years after the Party Time Prohibition Act? Bridgers were attacking Party Time dens with axes. A lot of pressure to marry the girl and shut the game down."

I considered Tony, pressured by Roy to marry me. I wasn't angry that he'd rather have married Gardena, or even that they'd had a son together. What really hurt was that he hid it from me. That he lied. That he never trusted me with his child.

Blitz said, "Mr. Anthony will be well. We'll see to that."

"I don't hate him, you know. Not really. It's just that —"

"You don't love him. You don't even need him. Everyone saw it but him." He rose. "I best get back to work."

He winked at me; recalling what he'd been up to, I laughed.

The Stunt

After all the excitement, I slept like the bird outside my window, waking later than I hoped. My carriage pulled up to the offices of Pike and Associates as the clock chimed half past ten.

"You're late," Doyle Pike said. "I trust you'll be punctual next time. We have much to discuss." He gestured to a chair on the other side of his desk. "I hope you're feeling well?"

"Indeed."

"Your little stunt might be useful after all."

I raised an eyebrow. "Stunt, sir?"

"Trying to drink yourself to death. You haven't told me everything, Mrs. Spadros, and I don't appreciate that."

"What would you like to know?"

"**Everything** about your relationship with Dame Anastasia. When you learned of her scam. Why you of all people were acting as her agent, and why you came to me for help. Why you left your husband, and why you tried to kill yourself. And those damnable letters! Why did you never tell me of the forgeries?"

"Sir, that was all over the papers."

"What do I care about the papers? I wasn't foolish enough to waste money on speculation, so I knew nothing of it. Until that blasted fool Freezout stood gloating about his letter collection."

Oh, dear. I suppose it wouldn't do to embarrass your lawyer. He would've been completely in his rights to demand payment up front. "Where should I begin?"

"At the beginning. But we have until half past noon. I will not delay my schedule for you or anyone else."

I let out a laugh. So the man liked his luncheon, did he? "Very well." I told him I met Anastasia Dame Louis at my engagement party to a man I didn't love. "Roy Spadros held a gun to my head and told me if I let my husband know of this I would die."

Pike leaned back, hand to his chin. "Which makes it interesting that he's forbidden his men to kill you now."

He knew about this but not my letters?

He waved it off. "My grandson Thrace has become obsessed with Family matters. Continue."

So I told him about the job Anastasia gave me, and how I learned of her scam. I also told him of my relationship with Joseph Kerr — which discomfited me no end — and how we planned to leave together. And how Tony caught us and I escaped, ending up at the zeppelin station alone.

"So you were brought to Clubb Hotel."

"Regina Clubb wanted me to betray my people to leave the city, which I refused. But she said she'd help me during the trial."

"In exchange for?"

"Not any of your business. Sir."

"It is if you want me to continue to help you."

The man was infuriating. "She wanted Gardena Diamond to see her son Lance. Gardena wouldn't see him. Mrs. Clubb wanted me to intercede on her son's behalf. That's all."

He chuckled. "You're right, that wasn't my business. So the Diamonds and Clubbs want to ally. Very interesting. Especially in light of the recent unpleasantness with young Master Jack." His eyes narrowed. "Yet you're friends with his sister. And his twin. And you're under Clubb protection, yet living in Spadros. You, of all people." He cackled, then leaned forward, resting his elbows on his desk. "We may need an untangler to sort this one out!"

What did he mean, **me** of all people? Such an odd man. "I thought you didn't read the news."

"Just not the details of an inquest which didn't concern me."

How had this **not** concerned him? "Yet not two months ago, you proceeded to blackmail me regarding your testimony in it."

He chuckled. "I had to have some way of getting the money you owed me." He leaned forward. "Did you know about Dame

Anastasia's scam when you came to see me?"

"No, I thought I was doing her some small assistance by sending letters to her debtors. I never imagined all this would happen." I felt weary. "Well, sir, I've done what you asked. The auction is this Saturday, and you're welcome to attend."

He gave his alligator grin. "Wonderful! We should get a rousing crowd. Where's it taking place?"

"Right outside my apartments." I gave him the address.

"I wouldn't miss it for the world."

* * *

Blitz opened the door with a flourish, wearing a black suit. He did a fair imitation of Pearson. "Good afternoon, Mrs. Spadros."

I laughed. "You're making a most proper butler."

He slouched against the door-frame and lit a cigarette. "Thank Mr. Pearson for that. He about talked my ear off with unsolicited advice." He followed me to my room once he closed the door.

I said, "I'm to return to Mr. Pike at half past ten on the 23rd, with a hearing the same day at the Courthouse at two. Would you arrange luncheon on Market Center?"

"Of course."

"And see if Master Jonathan Diamond may join me."

Blitz raised an eyebrow, but said only, "Very well."

I felt a twinge of regret. "Master Jonathan is our closest friend, Blitz. He means only the best for my husband and I."

He nodded. "Let me arrange these then."

"Blitz, how are we paying for all this?"

His eyes flickered to the side. "The Court gives you a daily allowance for food and essentials."

Which the quadrant was paying. But there was something he wasn't saying. "And?"

"And of course, you have your account at the bank."

There couldn't be much in that. "And?"

"And Mr. Anthony is obligated by law to pay for whatever else you might need."

"But? I know there's something you're not saying."

His shoulders dropped. "None of us want that, Mrs. Spadros, if we can do without." He glanced away. Taking Family money came at a price. "Mary and I have some saved. We'll make do."

I shook my head. "You keep tally of every cent! I mean it."

He chuckled. "Very well."

"Thank you."

That stopped him. "Why do you thank us?"

"Because you do a great deal for me. It would be rude and ungrateful not to." For an instant, I felt angry, but I pushed that aside. "I don't understand why the quadrant-folk treat you so poorly. Their horses are cared for better."

His eyes fell. "They say some are born high cards, some low." He shrugged, still not looking at me. "Thanks."

Blitz went off, and I sat with a cigarette, pondering his words. How could our peoples be so different after just a hundred years?

The *Bridges Daily* sat on my tea-table. The only item of interest was a full-column article describing Mrs. Regina Clubb's plans to attend the auction.

Well played, Mrs. Clubb!

Mrs. Molly Spadros wouldn't attend: she'd be a prime target for the rogues. Mrs. Judith Hart hated me. Mrs. Helen Hart, from all accounts, lay on her deathbed. Mrs. Rachel Diamond — who everyone thought dreadfully ill — would only attend if Gardena was allowed to bring her, which given the current climate between Spadros and Diamond, was doubtful.

Mrs. Regina Clubb could have quietly shown up, veiled, without telling anyone, and no one would be the wiser. But commissioning an entire article in the news declaring that she planned to attend? Now my auction was a notable social event! All the uppers in the city would rush to attend, for fear of missing the spectacle.

I wondered if Mr. Pike read the news that day. I imagined he'd be just as amused by this stunt as I was.

The Choices

Early the next day, Mr. Roman, a heavy-set olive-skinned man, examined my jewelry, affixing a certificate of authenticity and a minimum price to each. "A pity you had Dame Anastasia's necklace cut up, now that I consider it. It would have fetched a good price from the notoriety alone. But the rest of these are in as good a condition as when I made them."

"Wait," I said. "Isn't this moonstone hers?"

"No," he said. "I persuaded your husband to buy mine instead. It's as real as anything else you have here."

Tony's face as he placed the moonstone around my neck appeared before me. I pushed the memory away. He'd bought it to help me bear an heir, never knowing of my morning tea.

I couldn't allow myself to feel anything for him; it made things too difficult. "Do you believe the stories? About the moonstone."

He shrugged, picking up a bracelet. "I've worked with gems my entire life, Mrs. Spadros, and I've never found any particular benefit to them. Other than adornment, of course."

After Mr. Roman left, I decided to give the necklace to Mary.

She hesitated to take it. "This is too great a gift, mum."

"Do you and Blitz want children?"

"Of course, mum."

"This is said to help. It's real, not one of Dame Anastasia's copies." I handed it to her. "Wear it close to your heart. I wasn't able to be at your wedding, but I can give you a bride gift."

Her eyes filled with tears. "We're so grateful for your kindness, mum." She kissed the gemstone. "I'll treasure it always."

Suddenly, sawing and hammering came from across the street. Mary spoke from behind, her words almost drowned out by the noise. "The stands for the uppers, mum. I'd almost forgotten."

"I suppose this is to be expected. Our neighbors must hate us."

Mary said, "We'll find some way to make it up to them."

Hammering and sawing went on for many hours, stopping only at luncheon and tea-time. By dusk, the men had completed the stands, a set of stairs on each side.

The racket began again at dawn. As the day progressed, a low platform stretched across the remainder of the narrow street, with steps leading down both behind and in front on both ends. Once that was completed, the men began furiously sanding all that they'd done so far.

The barricades to my right had been moved another twenty yards to the end of the street, then reinforced with a thick wooden fence and gates which locked. Police checked the identifications of anyone who wished to enter, escorting them to their doors.

A tent pavilion ten yards long and five wide stood across the street towards the right barricade. Two men carried in a full-length mirror, others a carpet, which they unrolled inside.

This area would be for uppers to try on dresses or jewelry before bidding. A fifty-cent deposit was required to try on each item, which would be refunded should the lady win the item.

I'd invited everyone involved to tea so we might discuss the plan for the auction. The auctioneer, Benjamin Tops, and Gertie Pike, who'd be doing the book-keeping, arrived at the same time.

Gertie was an unattractive woman of twenty with lank blonde hair, who wore the same gray dress she always wore in public. Fortunately for her, the heavy material hid her four months' pregnancy: she merely looked stout, rather than scandalous.

Mr. Tops was a big blond man with a fine voice and graying mutton-chop sideburns. He shook my hand firmly, as if I were a gentleman. "An honor to meet you, Mrs. Spadros." He glanced around. "Is your husband not attending?"

"He had a prior engagement. But this is my property, and I have full permission from Mr. Spadros to sell it."

Mr. Tops gave me a smarmy grin, speaking a little too

enthusiastically. "I understand completely!"

"Please, sit, all of you," I said. Men were shouting, sanding, and hammering outside. "I hope you'll excuse the noise."

Right then, the noise stopped.

Everyone laughed, sitting around the low coffee table. Mary and Amelia brought in tea, sandwiches, and small pastries, then I began to pour as everyone took what they wanted.

Blitz, dressed in butler best, stood before us. "Viewing is from ten until four tomorrow, the auction at the same times the day after. Mrs. Dewey," he pointed to Amelia, "will take charge of the viewing. One maid per rack will show items to each group. These items are not to be touched except by those providing a deposit.

"Mr. Monarch has provided men to take viewing fees — a penny a person — and to stand overnight for security. He'll have locking canvas drapes to guard the racks from dampness.

"We have five locking money-bags, with boys hired to run them to the banker as they fill. Only the banker has the keys."

Mr. Tops said, "Will he be arriving shortly?"

"Our banker had a prior engagement," Blitz said. "He'll be here tomorrow with his guards. Once the money-bag arrives, Mrs. Pike will count and record, then the banker will verify amounts as he puts the money into the lock-box."

Mr. Tops gave Gertie a quick once-over; the smarmy smile returned. "Good idea."

Gertie stiffened, narrowing her eyes with a slight frown.

"On auction day: once a winner is declared, Mr. Tops will direct his man to bring the item and the customer to the payment table. Mrs. Pike will record the buyer's name, the item's name, and the amount, then write a receipt. Payment will be verified and stored by the banker. The item will be packaged and given to the customer or taken to their carriage." He gestured at Mary. "Mrs. Mary Spadros will take charge of packaging, transporting, and securing items which need to be held to the end of the auction. A guard and messenger will assist her. Afterward, the final monies will be tallied, and everyone paid. Any questions?"

I raised my hand. "What am I to do?"

"Nothing," Blitz said. "I'll stand here with you as your butler, and assist directly out front if needed. But the Court allowed this auction with the understanding that you would neither leave the building nor show yourself to the crowd."

I felt crestfallen: I wanted to watch the auction!

"You'll be able to watch from upstairs, mum," Mary said. "Just don't go to the window, and you'll be fine."

The sound of men moving about outside resumed. I said, "Would anyone like more tea?"

"I think we're done here," Mr. Tops said, rising.

"I'll see you out," Blitz said, and the two went off.

Gertie Pike took another small sandwich and a cup of tea.

Blitz returned with Jonathan Diamond.

"I thought I'd see how you fared," Jon said.

I rose, offering my hand for him to kiss. "Master Jonathan Diamond, may I present Mrs. Gertie Pike."

Gertie rose, and Jonathan offered his hand, which she shook and resumed her seat.

Jon stood there, his face perplexed.

I said, "Would you care for tea?"

"No, thank you. But I'd be glad to sit with you." Jon sat, then turned to Gertie. "How are you acquainted?"

"Mr. Doyle Pike is my husband's grandfather."

"That's excellent," Jon said. "Mr. Pike has a fine record in large cases such as this one."

Gertie pressed her lips together, crossing her arms.

I said, "Would you like to tour the racks, Mrs. Pike? When you're done, of course."

"Why-ever would I want to view your clothing?"

I shrugged. "Many will be out front tomorrow to do just that. I thought to give you first view."

Her face turned skeptical. "I'm not sure why you sell them."

I felt sure she'd been told. "I have things I no longer need, and I wished to benefit the poor."

"Really," Gertie said flatly. "What's your interest in the poor?"

Jon said, "Mrs. Pike, is something amiss?"

"I'm perfectly well," she said. "But I find a woman with such wealth wishing to rid herself of it so quickly odd in the extreme."

I smiled. Envy did not become her. "Have you never wanted to make a new life, Mrs. Pike?"

"I did," she said sharply, "when I married my husband and had his children in his home."

Her intent was plain. But I needed her help, so I said, "Then perhaps you understand I might wish to benefit others as well."

Jon said, "Would you like an escort to the taxi-station, Mrs. Pike? Mrs. Spadros is recently ill, and needs her rest."

Gertie put down her cup and rose. "I would appreciate that, sir." She turned to me. "Good evening."

I rose also. "Shall I see you on auction day?"

She hesitated. "You shall." Then she and Jonathan left.

Mary stormed in with a large tray. "The nerve of that woman!" She began filling the tray with dirty plates and cups.

I laughed. "You listened. Shame on you."

"She has no right to speak of what she knows nothing about. She best watch her tongue on auction day, or I'll have it out!"

I remembered the poor tongueless servants at the cottage, and I felt a sudden melancholy. "Don't say such things, Mary."

Her head drooped. "I'm sorry, mum."

I never expected such ferocity. Perhaps this tabby was a secret lioness. "I feel grateful for your support." I went to the door and peered out front. To my surprise, Jonathan Diamond and Gertie Pike faced each other in the late afternoon's glare, arguing in whispers, fingers pointed! I said, "Whatever are you two doing?"

Gertie flushed crimson. "Nothing, mum. I was just leaving." She hurried away, leaving Jonathan to gape at her.

The men had hammered a black skirt round the platform and the edges of the stands, and were painting the exposed wood a dark green. "Come inside, Master Diamond. Leave her be."

Jon pushed in past me. "The woman is incorrigible."

I shut the door, amused. "Oh?"

"Opinionated, rude, and altogether too harsh." Jon stopped, took a deep breath. "How did the meeting go?"

"It went well. Would you like to see everything?"

Jon laughed. "In this, I agree with Mrs. Pike: browsing rooms of ladies' clothing is not my idea of entertainment."

"Very well, then. No tea, no last view of my worldly goods before they're gone forever. What would you like to do, then?"

"Let's sit upstairs for a bit."

So we went upstairs, where a table and chairs had been set, I suppose, for me to watch the auction. Jon ignored the hats and jewelry and plopped himself down.

The sun blazed off to the left, a red ball low in the sky. The rooftops stretched as far as one might see, and in the far distance, a hint of Market Center. I sat beside him. "Would you like to visit for Midsummer? We can see the fireworks from here."

"Alas, I must attend the spectacle in person. My father would be annoyed if I missed it, especially if I were here instead." He put his hand on mine. "But your invitation pleases me."

Jon leaned back, gazing out of the window as we watched the sun set, his hand touching mine. A twinge of grief regret heartache, then that day, for the first time, out of all the choices, I chose peace. In the end, I believe that's what saved me.

The clock struck six. Jon kissed my hand. "I must go. We have guests tonight, and I dare not be late for dinner."

I stood, taking his arm. "And who might these fine guests be?"

Jon looked at me sideways, and at that instant, he reminded me of his sister Gardena. "You know I can't say. But it will at least not be boring." He chuckled as we descended the stairs.

We went to the door, where Blitz stood with Jon's top hat.

I straightened Jon's cravat. "Well, my dear, enjoy your not-boring dinner."

Jon beamed, stepping back to give me an extravagant bow. "Until we next meet."

I laughed. "Go on, before you're late."

He took his top hat from Blitz, chuckling as he bounced down the steps and to the right, where I imagined his carriage waited beyond the barricade.

Blitz stood gaping. "I've not seen him do that in — well, ever."

I leaned against the door frame. "Neither have I."

* * *

Before the sun had risen fully, a knock came at the door; Mary answered. A woman spoke to her.

I leapt from my bed, rushing to the door without a robe. "Eleanora? Please, come in."

Eleanora Bryce, a brown-haired woman of middle age wearing widow's brown, entered quickly, glancing behind her. "I'm grateful your man brought me."

"Mary, this is Mrs. Eleanora Bryce."

Mary curtsied low. "A pleasure, mum."

I escorted Eleanora to my room, putting on a robe. Mary brought in tea. Then we sat at my tea-table.

"I'm sorry it took so long to visit," Eleanora said. "Since that Diamond man came, people have been afraid to stay at my home. But David's safe. I'm here as long as you need me."

That was a relief. "Has David's condition changed at all?"

"Well, mum, I didn't want him to know you were still in Bridges. He got very quiet when he first heard — for a whole day, he didn't rock at all! He didn't speak; it seemed he was deep in thought. Then he heard about the trial and how they mean to hang you, and it upset him no end. He cried for hours. Now he just lays in bed staring, except when he hears a noise outside. Then he jumps at the sound, and rocks again for a long time, just like he used to." She sighed. "I don't know if this is good or bad."

"I think it's good. He's taking notice of the world outside."

"You think so?" Tears came to her eyes, and I took her hand.

David was all she had left. Her oldest son Nicholas (we children called him Air), my best friend as a child, was murdered in front of me when I was twelve. For a long time, Eleanora blamed me for his death. His sixteen-year-old brother Herbert was killed in January by the Bridges Strangler.

How did she bear it?

"I think he will," I said. "The doctor said so, and I trust his judgment." We sat silent for a moment, then I said, "Tell me of the man who came. I'm astonished he would have the temerity to return to your home after all he's done!"

Eleanora peered at me. "It wasn't him, mum."

I felt so shocked that for an instant, I couldn't speak. "**What**?"

"He was **dressed** like the man who came to see us before David was taken: dark skin, wearing all white, his head shaven. But this man was taller, more slender. And much younger — why, not much older than you. He cried out as the men beat him, asking why I told people he took my son."

I sat there so astonished I wondered if I were in a dream. "You're **sure** this was a different man?"

"Yes, mum. He came in courteous as you please, and inquired as to my son's health. He wanted to learn the truth of David's taking, and was confused when the men attacked." Her face turned disapproving. "Not at all like the other man. That man was at least forty, and he came to make mischief. When the men threw bricks at him, he knew why. He just wanted to escape."

Someone else took David.

It wasn't Jack Diamond.

How could it **not** be Jack Diamond? "Are you **certain**?"

Eleanora said, "I swear on the Cards." She made the sign of the Board, crossing her arms to clasp her shoulders. "May mine be burnt for a lie."

Jack Diamond didn't take David.

Could the Red Dogs be trying to frame him, too?

I sat stunned at the revelation while Mrs. Bryce drank her tea. Then I truly looked at her.

She'd always been quite pale. And grief had taken its toll on her, even in the few months since David's kidnapping. But today she seemed almost happy. "You look well."

Mrs. Bryce smiled. "I am." After a moment, she said, "I never thanked you properly for the money you gave me."

It was less than a dollar, and she'd thanked me once already, but I kept silent.

"It may not seem like much, mum, but I got new cloth, and paid my bills and fees. And I was able to send a letter." At this, she beamed. "And he answered!"

"Who answered?"

This sent her into an outpouring of story about her dead husband and the terrible things he'd done. Several men in Dickens harassed her after he died, yet another helped when all seemed lost. "He's been trying to find me. He wants to come here." Her eyes filled with tears. "He's coming here!"

"Oh! That sounds good!" I smiled, sobered by the look in her eyes. "You love him."

Her cheeks colored. "I do. And I think he loves me. That some good might come from all this seems too much to hope for."

I considered this. "He's coming here; that's got to be good. Did you tell David?"

"I didn't want to get his hopes up. Besides, he barely knows the man." She pondered this. "No, I'll wait until he's here. Until he tells me of his intentions. Until I'm sure."

"That sounds wise." I was reminded of how Roland asked for Lance, who it seemed Roland already loved. If Gardena decided to end her courtship with Lance, it would break the boy's heart.

David Bryce had gone through enough for one lifetime already.

Eleanora set her cup down. "Now what can I help with?"

"You and my maid Amelia can oversee the viewing."

Eleanora nodded slowly. "How is it to be run?"

"Amelia has it planned out, never fear."

At that moment, the side door opened and shut. Amelia came to the open doorway wearing her maid's uniform. "Mum, you need to —" She stopped when she saw Eleanora and curtsied. "My pardons, mum, I didn't know you had a visitor."

I rose, as did Mrs. Bryce. "Mrs. Eleanora Bryce, may I present my lady's maid, Mrs. Amelia Dewey."

Amelia curtsied low.

"Mrs. Bryce is here to help you with the viewing."

Amelia peered warily at Eleanora, then back at me. "I'm sorry, mum, you wish me to direct — her?"

Oh, dear. Eleanora, though she lived on the worst street in Spadros quadrant, was a merchant, and of much higher standing.

Eleanora smiled, taking Amelia's hand. "My dear Mrs. Dewey. You know best what Mrs. Spadros wants. Let's discuss how to proceed in the parlor, so our Lady can prepare herself."

With a stunned backwards glance, Amelia let herself be led out. Good thing I knew how to run my own bath.

Since I wasn't allowed out, getting ready was merely a matter of quickly bathing, putting on a house dress, and fixing my hair.

A bit later, Amelia knocked. "Mum, do you need anything?" Her eyebrows rose when she saw me. "You're making excellent progress, mum! Would you like some breakfast? I know it's early yet, but the men will be here soon."

Eleanora and I had just set down to eat when the bell rang. Men began moving racks to the street, and Amelia hurried out to direct their placement.

"Mum," Mrs. Bryce said, "may I ask why you sell everything?"

The way she said it moved me as Gertie's sarcasm could not. But I couldn't break down, not now. "I left my husband, and I'm in terrible debt. I may never wear any of this again." I shrugged, discouraged. "He wants nothing of me in his house, so —"

"I'm so sorry, mum." She reached across the table to take my hand. "If I can do anything to help, I will."

A rack went by out in the hallway, and I called out, "Stop!"

I rushed over to them. My red dress of crushed taffeta I wore the night Tony was attacked, the dress which Tony liked so well. My forest green gown that I wore at the Grand Ball this year. The matching coat, my favorite, beaded and trimmed in black. These things held memory. How could I let them go?

"Not these yet," I said. "Put them aside."

The men draped them on a chair in the parlor. I returned to my seat. "This is more difficult than I thought."

Mary came in. "Things will get better, mum. You'll see."

I smiled at her. "Mrs. Eleanora Bryce, may I present my housekeeper, Mrs. Mary Spadros."

Eleanora's eyes went wide. "Such a lovely girl!" She held out her hand. "A pleasure to meet you."

Mary curtsied. "And you, mum."

Introductions completed, I finished eating, as everything I had in the world was wheeled out to be sold.

The doorbell rang and after a moment, Blitz came in. "A Miss Tenni Mitchell to see you?"

"Oh! Yes! Please send her in at once."

Tenni was taller than I remembered, and had filled out since I'd seen her last. The days of her being my body double on cases had passed, it seemed. "I'm working at a dress shop down the street from Madame's," she said. "They pay a penny extra a day, since I can take measurements and figure." She beamed. "I can get meat for my sisters on Sundays!"

"I'm so glad. It's good to see you!" I felt an instant of melancholy. "How is Madame?"

Tenni seemed confused. "I hear her shop does well."

Of course. She was just a shop maid, not Madame's confidante. "I'm glad to hear it. Come, now. I'll need you at the fitting booth." I brought her to the parlor window to show her where she was to be stationed. "Would you like some tea before you begin?"

"I'd like that, mum."

"Amelia, get Tenni some tea in the kitchen, please."

I went to the front door, peering out. The barricades had been moved to the end of the street, and guards stood watch. The most valuable of my dresses and all my jewels were set close to the house. I caught a glimpse of my wedding ring.

I couldn't become sentimental, especially when the ring only reminded me of grief.

Blitz said, "Mrs. Spadros, you must stay inside."

I closed the door regretfully. "I know."

I went upstairs, but all I could see was the stands for the uppers. With no curtains on this picture window, they could see me clearly. And with the possible exception of Mrs. Clubb, they would have nothing for me but scorn. So I went downstairs to my room, opened the window, and drew the thin lace curtains closed.

Not much happened at first, but then a line formed outside the fitting booth. One party at a time, they were allowed to enter. Sound ebbed and flowed: most of it past where I could see.

It reminded me of my childhood, waiting for the Cathedral to open. Since I wasn't allowed to take part, I didn't wear the pretty gown of a whore, and I never escorted the men to their booths. Instead, when the Cathedral was open I would run back and forth with messages like a tiny child as the other girls snickered.

But waiting each night, hearing the sound rise and fall — it felt exciting, like something new might happen. Once I grew older, after Ma fell asleep I'd go outside, and Joe would come to me.

Where was Joseph Kerr?

I'd known Joe all my life. If he were alive, he must have some reason for allowing this. Something so vital to his person — or his family — that his only choice was to let me suffer. This I could understand, perhaps even forgive. But even so, it hurt too deeply.

Joseph Kerr had to be dead. And could he possibly have seduced all those women? When would he have had the time?

The day wore on. After luncheon, men set a dark wooden podium on the platform. They placed two sturdy rectangular tables and two awnings behind the platform along my side of the street. Finally, it was over. Children swept the street; maids straightened racks. A man hammered a bit of drape which had come loose; others began to take down the fitting booth.

I went out as canvas covers were put on the racks. I stood in the late afternoon sun, feeling as if I were selling my entire life.

He will not support you once the hope of money is gone.

What did I sell my things for?

Not for Mr. Pike. To be free.

Each thing I sold brought me a step closer to being free of all of them. An independent woman. Perhaps not of means — this would hardly pay what I owed Doyle Pike — but free to choose my way.

I went to my dresses and coat draped over the parlor chair. Yes, these had memory: the red taffeta, of the horrible night Tony was attacked. His pale face. The terrible bruises on his side. The green dress and overcoat reminded me of the Grand Ball, the night I saw Joe again after so long. How miserable I felt!

Eleanora came up to me. "I must return to David."

"I want to put these out as well."

She put her arm round me. "I remember how hard it was to let go. With Nicholas, we had no choice: we had to leave so suddenly. When my husband died, it was an agony. Each piece of clothing, each book. But again, we had no choice: it sell or starve. And the same with Herbert." She sighed. "Be grateful you can choose."

The Auction

The banker, Mr. Myriad, and Mr. Tops arrived at nine the next morning. Mary and Amelia got them tea. "I'll let you know when Mrs. Pike arrives."

"If I'd have known a woman would be doing this, I'd have brought my own accountant," the banker grumbled.

I paced and peered out for an hour, watching for her. I didn't dare hire his accountant — I'd promised to pay too much already.

Doyle Pike arrived with Gertie as the auction began. To everyone's surprise, her baby was with them.

"I had no one to watch her, mum." Gertie and Mr. Pike carried her pram up the steps. Her manner seemed strained, and she made no further attempts to greet us.

"I'll have no more excuses," Mr. Pike snapped. He turned to me. "My apologies, Mrs. Spadros. Best of luck today." As he opened the door, Mr. Tops began his introductions.

Gertie stared at Mr. Pike as he went, face sour.

"Mrs. Pike," I said, "I have the ledger here."

Gertie's baby began to cry.

"I'll take her, mum," Mary said. She went to pick up the baby.

"No," Gertie snapped. "I'll have her with me."

"But Mrs. Pike, you'll be busy —"

Gertie said, "I'll not leave my child with strangers."

Mary and I glanced at each other. Then Mary and Blitz brought her — and the pram — back down the steps to the tables. Mr. Myriad sat there already, his guards beside him, with two heavy lock-boxes on the table. One had slots for cash, the other for coin.

Mary introduced Gertie to him and settled her baby beside her, who continued to wail. Gertie opened the ledger. Then she picked up her child, a babe of seven months, who struggled to win free.

I turned to Amelia. "Keep watch over Mrs. Pike."

"Yes, mum." She went outside.

I retreated to my room to watch the show. The racks had been moved behind the auctioneer's platform and arranged in order, the least valuable items first.

Mr. Tops spoke rapidly. The baby wailed. Amelia cooed to her. Ladies trundled past with carts full of packages.

I felt grateful for the money, but the smugly satisfied looks on their faces made me cringe.

One day I'd be a lady of means, and I'd remember.

Finally, the baby cried itself to sleep, and Amelia came inside.

The auction paused for luncheon. Mrs. Pike ate at her table, not willing to wake the baby by bringing her pram up the stairs again.

I asked Mr. Myriad, "How is it proceeding?"

"Rather well, if not for the howling brat."

"I apologize, sir. Hopefully the baby will sleep."

As if in answer, she began wailing again. "One can only hope," the banker said. "This is why women should keep to their rightful place." He glanced over at me. "No offense, madam."

"None taken." I wasn't any happier with the situation. I wouldn't have minded the baby if Mrs. Pike were in better humor.

Amelia spread a thick bed-cover on the ground; the baby, finally happy, crawled around on it. Yet this seemed to distract Gertie even more, and a line formed beside her station.

"If I weren't forbidden to show myself I could take this over," I groused. "But she won't let anyone else do the work." Mary was busy with the packages, Amelia entertaining the baby.

Blitz had offered and been rebuffed. "I'll go out again," he said.

"Tell her she must choose her work or her child."

Blitz snorted. "I doubt saying **that** would play out well." He left, closing the front door behind him.

I moved to my rooms, peering out. Blitz leaned over, speaking in Gertie's ear. She retorted angrily, then he spoke again. She slumped a bit, then nodded.

Amelia brought a chair and sat beside the baby, who at this point was the happiest of them all.

When Blitz returned, I asked, "Whatever did you say?"

He grinned. "I reminded Mrs. Pike that Mrs. Dewey has three children of her own and can well handle a babe at its mother's feet. Also, that her husband's grandfather was watching."

Ah. "She did seem to be here coerced."

"Indeed. One might hope things will improve."

And so they did. The items were sold, the people left content. Men began taking down the platform. Gertie tallied the amounts, the banker checked them. A line formed of those to be paid: the workers, the merchant who sold us the packages, the auctioneer.

Once they'd left, Blitz brought the ten percent for Family fees to Mr. Monarch at the Backdoor Saloon. Then we figured the remainder to be split between those who'd helped: Mary, Blitz, Amelia, Gertie. Even split four ways, it came out to a nice sum.

Gertie balked. "Why should I take money to help the poor?"

I replied, "Surely you wish to be paid for your work! Don't you wish to help your household as well?"

She drew back. "My husband is a law clerk, not some rabble in the slums! Did you bring me here for charity?"

"Of course not. You've been a great help to us."

"I'm a respectable, married woman," she said. "I did this to help the poor, not to take outside employment like some servant."

Amelia flinched.

"If you don't want the money," I said, "you certainly don't have to take it. Here," I told Mr. Myriad, "put it in with the rest."

Gertie nodded, satisfied.

Doyle Pike had stood aside watching this exchange, an amused smile on his face. He said to Mr. Myriad, "Deposit the remainder in my account minus your fees and send me the receipt."

"By all means, sir." The banker closed the boxes and stood.

Amelia raised an eyebrow. Gertie stared in horror. "**What?**"

Mr. Pike appeared unruffled. "Collect your things, my dear," he said to Gertie, "it's time to go."

"This was all for **your** benefit?" Other than a few workers dismantling the stands or sweeping the street, the rest had gone. "This is an outrage! I came here to help the poor —"

"Which you have. Mrs. Spadros has no funds —"

"Look at the luxury she even now lives in! To think of all those people you charged a penny to — to look at her clothes!"

"No one forced them to do so," Mr. Pike said. "They lined up for miles. And I'm sure they found it fine entertainment. No need to make a scene, my dear. Come on, collect Harriet and let's go."

He put his hand on her shoulder, but she shrank back. "I'll do more than make a scene, you puffed-up grifter!" Then she said to me, "You two deserve each other." She picked up her baby and put her in her pram. "I can make my own way home."

Mr. Pike sighed. "Forgive my grandson's wife. She has more fire than sense." He snorted. "She'll settle down eventually."

I hoped so. I was beginning to regret including her.

Once he left, Amelia said, "What in this benefits the poor?"

From her, it stung. "Donate to the poorhouse, if you wish."

"But why lie?"

Mary glanced over but said nothing.

I said, "Would anyone have come if it was for my benefit? And it would have shamed my husband as well."

Amelia's cheeks flushed red. Then she hurried inside.

Mary and I carried the empty racks back into the apartments. A coat-hanger lay on the floor, tissue-paper wafted from a shelf.

"I think we did rather well," Mary said from behind. "Don't fret about all this; I'll clean up and have the racks returned."

"Thank you, Mary."

But my heart felt like these rooms: cold, empty. "Do you ever wonder if you've done the right thing?"

"Don't let Mrs. Pike upset you, mum. She dislikes her grandfather, that's all. Come on, it's time for tea."

After dinner, I couldn't sleep, so I lit a lamp and sat writing in my journal. A loud thump on the door startled me.

I went to the door with the lamp, Blitz meeting me in the hall. We peered out.

Mr. Sticks Monarch lay crumpled on the steps, dead.

The Distress

Blitz drew his revolver and moved past the body, searching the street on both sides. "Hey there! You!"

A police constable younger than I was came over, shock crossing his face as he saw the body. "How'd that get there?"

"I heard a noise at the door not two minutes ago," I said.

By this time several police constables had hurried up. Blitz and I retreated into the house to let them do their work.

A few minutes later there came a knock; Blitz opened the door.

One of the constables stood there. "Sorry to bother you."

I came up beside Blitz. "How'd he die?"

Men were loading a body wrapped in a sheet into a wagon.

"Shot, less than an hour ago." The constable handed over a business card. "You know anything about this?"

A white card, blank on one side, the stamp of a red dog on the other. "The Red Dog Gang. They're the ones who framed me."

Amusement crossed his eyes for a brief instant, then his face went carefully neutral. "If you say so, mum."

Even they don't believe me. "He's a Spadros man, Constable. Make sure he's cared for. Sawbuck will know what to do."

I locked my window, drew my curtains, and huddled under the covers, but I couldn't sleep. The man guarding my street was shot then dumped on our porch — without anyone knowing?

An hour later a knock came at the door. By the time I'd gotten into my robe, Blitz had answered it. I opened my door to the hallway; Sawbuck stood there.

I'd only ever seen Sawbuck dressed as a gentleman: suit,

topper, shoes shined well. But that evening, he wore a cap and long-coat, with a working-man's vest, pants, and boots, spattered with mud. He peered at me. "Are you well, mum?"

"Ten, what happened?"

Sawbuck smiled as one might at a child. "An excellent question, Mrs. Spadros. Perhaps you might dress, then we can discuss it?"

Chagrined, I hurried back to my room and put on a house dress and a shawl. When I returned to the parlor, it was dark and empty; a light showed under the kitchen door.

Sawbuck and Blitz sat talking. They rose when they saw me, but I waved them to sit. "I need no formality." I filled the kettle and put it on the stove. I wanted a drink, but tea would have to suffice. Then I sat, making a perfect triangle of us three. "I just want to know what happened."

Sawbuck snorted. "Is it not obvious? I thought you more capable than this. These Red Dogs send a message: no one is safe from them, not even our Button Men. Most certainly not you."

It was obvious, when put that way. "And they put the Red Dog card on him in case we didn't get the picture." I leaned forward. "Yet how did they put him there without anyone seeing it?"

"Well," Sawbuck said, "that's the real question. The street's not lit. Only a few men guard at night, but even so someone must have seen two men carrying a body. Or perhaps three; Monarch's no lightweight." He shifted in his seat. "I've sent for new constables; these ones will be questioned."

I remembered the shocked face of the young constable who first came to the door. "You mean to have them tortured?"

Sawbuck chuckled. "Not everyone merits the tender attentions of Roy Spadros. But I assure you, there will be no repeat of this."

I sat there for a long while, my mind blank. The kettle began to whistle, and I took it off of the heat. "Tea, anyone?"

"Coffee," Sawbuck said, "if you have it."

"And I," Blitz said. "Mary's asleep, but I won't any time soon."

So I brewed coffee as I considered the matter. How did killing Mr. Monarch benefit the Red Dog Gang? "Could this have been meant to goad your men into some rash action?"

"I considered this," Sawbuck said. He sat quietly as I poured coffee, set out sugar and cream. "And you may be right." He relaxed, sipped his coffee. "I don't know what it means, but —"

I'd been pouring water over my tea-strainer, but at this I put down the kettle. "What?"

"Do you recall the man sent about Master Rainbow's jacket?"

"Vaguely," I said. "I was ill. Tony let him in, asked him to sit."

"Sit?" Sawbuck rolled his eyes and chuckled. "My cousin. You're a bad influence over Mr. Anthony, I must say."

"What do you mean?"

Sawbuck shook his head. "Nothing. In any case, before he ran off with the so-called 'Ten of Spades,' he told me the name of the black-haired woman who bought the other jacket."

"Why, that's wonderful! Who is she?"

"Well, that's the thing. On the invoice, she signed her name Maria Athena Spa-day."

"Spa-day? I've not heard that name before. How is it spelled?"

"S-p-a-d-e," Blitz said. "Like the Holy Symbol, The Spade. It's Italian." He snorted in amusement. "They say the Spadros family 'never changed its name.' But of course it did. Perhaps the Spadros brothers needed to change their names for some reason."

"Ohhh," I said. "And this is important how? Other than now we can find her, which of course is excellent."

Sawbuck hesitated. "There **is** a young woman in Bridges by that name. But she's disappeared. Given all else that's happened, I think the Red Dog Gang used this woman for another reason."

Blitz began to laugh. "Oh, if I could have seen his face!"

Sawbuck gave Blitz a disapproving glance. "This isn't funny."

"Wait," I said. "What — who is this woman?"

"It's not the woman," Sawbuck said. "It's the name. Someone else was named Maria Athena Spade: Mr. Roy's mother."

This perplexed me. "I don't understand."

Sawbuck said, "They called Maria Spadros the Death Card —"

One of the many names this black-haired woman working with the Red Dog Gang used.

"— but not simply for her title as Queen of Spades. From what I hear, Mrs. Maria made Roy Spadros look like a good, kind man."

"Oh." The thought dismayed me.

"Yes," Sawbuck said. He kept his voice low. "It's no secret Mr. Roy hated his mother. He seldom speaks of her, but when he does ...." At that, Sawbuck shuddered. "But there is one thing very few know." He hesitated. "From the rumors — **very** quiet rumors, mind you — Mrs. Maria Spadros took an inordinate interest in her only son. An unnatural, unseemly interest."

"Good gods." Blitz and I spoke at the same time.

I said, "This is horrifying."

Sawbuck nodded. "Whatever the truth, she disappeared on the way home from Mr. Roy's wedding and was never seen again."

I remembered the letter Roy gave me, the one he claimed this black-haired woman sent him. How could the Red Dog Gang have possibly learned something like **this**? "They intend to cause **him** distress, perhaps to goad him into some rash action."

"I believe so. Although I applaud their intent — I'd torment Mr. Roy myself given the chance — right now is the worst time for it."

I nodded. A revolt in his own ranks. His son — no, brother — almost killed by men he trusted with his safety. "These Red Dogs know far too much. Someone old is behind this. Very old. Someone gathering information for decades."

Blitz blinked. "What do you mean?"

I recalled the ancient women in the Cathedral, how they spoke to the others. "The very old like to talk, yes, but never about anything truly important. That, they reserve for those they consider trustworthy."

Sawbuck and Blitz stared blankly at me.

"They're so old that all others look as children to them." I pondered this idea. If true, this changed everything. Then I peered at Sawbuck. "What do we know about Freezout?"

"Other than what we read in the papers? Ambitious in his business life, yet content in his marriage. Children, grandchildren. No scandal that I know of."

I had an idea. "Might Mr. Blackberry of the *Bridges Daily* visit? He'd be willing to look for information on the man."

Sawbuck gulped down the rest of his coffee. "I'll ask in the morning. But it's getting late."

"We must find this woman," I said, "if only to learn what she knows." I held out my hand, which Sawbuck took briefly. "Thank you for your help, Ten. I truly appreciate it."

Once he left, Blitz said, "I forgot to tell you: Inventor Call sent a Memory Boy during the auction. The boy refused to come inside, yet the Court guards refused to bring you out." Blitz sounded disgusted. "The Inventor says he only reports to Spadros Manor. Since you're no longer part of the Family —"

"I have no right to his words." This after I gave him my map!

"I'm sorry, Mrs. Spadros."

* * *

The next day was a Sunday, yet I woke to a commotion of police outside. When I peeked past my curtains, it appeared they were examining the entire street.

A pity they became involved, I thought. Sawbuck and his men were ever so much more discreet.

I considered our conversation the night before. Someone who knew the Spadros Family intimately had spoken of things they should not to the wrong person.

And I remembered the tongueless, thumbless old servants at the cottage. They were the right age to know the truth.

It was well after luncheon before the police left, then the neighbors emerged to look up and down. They stood in groups talking, from time to time glancing my way, then went inside.

Dr. Salmon came to visit a bit later, sitting with me at my tea-table. "I'm sorry I didn't come earlier. But your people have given me reports every day."

"Is that so?"

"It's good to see you improved. You've held your auction?"

"With a great deal of help."

"I'm glad to hear it. I'll leave more tonics, with specifications to concoct your draughts. Continue to take one every day."

"For how long?"

"For the rest of your life. It's fortunate the liver can regenerate. But in its weakened condition, we don't dare relax our guard."

For the rest of my life?

What had I done?

* * *

After Dr. Salmon left, the Court guards returned the barricades to their previous places ten yards from each side of my front door.

Tony's piano-black and silver carriage pulled up right at four o'clock. I ran to find Blitz. "I'm not 'at home.'"

Blitz gave me a skeptical look. "You're not serious."

"I don't wish to see him." The doorbell rang.

"But why?"

"I won't have him in here."

Blitz sighed. "Very well." He opened the door just wide enough for his body to show. "Mrs. Spadros isn't 'at home,' sir."

"Nonsense. I receive her schedule before you do. Stand aside."

"She doesn't wish to see you, sir," Blitz said. "I'm sorry."

"Are you really going to keep me from my wife?"

"As her butler, yes, sir, I must allow in only those she wishes."

"And why is that? Has she seduced you too?"

Blitz recoiled, and I could tell from his stance that he felt hurt.

I pushed Blitz aside. "How dare you speak of me so!"

Tony's face turned red. "Jacqui —"

"No. I want you gone."

"I need to talk to you —"

"By insulting me and threatening my butler? Your cousin! And you've insulted him as well. You're behaving like a scoundrel!"

"Jacqui —" He glanced around; several of the neighbors peered out. "Can we at least go inside?"

"Anything you want to say you can say here." I could imagine his reaction to my parlor, my tiny rooms, my one kitchen. "Well?"

Tony straightened. "I came to help. To see if you were well."

"Since you receive my schedule, you know the doctor's just been here. I'm perfectly well, and I neither need nor want your help. I thought I made that clear."

His face turned to ice. "Good day." He put his top hat on, got into his carriage, and pulled the curtains.

Blitz said, "Why do you agitate him?"

"He doesn't own me! And I'm not afraid of him. If he wishes to enter my home, he must behave like a gentleman. Until then, he'll remain in the street."

* * *

Jonathan visited the next afternoon, claiming he'd just heard of Mr. Monarch's death. "I went to your husband as soon as I heard of it. He said he'd been here, but little more."

"He did visit, Jon. He acted very rudely, so I didn't let him in."

Jon's jaw dropped. "That doesn't sound like him at all."

"No, it's not."

"He's hurt, Jacqui. He's in great distress. He needs you by his side. I —" Jon clapped his hand over his mouth.

"You what?"

"I don't like you being here either. I wish I could've been here during the auction, but my father forbade it. The thought of all those people so close by was terrifying. Any of them could've come to harm you, like they did your man out there."

It surprised me that his father allowed him to visit as often as he did. "I understand. But the auction went well! Everything sold, which should more than cover my attorney's fees."

"Well, that's good news, then! You must feel quite relieved."

I considered this. "I suppose I do."

"I'll not be by much this week," Jon said. "My brother Beloty sat for me as Keeper whilst you lay ill, yet he neglected much of the work." He grimaced. "And left me all the papers to complete."

"I thought Cesare was doing that."

Jon snorted. "For your case only, and that after coercion from my father. Cesare considers Keeper of the Court beneath him."

I chuckled at his expression. "Be at peace; care for your duty. You've helped me beyond what anyone might expect."

* * *

The next day after breakfast, Blitz handed me a cheap envelope holding a quarter-sheet of paper with large childish print on it.

Deer Missus Spadros —

I am sorry it took so long to Rite.

I asked Daddy if I could Rite to you, & he said No.

I didn't no how to rite, so I learnt how.

Miss Ann tot me words & to hold the Pen.

But I had no Money for Paper.

So I did extra Work. & extra Work for the Boy to take this to you.

I miss you very much.

Every on is Very Sad. Men shot Holes inside.

They are Scared too.

They said you were Sick.

I hope you really get this.

Your Frend,

Pip Dewey

The page was speckled and blotted, and for an instant, it broke my heart. *I hope you really get this.*

"Amelia!"

Blitz put his head in. "Mrs. Dewey won't arrive until after morning meeting."

"Very well. When she arrives, I want to see her at once."

"Of course." He shut the door.

I smoked three cigarettes waiting for her. Before she could say a word, I said, "You should be ashamed of yourself."

Amelia's eyes went wide. "What happened?"

"You refused to teach him to write, you made him work to buy the paper, and you couldn't even bring me his letter? You made him work for that too? How could you?"

"Who?" Amelia seemed genuinely perplexed.

I held up Pip's letter but didn't give it to her. "From your son, who had to go to others to learn to write, had to do extra work to buy paper, and more to hire a messenger. When you come here every day!" I shook my head, disgusted. "How can you live with yourself, treating your own child like this?"

Amelia came in, shut the door, leaned on it. "I had no idea he even wanted to write to you."

I read from it: "I asked Daddy if I could write to you and he said no. I had no money for paper so I did extra work, and extra work for the boy to take this to you."

Amelia said nothing.

"You've made it so your own child —"

Amelia held up her hand. "Wait. I know what happened." Color lay high on her pale cheeks as she stared straight ahead. "Mr. Dewey doesn't know how to read or write."

I felt chagrined. "Oh. I'm sorry."

"Pip doesn't know that. None of the children do. Mr. Dewey pretends to read when he's given something, and fortunately has never been asked to write anything." Amelia closed her eyes. "He did all this — to write to you?"

"It seems I'm one of the few people who've been kind to him."

She opened her eyes and they were red. "They were kind to him. We have to pay for paper, yes, but also the envelope and the sealing wax. Whoever gave him those — even Jane or Mr. Pearson — would be brought out back and whipped if they were caught stealing. They probably paid from their own money. Mum."

I sprang to my feet, horrified. "Whipped? This is unbelievable! How do you live in such a terrible place?"

Amelia gaped at me. "Mum, it's Spadros Manor … it's the best place any servant in the city can hope for."

I felt as if the words I said were in some other language that no one here understood. "This is wrong."

"We have food, mum, and good clothing. We have warm beds. We won't starve." She hesitated. "At least it's not the Pot."

"No one is whipped in the Pot!" I sat heavily. What these people endured seemed unbelievable. "You quadrant-folk keep the Pot in ruins precisely so you can point to it and feel superior, whilst undergoing deprivations and inhumanity we'd shudder at." I put my head in my hands. "How did this happen?"

"Begging your pardon, mum, but it was your Pot's doing. We was thrown outside the fence like trash to fend for ourselves."

Left to fend for themselves. And they let the Families create — what did Thrace Pike call it? A "self-appointed monarchy," in which the kings felt nothing for their low cards. No responsibility, no respect, no love. No duty to care.

I felt like crying. "It may mean nothing to you, but I'm sorry."

The Options

Sawbuck came by late that afternoon, dressed as a gentleman this time, to as many hoots and whistles as had plagued Jonathan on his visits. Blitz had put him in the parlor, and he rose when I entered. "I hope you're well, Mrs. Spadros?"

I sat across from him. "Indeed."

Sawbuck settled himself on the sofa. "Mr. Blackberry's legal team advised him against visiting. They felt it best if he at least appeared impartial."

I chuckled. "Very well."

"But he will look into Mr. Freezout for us. I asked him to look into Miss Spade as well."

For a moment, I couldn't decipher who he meant. Then I remembered. "Maria Athena."

"Yes."

"Well, that's good!"

Sawbuck leaned forward. "Are you sure we should trust him? He's worked for the Clubbs the majority of his life."

"Ten, I've known the man since I was five years old. He's only ever helped. Besides, I'm sure the Clubbs want to learn these things as badly as we do."

"That's what I'm afraid of. His search delves into both Spadros and Hart quadrants. Can we trust him not to share his findings?"

I considered this. "The Red Dog Gang is a threat more serious than our quadrant differences. But if it makes you feel better, you can warn him not to share what he finds with them."

Sawbuck nodded, but he seemed skeptical he'd be heeded. "I

truly hope we don't need a new editor so soon."

Fear spiked through me, recalling Tony's assassination of the previous editor, but I forced myself to stay calm. "Mr. Blackberry is a wise man, Ten. He won't do anything to cause trouble."

When I woke the next morning, a newspaper had been slid under the door: the *Bridges Daily*.

Its top story:

Our Queen of Hearts Folds

Wife of Hart Family heir succumbs to long illness

Why did the paper call Helen Hart "Our Queen of Hearts"? What must Mrs. Judith Hart feel, to have her son's wife receive the title which rightly belonged to her?

As I gazed upon Helen's portrait, I felt deeply sad that I'd never known her. She invited me to luncheon once, yet was told I had another engagement — without anyone even asking me!

But according to Master Blaze Rainbow, her invitation was forced on her by Mr. Charles Hart. This brought Mr. Hart's recent visit to mind. If he were enamored with me, you'd think he'd want it kept secret. Why would he want me to become acquainted with his daughter-in-law?

As I read further, I noticed that the entire first part of the paper had been devoted to Helen Hart, pushing all news about my troubles onto the bottom of the second to last page.

Was this deliberate? If Mr. Blackberry wished to make people forget about me, the zeppelin explosion, and the economy, this seemed the best option a news-man might have.

* * *

Later that morning, Tony's carriage pulled up. I rushed outside before Tony rang the bell, shutting the door behind me to avoid another argument between him and Blitz. "Yes?"

"May I walk with you?" Tony hadn't removed his hat, didn't take my arm, nor did he offer his.

What could he possibly have to say to me? "Very well."

I descended the steps. "I wouldn't suggest approaching the

barricades, unless you wish to be hit by rocks."

Tony flinched, then nodded.

The day was warm and pleasant. We strolled five yards to the left then turned right to cross the street. The men crowding against the barricades just watched us.

Tony strolled along as if on promenade, yet he never looked at me. "Ten told me what you planned."

I shrugged, turning to the right a few feet before the doors across the street. I didn't know anyone there, and I feared they might come out here to shout at me too. "It was all in my letter."

"Perhaps I should have believed you," he said. "But it seemed inconceivable for you to be so very false."

That stung.

He sounded weary. "I don't wish to be enemies." He stopped, faced me. "I never once intended you harm. Not even that night."

The horror on his face the night he caught me and Joseph Kerr together swam before me. I struggled not to cry. "I know. None of this was your fault."

"Unfortunately, you've left me with very few options." He continued to walk, shoulders slumped.

I followed, miserable. I'd let him believe a lie for so long. But what could I have done differently? How could I possibly make this right?

I knew what he'd say should I ask: *come home.* But it was impossible. I'd lose everything I'd worked so hard for, betray everyone who'd died trying to free me from the Family.

We turned right perhaps six yards from the other barricade, crossing the street towards my apartments. We turned right again, towards his carriage. As we neared the carriage, Tony said, "There was one flaw in your plan."

Curiosity pushed aside my misery at once. "Oh?"

"Gardena will not have me either."

Oh, Tony …

Honor opened the carriage door. Tony removed his top hat, climbed in, and the door shut behind him. They drove away, stopping briefly at the barricades. The men there bowed as his carriage passed, glancing at me with fear on their faces.

*Gods, Tony! I **never** meant to hurt you!*

The front door had locked behind me. I sat on the steps hugging my shawl to me for a long time, feeling numb, until Blitz found me outside and took me in.

* * *

The next afternoon, Mr. Doyle Pike came calling after tea. "I'm sorry to disturb you, madam, but —"

"Not at all, sir. Please, come in and sit down."

He hesitated. "Very well." We sat. "Are you acquainted with a Master Tim Keycard?"

"No," I said. "Should I be?"

Mr. Pike frowned. "Mr. Freezout has put Master Keycard on his witness list. But there's no man by that name registered in the city. I have an investigator looking for him, but so far we've not had much luck. Do you have any idea who this might be?"

"Keycard .... The name sounds familiar. Could it be an alias?"

"Not if the District Attorney wants to remain within the law. He's required to provide the full legal name of every witness he plans to call."

"Hmm," I said. Then I recalled questions Mr. Freezout asked during the inquest: my birth name, my parents' names. If what Mr. Pike said was true, he already knew these things. Why ask?

Unless he didn't know. "Are people registered in the Pot?"

Mr. Pike got a stunned look on his face. "I don't believe so!" He sat in thought for a while, then began to stand.

I realized where I'd heard the name. "I know where he's from."

Mr. Pike sat. "Oh? Where?"

"Just east of Stud Street, off Snow, Spadros quadrant, there's a brothel called the Keycard Cafe. That's likely where he was born."

Mr. Pike seemed confused. "Stud and Snow. The Pot?"

"Yes, sir. The Spadros Pot. Have your man ask there, but tell him not to dress well, and don't go alone. That's a rough area even for the Pot. But he'll find someone who knows the man."

* * *

Midsummer Day came, and since I couldn't leave, it was much like any other day, except fewer shouting men at the barricades.

Didn't these men have anything better to do than to shout and wave their signs? Did they not have jobs, families?

I seldom glimpsed women and never children, other than messenger boys. And after that brief time my neighbors stood talking after Mr. Monarch's death, I saw little of them either.

Another apartment building sat across from mine, sporting a flat roof-top with a small garden. To either side I could only see doors. A bit more comfortable and infinitely safer, yet for now this was a prison just the same.

Twilight fell. Amelia went home. Blitz and Mary sat in the parlor. I went upstairs to the table in my big room.

The sky darkened, and the Midsummer fireworks began. I missed Jonathan. I missed Joe. I even missed Tony.

I pushed the feelings back. I couldn't reach for Tony, not now. Even to send a note for his birthday would cause him pain.

What I really missed was drinking. Everyone drank at least one toast at Midsummer — even Blitz and Mary had a bottle downstairs they thought they kept secret from me.

But there was no help for it. I chose this life. And now that time had begun to heal me, I found I wanted to live it.

* * *

On the day I met with Mr. Pike, Amelia arrived early to get me ready. She'd been told to select a plain, modest dress of a dark color for me, no jewelry, and nothing of great value. We chose a charcoal gray walking dress with a white lace collar and matching hat. Getting ready took longer than usual as I kept asking Amelia how she did my corset, my hair, my makeup.

I'd barely gotten ready when the doorbell rang: my carriage from Spadros Manor sat outside. I looked to Amelia. "I thought we weren't expecting the carriage until ten."

Amelia went to the door, returning a moment later. "The footman wishes to speak with you, mum. Should I —"

"No, I'll speak with him." I'd thought my former day footman Skip Honor might want to speak with me after all that happened. I was surprised it took him this long to do so.

Honor was normally a man of calm demeanor. Today, he seemed nervous. "May I enter?"

I took a step back. "Of course." I sensed rather than saw Amelia come up behind us. "Would you care for tea?"

"No, mum, but if we might speak in private?"

I turned to Amelia. "All's well, you may return to your duties." I gestured to Honor. "Come to the parlor."

He followed me to our parlor. I thought it might make him nervous to sit, so I stood facing him. "How may I assist you?"

"I feared to speak, mum, but with what's happened we felt we must, if only —" Honor hesitated, casting about as if not sure where to begin. "I grew up in Bridges, mum. Not far from here, if truth be told. I was ten when my mother got trampled by a runaway horse-and-carriage. She never woke, so —"

"Oh, I'm so sorry."

"No, mum, she still lived, she just never woke. So they sent me to an orphanage. In Dickens, mum. That's where I met Jacob."

He peered at me expectantly; for a moment I felt confused. "You mean Jacob Michaels? Mr. Anthony's manservant?"

Honor glanced at the floor, then at me. "Yes, mum."

I nodded, wondering where this story was going.

"Well, mum," he took a deep breath, let it out. "We — we formed … an attachment, if you will."

"I see."

"Four years later, Jacob was sold to the Spadros Family as manservant to Mr. Anthony. We thought we'd never see each other again. But eight months later, my mother woke and sent for me." He smiled, his cheeks coloring. "Jacob spoke for me, mum. He got me the job here."

"I'm very glad of it. You've been a fine footman."

"Thank you, mum. But that's not why I came here." He seemed torn between options, as if he'd made a decision yet feared to start the round. But then he straightened, holding out his right hand, palm up. "With this hand, I burned the Holy Card and made blood oath to the Spadros Family. Jacob did the same."

Burned a Holy Card? Blood oath? What blasphemy was this?

He dropped his hand to his side. "We didn't understand why you were betrothed to Mr. Anthony. Why you were married to him. But when you put my Jacob at table with you, mum. After

Mr. Anthony was attacked." His eyes reddened. "Making him your equal ... I — in my heart I became your man." He took my hands, dropped to one knee. "We've decided to swear to you."

"What does that mean?"

"We'll be your eyes and ears in Spadros Manor." He said it as if this seemed obvious. "Jacob serves Mr. Anthony himself, mum. We'll tell you of anything which puts you at risk."

"Please, stand up."

He did so.

I let go of his hands. "This ... I'm quite touched by your allegiance. And I accept. But I don't want you to betray my husband's words told in confidence. He should have privacy."

"I completely understand, mum." He said it as if he approved. "And I would like to remain your footman. When you go out, mum, I mean." His cheeks flushed. "I must attend Mr. Anthony most times, but I sincerely wish to serve you. When I can."

I smiled at him. "I'd like that too. But I have a question. Who guards him at night?" Blitz used to be our night footman, but of course, he couldn't be, now that he lived here.

"Pearson's youngest son, Alan. He prefers to sleep the day away, so the job suits him."

I felt relieved. "Very good. I may not live with Mr. Anthony, but I wish no harm upon him."

At this, Honor clearly wished to ask something, but hesitated to say it. So I did. "I left Mr. Anthony because I was married to him against my will," at this I felt sad, "but he just learned of it."

Honor looked appalled. "Good gods!"

"I don't regret telling him the truth, but I do regret not telling him sooner." I'd felt so afraid — of Roy, of being defenseless, of having no means — that I hurt the one person, it seemed, who'd loved me. "Please tell your Jacob I'm grateful for his offer."

"I will, mum."

"Is Pip well?"

Honor seemed surprised. "Pip Dewey?"

"Yes. Is he well?"

He glanced past me. "I had no idea you knew him."

I chuckled at that.

Honor's cheeks colored. "He's well, mum."

"Please tell him I received his letter."

"I will, mum."

I glanced at the clock. "I suppose we best go, before we're late."

I followed Honor out to the carriage, which was now ringed with horsemen from the Court. We arrived on time for the meeting, and I was shown up at once.

But Mr. Pike didn't rise. Rather, he gestured for me to sit.

Mr. Pike clasped his hands together near his face, gazing out of the large windows to his right. "The District Attorney has a great pile of evidence against you."

"Yes, I know."

"He wants to make an example of you, so that others involved with the Families will know they aren't safe from prosecution."

"I guessed as much."

"The city's in an uproar. They believe you're involved in both Dame Anastasia's scam and the bombing."

"I see."

"However, the people who matter are more upset by the financial scam. Dame Anastasia's men are dead —"

I felt appalled. "**All** of them?"

Mr. Pike gave a dismissive wave. "That villain loose in the city. The Bridges Strangler?" He shrugged. "In any case, Mr. Freezout is under tremendous pressure to find someone to prosecute. Anyone would do. But he's running for Mayor on a promise to rid Bridges of the 'criminal element' — by which any fool can see he means the Four Families. He's always hated them." He let out a cackle. "I can only imagine how high **his** Family fees are!"

Giving ten percent to a Family would be a monthly reminder of what his family had lost in the Coup. This reinforced my idea that Mr. Freezout was behind this frame-up.

Mr. Pike pursed his lips, giving his head a small shake. "The only way Freezout has to strike at the three Families suspected of being associated with her in the financial scam is to go after you." His shoulders slumped. "And it looks as if he's succeeded."

"What do you mean?

"Well, he doesn't want to be the man responsible for hanging a young woman, especially the 'Lady of Spadros.'"

The Lady of Spadros, huh? I wondered what my mother-in-law Molly thought of that.

"While rousing the people helps his campaign for Mayor, this card has two sides."

"What do you mean?"

"A crowd emboldened can turn from cheering to rage in an instant. If he harms you, he risks putting a quarter of the city into riot." He took out a paper and laid it in front of him. "So he's making an offer you dare not refuse."

"What kind of offer?"

"You plead guilty to the gem scam. You go to the Prison —"

Where Jack Diamond — who'd vowed to torture me to death after my father murdered his manservant — had complete control.

" — and the zeppelin bombing charge goes away."

"What else?"

"Tell Mr. Freezout everything you know of the Four Families."

Ah, what he really wanted. "You want me to betray the Families to gain a berth in the Prison?"

Mr. Pike leaned forward. "I want you to forgo a long, costly trial which you can't win."

"By which you mean **you** can't win."

"I can counter every evidence they offer. But in Merca, the jury decides. The District Attorney will dismiss anyone living in Spadros quadrant, claiming undue influence. So at best, we face a jury with no loyalty to you. One which knows you came from the Pot, is jealous of your 'unfairly gained' position, and believes you'll get every advantage due to your marriage. Everyone knows Roy Spadros has pardoned you, and are suspicious of the Spadros Family's protests that they wish to be uninvolved." He shifted in his chair. "At worst, the jury will be openly hostile, eager for your execution. I can work to get you the former sort, but ..." He glanced away. "It's too much risk. I advise you to take this deal."

"What about the Clubbs? They said they'd support me."

"They can only do so much. The city believes you'll get an unfair trial —"

"I am!"

He looked at me sideways. "You know what I mean. Any interference will be seen as proof of that. No witness can be intimidated or killed, no evidence tampered with. Well, at least, not openly." He leaned forward. "My dear, you risk the gallows! And even if you **are** acquitted, you'll be open to every crackpot would-be assassin in Bridges. Better to take the lesser charge and disappear from view until this calms down."

If I went to the Prison, fell into Jack Diamond's hands, the gallows would be a mercy. I rose, feeling agitated. "And yet you said you could help me!"

"I'm trying to help you now."

"You want me to lie? To say I did things I never did? Betray people who've died trying to help me? But I'm innocent!"

"I'd like to believe you, madam." Mr. Pike spoke bitterly. "I used to believe there were innocent people in this world, then I learned otherwise."

I sat heavily. I'd told him everything. *Even he doesn't believe me.*

"I'm trying to save your life, Mrs. Spadros."

Two options, neither of them good. "Thank you for telling me. I'll notify you of my decision before the hearing."

I went to my carriage in the light rain. The meeting had been short, and we had time to spare. "Twice round the Plaza," I told Honor, "before we go to luncheon."

I needed to think. This would be the biggest decision of my life.

* * *

I went to luncheon with Jonathan Diamond, my guards following. This restaurant's walls were paneled in a warm brown. Large windows displayed an equally large patio area, its canvas umbrellas closed and tables empty due to the rain.

I felt cold, shaky.

Jon was already at our table when I arrived, and to my surprise, Charles Hart accompanied him, dressed in mourning. I'd expected Mr. Hart to be home with his family, in light of the recent death of his daughter-in-law.

They rose, Jonathan offering his hand. "Are you well, Jacqui? You look quite pale."

My guards went to a nearby table and sat facing me, I suppose to watch in case I might try escaping. Being surrounded by police wasn't the most comfortable feeling. And I didn't particularly want to speak to Jon about Mr. Freezout's deal with Mr. Hart here. "I'm well, thank you."

Jon waved a waiter over and asked for a glass of water, so as to take what I suspected to be tonics of some kind. He'd done this several times a day for as long as I'd known him. Each time I asked, he'd reply that they were "for his health."

He unfastened the brown velvet pouch which invariably hung on his left hip, then lined up the long thin glass vials inside it. He selected the vials which had the number 1 engraved upon them, three in all, returning the rest to his pouch, each in its own velvet niche. He produced a thin glass dropper from the pouch, putting six drops from each vial into the water, which he drank. Then he returned the vials to his pouch and smiled at me. "I suppose I provide some entertainment?"

"I find it gratifying that you care for your health. I shouldn't wish you to fall ill."

Jon gave a fake smile, glancing away.

"I understand the trout here is excellent," Mr. Hart said, obviously wishing to change the subject.

I browsed the menu, heart pounding, yet didn't really see it. Was Jon's condition serious? He fell ill often, at times even needing a cane to walk. This was the longest stretch he'd been well in quite some time. Gardena would only say Jon had a "delicate constitution." Yet he seemed distressed every time I brought up the topic of illness.

Jonathan's mother was ill, yet had kept everyone believing her condition was much worse than it was, so that she might both protect herself and spy.

Had Mrs. Diamond kept her true condition from all her children? Perhaps Jon's care for his health — which seemed obsessive — was due to worry about likewise becoming ill.

But I wasn't sure, and it bothered me.

"Excuse me." Jon left, I suppose, to the Men's Room.

"I hope you're well," Mr. Hart said, in an offhand manner. He sat to my left, scrutinizing the menu.

"Did you get my letter of condolence?"

"No." He glanced away. "Judith threw it in the fire before I might read it. But I thank you for your kindness."

"Why does she dislike me so? I've only —"

His eyes flickered to the guards sitting at the next table. "Let's not speak of her now."

"Of course, sir."

He pulled out a fist-sized red velvet box. "I'd like to offer a Midsummer gift, if you'd accept it."

Midsummer gifts in Bridges were usually flowers, or a small pin. But inside sat a silver necklace with a half-dollar sized pendant bearing a silver cabbage-rose in full bloom with a gem of deepest red at its center.

"My word," I said. "This is exquisite."

"It was my mother's. Alas, my wife has refused it, and my grand-daughter, poor dear, would only lose it. I meant to give it to Helen upon her bearing Etienne an heir, but —"

"I'm so sorry for your loss, sir. I wish I might have known her."

We sat in silence as talk from the other tables buzzed around us. But then he smiled. "It would do me a great honor should you accept this. As a token of our friendship."

It was his mother's, and costly. Should I accept it?

But then, remembering my dresses, I felt compassion for him. Mr. Hart likely felt it too much a reminder of all he'd lost. "I shall treasure it. As a token of our friendship."

Once I took it, he seemed to relax. Since Mr. Hart had waited for Jon to leave before offering the pendant, I thought it best to put it away in my handbag. It barely fit.

The waiter approached. "May I take your order, sir?"

Mr. Hart said, "We await one more."

I glanced at the menu. "Jon likes lamb roast, medium rare."

Mr. Hart peered in the direction Jon went. "Very well."

The longer we sat, the more I thought about Mr. Pike's offer. I felt torn. Either option seemed bad. I didn't know what to do.

Jon returned a bit later. "I hope you weren't kept waiting."

"Your friend seems to know your tastes," Mr. Hart said.

"I had Mr. Hart order lamb roast for you," I said.

Jon's face lit up. "I haven't had that in some time!"

I smiled, but I didn't feel it.

Jon's face turned grave. "Jacqui, what's wrong?"

I desperately needed Jonathan's counsel. Yet I feared speaking in front of Mr. Hart. Could I trust his discretion? At the time, I didn't know what else to do. "I have terrible news."

I told them what Mr. Pike — no, Mr. Freezout — had offered.

Mr. Hart put his hand to his chin and gazed to the side.

Jon's expression didn't change. "What did you decide?"

"I don't know what to do. It's bad or worse, in my view."

He nodded slowly. "Because of Jack."

I took a deep breath to stop my voice from shaking. "Yes."

Jon sat peering at me for some time. The waiter arrived with our tea, asked us something. I didn't even hear what Jon said.

When the waiter left, Jon placed his hand on my arm, and I jumped. "Jacqui. Look at me. All will be well. I promise."

I nodded, although I wasn't entirely convinced.

Mr. Hart leaned forward, resting his arms upon the table. "You're sure you don't want to return to Spadros Manor?"

What sort of question was this? "Yes, I'm sure."

Mr. Hart leaned back in his chair. "Your husband and I discussed something after you were first arraigned." He sat regarding me for some time. "There may be a third option."

The Plan

I gaped at him. "Whatever do you mean?"

"Forgive me if I'm wrong," Mr. Hart said, "but it's my understanding that you both wish to travel."

Jonathan froze.

I shrugged. What I really wanted to do was leave Bridges and never return. Was that travel, or just flight?

Jon's face turned alarmed. "May we speak privately, sir?"

Charles Hart blinked. "By all means."

They moved out to the patio, standing in front of me not ten yards off. I couldn't hear what was said through the glass, but I knew Jonathan: he'd been my closest friend for over a decade. Jon was angry, outraged, dismayed. Mr. Hart seemed to be trying to persuade Jon of something Jon both wanted and feared.

Mr. Hart put his hand on Jonathan's shoulder as a father might his son. Then Jon gave him an anguished, vulnerable look, something in it I'd never seen between Jon and his father Julius. I can't explain those few moments any better, but I felt I invaded their privacy, watched a scene I should not. It puzzled me. How could a Diamond and a Hart possibly know each other this well?

Jon's face turned resigned, and as Mr. Hart spoke, hopeful.

My heart pounded, and I felt ill. Even though Mr. Hart claimed Tony agreed to it, I felt afraid of whatever made Jon so dismayed. And though Jon seemed to trust Mr. Hart, I didn't know him. I didn't trust him to have my best interests in mind.

Finally, they returned, but Jonathan wouldn't look at me.

What had Mr. Hart just persuaded Jon to do?

Jon turned to me and took my hands in his. His hands trembled as he stared at them. Then he took a deep breath, let it out. His head raised, his gaze steady, earnest. "Come with me."

I stared at Jonathan, stunned, too astonished to reply.

"Let's leave Bridges, Jacqui, just as you wanted to."

"It's quite simple, Mrs. Spadros," Mr. Hart said. "Take the deal. Let them 'send you to the Prison.' But instead of going to the Prison, you and Master Diamond leave the city together until your 'sentence' is over. A sleight of hand, if you will."

Jon glanced away. "If I do this, I may not be able to return. But if you want to come back, you'll be free to do so. You won't set foot anywhere near my brother, I promise."

The waiters placed our food in front of us. Nicely browned pork roast and mashed potatoes, my favorite. The smell was tantalizing, but I feared if I ate anything I might be sick.

Of course Jon wouldn't be able to come back if he did this! He'd be dismissed as Keeper of the Court, perhaps face charges. And his father would be furious! Jon might even be disowned for helping someone in the Spadros Family this way.

Could I allow Jonathan to throw away his life, his title, his money, his position — for me?

This was clearly Mr. Hart's idea, a man who'd been in a bitter personal battle with the Spadros Family for more a generation.

Mr. Hart had moved to my side much too quickly for my liking. Why did Mr. Hart want Jon to do this? Was this some way to strike back at Roy Spadros? What did it gain him?

Whose side was he on?

"Please, Jacqui." I'd never heard such urgent fear in Jon's voice before. "Please. I beg you. Take the deal. Come with me."

I wanted nothing more than to walk out of the door, get on a zeppelin with Jonathan Diamond, and never look back.

But the smug smile on Mr. Freezout's face lingered in my eyes.

Mr. Freezout was an aristocrat ... wealthy ... persuasive ... with motive to destroy the Spadros Family ... in a position to harm me in a way **none** of them could counter ...

Could Mr. Freezout have **planned** all this? Could he be the man directing the Red Dog Gang?

I remembered the note I found in Marja's dying hand:

YOU'RE MAKING THIS A CHALLENGE.

Could **he** have written it?

"No," I said. "I won't lie. I won't confess! I didn't do it."

And then I realized what was going on.

"This is exactly what they want me to do."

"Who, Jacqui?" Jon sounded in agony. "Why would you not **save** yourself?"

And I realized then that while Jonathan knew all about my private investigation business, about Air, and of course Joseph Kerr, he knew nothing about the events of the current year.

I didn't want to reveal these things in front of Mr. Hart. But we only had a few minutes before I must leave for the courthouse: at this point I had little choice. So I told them about the search for Air's little brother David Bryce. I told them of the break-in at Madame Biltcliffe's shop and the forgeries. I also told them in the most general terms about the attacks on Tony and our men, all from a man calling himself Frank Pagliacci.

Jon stared at me, mouth open, impatiently waving away the waiter who came asking if our meal was satisfactory.

Neither of us had touched a thing.

Mr. Hart sat eating as if alone, but I felt he weighed every word. Scrutinized it. Memorized it. And it frightened me.

Tony and Jonathan trusted Mr. Hart to get me out of Bridges if we lost the round. But every time I looked at Mr. Hart, I felt he hid something vitally important.

I hoped I was doing the right thing.

I told them about Anastasia's job, how I learned of her scam, and that she had been Frank Pagliacci's lover. And I told him about the murder of Marja, one of the women who raised me.

"I'm sorry Marja's dead," Jonathan said. "She used to save sweets for me when I'd visit the Cathedral."

For a moment I struggled to focus, to push through my grief. I needed Jon to understand.

So I told them everything — except my belief that Jon's twin brother Jack was involved. With what Eleanora had said, I wasn't sure anymore. And after his sister Gardena's reaction at the yacht launch to my even implying it, I felt afraid to speak of it with Jon right then. I merely said that Frank Pagliacci and his associates were calling themselves the Red Dog Gang.

Jon nodded. "I've read of the attacks on the Clubb merchants. You mean they're responsible for the strangulations as well?"

"I believe so."

And then I knew what I had to do.

"At every step, they've tried to distract me, divert me. They kidnapped David. They murdered my informants. They've killed, attacked, and threatened my family. And now this frame-up. They've done all this for one reason: to stop me from investigating what these Red Dogs are doing." It was all so clear. "They might even be spreading these tales about Joe being alive!" That one almost killed me. "I believe this District Attorney is in cahoots with them. It's likely he's being paid a great sum to do this. He may have planned it. He may even be leading them. In any case, I'm not having it. I refuse to run away and let them win, let them destroy everything, when I know I'm innocent."

Mr. Hart didn't have much of a tell. But as he studied us just then, I got the impression he felt sad.

Why sad?

Jon's face fell. His hand resting on the table shook, and he quickly hid it in his lap. "Jacqui, you know ... how ... very much ... I care for y — your well-being." He took a deep breath, squeezing his eyes shut, not moving. Then he opened his eyes, faced me. "But —" he let out a breath, straightened. "I'll support any decision you make in this."

"Thank you. Now," I put my hand on his shoulder, "you must eat. It's almost time to go."

Jon picked at his food until it was time to leave, but I ate with relish. I was no longer afraid.

No matter what happened, the Red Dog Gang was not going to beat me this time.

The Play

I strode into the hearing chamber, Jonathan and Mr. Hart trailing behind. Mr. Pike met me. "So what have you decided?"

"I admit to nothing," I said. "I'm innocent."

"Very well," Mr. Pike had an air of resignation. "So be it."

Mr. Trevisane was at our table; Tony sat a few rows back. Jon sat beside Tony, shaking his head.

Mr. Pike, Mr. Freezout, Mr. Trevisane, and a black-haired man who appeared to be a Hart left through a side door with the judge.

I glanced back at Jonathan and Tony. Tony didn't look at me; Jon merely shrugged.

After some time, the men returned. Mr. Freezout spoke first, quite confidently, and if I didn't know I didn't bomb the zeppelin, I might even believe I did. He brought out my letters and the forged invoices. He summoned witnesses who heard Dame Anastasia say I gave her the package which killed her.

Mr. Pike, however, was not idle. He demanded to know who determined that these letters and invoices were in my hand. Mr. Pike questioned each witness mercilessly, and requested his own writing expert, a request Mr. Freezout claimed wasteful, but that the judge granted. Yet Mr. Pike never once mentioned Ma.

Afterward, the judge determined that the case should go to trial. People began to stand and walk towards the exit. I turned to Mr. Pike, who now sat beside me. "Why did you not tell the judge my mother was aboard the zeppelin?"

"Tell me the truth, now. Was she really on the zeppelin?"

I glanced away.

"As I suspected."

"But I did believe she was. I swear it." I began to be afraid. "You must never tell anyone. It would put several people in danger should they learn she's alive."

"Then I made the right play. This gives Freezout less time to produce her." Then he gave his alligator grin. "Plus, I relish the thought of his reaction when he hears it in front of everyone." Then he sobered. "I hoped you'd decline to go to trial, simply for your own sake. But now, I feel relieved. The Families have each sent a representative, urging me not to interfere with this trial, and to inform me of the consequences should I fail to acquit you."

I felt astonished. The Families **wanted** this to go to trial?

But then I remembered what Roy had said: *we must not be seen to interfere with the investigation in any way*. They wanted it to play out, even if it ended badly. Why?

Mr. Pike glanced in the direction of Jon and Mr. Hart, who stood talking. "Make a list of anyone who believed your mother to be aboard. I'll stop by later for it."

* * *

When I returned home, the clock struck five: it was tea-time. As Amelia brought in my tea and sandwiches. I pondered Mr. Pike's question: Who knew Ma was going on the zeppelin?

Mrs. Rachel Diamond, of course, but I couldn't bring her into this. Not only would that endanger her, but having pretended to be so terribly ill all these years made her easy to discredit.

But Gardena Diamond knew, because I asked her to smuggle Ma out of Bridges in the first place. She asked her oldest brother Cesare to talk to Lance Clubb about it, and Lance arranged the carriage to take Ma to the zeppelin.

But according to Tony's mother Molly, Ma never left the Cathedral. So either Molly got into that carriage herself, or she hired someone to go to the zeppelin station that night.

This raised an interesting question. Molly said Mrs. Rachel Diamond contacted her — at great risk to her person — to keep my mother from getting on the zeppelin. How did Mrs. Diamond know there was a danger?

I pondered this but could deduce no answer. Mrs. Diamond

obviously had access to information — at the very least, the night before the bombing — that she didn't care to share with the Clubbs. Why would she not contact them? Did she not trust them?

Her husband planned to give the Clubbs both her only daughter and her grandson. Why would she agree to that if she didn't trust the Clubbs with information which could save hundreds of lives and their station?

The only way this play made sense was if not telling the Clubbs benefited the Diamond Family in some rather vital way. As the saying went: *Diamonds only protect their own.*

Then why protect my mother? Who was she to Mrs. Diamond?

While considering the matter, I realized there might be a driver who brought a woman fitting Ma's description to the zeppelin. Someone Lance contacted to arrange the affair who never got aboard. Men at the dock who saw the group from the Pot enter the cargo hold. Perhaps Mr. Pike could investigate that angle.

By the time I'd written this list, put it into an envelope, and sealed it, the sun had set, although the sky still was blue.

But I finished just in time: the doorbell rang, and lo! and behold! it was none other than Mr. Doyle Pike, his dark brown and brass carriage outside in the twilight. I put the envelope in my pocket and answered the door.

He seemed surprised to see me. "Do you always answer the door yourself? Seems a bit dangerous, all things considered."

I shrugged. "My butler and housekeeper are newlyweds, sir. I'm sure they're occupied."

He chuckled at that, and let me lead him into the parlor.

"Would you like some tea, sir?"

"I suppose so."

"Amelia!"

Her voice was muffled in a back room. "Coming, mum."

I gestured to the sofa. "Have a seat." I seated myself in a chair across from him. "What news?"

"Well, I just came from the courthouse, where I've looked through several large boxes of information about your case. I also had the inquest notes collected. I'll look over them later."

"You sound busy."

"Indeed."

Amelia came in, glanced at us, then rushed out, coming back a few minutes later with tea. After she left, I handed him the envelope. "I think you'll find this interesting."

He opened the envelope, reading through it. "You're right. This will make a daunting list of witnesses." He grinned his alligator grin. "I love it."

Was this a game to him? "You sound as if your primary interest is in beating these men."

He leaned forward, picked up his teacup and saucer. "It's why I do it." He took a long drink. "Well, and the money doesn't hurt."

"But you don't believe any of us to be innocent. To you, we're all scoundrels."

Mr. Pike grinned. "Even scoundrels deserve justice."

I'd never considered that, but it made sense. "Why is Mr. Freezout doing this? I'm not guilty of these things." Except the perjury. They'd caught me in lies during the inquest. "What could his motive possibly be for this trial?"

Mr. Pike's eyes narrowed. "That's an excellent question. He leaned forward, elbows on his knees. "It's a pity women aren't allowed to become lawyers — you'd make a fair decent one."

I snorted. Women weren't "allowed" to do much of anything in Bridges. It was just one reason I wanted to get out of here.

"I don't wish to speculate. I'd rather talk about your defense."

"What about it?"

He glanced past me. "Are your people trustworthy?"

I shrugged. Amelia would report to Tony and Pearson no matter what, and probably let at least some slip to her husband Peter, which meant Roy knew much. Mary likely spoke with her parents — again, which went straight to Roy. I expected Blitz spoke with Sawbuck at the very least.

That actually wasn't so bad: Sawbuck hated Roy and wanted nothing to do with him.

"Well, then," Mr. Pike said, "what we discussed earlier. We have to reveal that eventually. But how I plan to play this is to order the witnesses so you testify before many of these others.

That'll be unusual, and some of the press will attend just for the spectacle. But they'll all come out if we let it slip that your testimony holds some special item. You have a flair for the dramatic. I feel certain you'll know when to show your cards."

"Won't the District Attorney be upset we didn't tell him?"

He shrugged. "I don't have to tell him anything at the moment. He knows our defense is that you have an alibi. And that we suspect intent to frame you. I must notify him five days before I use the materials or witnesses we gather, but it's his job to learn the details and meaning of each. He already knows from the inquest that we have evidence of forgery and theft of your letters." He set his cup down. "The real trouble is the jury. Many of them will have prejudice towards you, and I can only do so much. If they don't believe your testimony, or doubt your witnesses speak true, or believe any of the witnesses have been pressured to testify for rather than against you, there's not much I can do." He glanced away. "Which is why I advised you to take the offer."

* * *

Two weeks later, back I went to the court. It was much the same as the first time. However, Mr. Freezout added a charge of "conspiracy" involving the financial crisis. He also added another hundred or so to the list of those I'd supposedly murdered: the people from the Pot who were being smuggled in the hold.

At least **someone** remembered them.

Watching Mr. Pike and Mr. Freezout was like the theater — each had speeches to persuade the judge, who sat as if the whole matter bored him. I have to say the whole thing would have bored me, if I wasn't the one on trial. But at last one or the other would prevail. The judge would hit his small hammer — Mr. Trevisane said it was called a gavel — and the next part would begin.

Mr. Pike seemed particularly upset about Mr. Freezout's plan — which the judge allowed — to display the portraits of the dead quadrant-folk every day throughout the entire trial.

Finally, it was over, and we all rose as the judge left.

"Impressive," Mr. Trevisane murmured next to me. "Mr. Pike got the judge to agree that this is a hostile venue. Although in this case, it matters little."

"Why? What does it mean?"

"My dear, surely you can't imagine you'll be allowed to leave the city? But he's actually given a delay in the trial date, which should give time to settle the negative publicity." He leaned over to speak in my ear. "Give the Clubbs a chance to help you."

I smiled at him. "That is encouraging."

"Indeed. This judge isn't known for such things."

Mr. Freezout didn't look perturbed in the slightest by the decision, and I wondered how much of this really was like the theater, an act.

Jonathan Diamond and Mr. Hart followed me, Mr. Pike, and my guards to the hallway and outside. Mr. Freezout stood on the steps; there must have been a hundred reporters with him.

"Oh, gods," Mr. Hart drawled. "Here come the dramatics."

"The judge feels he can delay the trial without any protest from you, the people! And why? So this woman has more time to lounge about? We demand a speedy verdict!"

"Come on." Mr. Pike appeared at my elbow, hurrying me past them. "Let's get you to your carriage."

But the reporters immediately abandoned Mr. Freezout. "Mrs. Spadros! Do you feel you can get a fair trial?"

Mr. Pike took my arm. "Say nothing." We hurried down the steps, the others close behind, and Honor opened the door.

"Mrs. Spadros! You've admitted to being from the Pot! Do you feel you've been judged guilty already? Do you think you're held to a higher standard because of your birth?"

That a quadrant-man would even consider asking such a question surprised me. The answer seemed obvious.

Mr. Pike shoved me inside, shutting the door.

The crowd of reporters rushed up behind us so fast some of them pushed the carriage when they slid to a stop. The horses whinnied; I grabbed hold of the door handle to keep from sliding down the bench seat.

The curtains were drawn, but thin enough to see out. Mr. Pike turned to the reporters. "Mrs. Spadros will not get a fair trial in Bridges. Your District Attorney would rather hound a young woman than find the real culprits."

"You're saying Mrs. Spadros is innocent?"

"We've maintained that the entire time. The ruthless men who would murder hundreds then frame a young woman deserve our undying scorn. You might ask yourself why the District Attorney isn't spending your hard-earned money searching for them." Mr. Pike climbed inside the carriage, pulling the door shut. "That ought to give them something for their columns."

"So what happens now?"

"I'll speak to the press. You stay inside, keep a sober demeanor, and," he pointed at me, "don't. Talk. To **anyone**."

I took this to mean "don't talk to anyone" about the trial. Which he must have seen in my face, because he said, "If someone you don't trust with your life comes asking about what tea you prefer, don't talk about how wonderful a day it is. Because those men out there," he pointed his thumb towards the windows, "will report that you think it was wonderful all those people are dead."

* * *

Even though the trial would be delayed, there was still much for Mr. Pike to do. Yet there was little for me to do. I spent many a day pacing, peering out, trying not to think.

I saw now why Tony warned against suicide. Locked in my apartments with a daily stream of curses and slander, life soon became unbearable. I closed my window so I might not hear so clearly, but my room became stifling, forcing me to open it again.

Blitz bought an ice block, and a fan was set atop it. But even with all the fans on, the heat was oppressive, the humidity, worse.

I wrote to Pip, sending an extra sheet and envelope each time, and Amelia agreed to bring the letters back and forth. Jonathan came as often as he could, usually after tea, when the crowd tended to tire. He often brought books, or a painting.

One day, when we sat admiring a painting he brought, I lowered my voice. "It's very dull when you're not here."

"Dull? I always thought your servants quite entertaining."

"It's just — there's nothing to do. I've read every book. I don't even have my piano. Not that there's anywhere to put it."

Jon rose, peering down the hallway. "I can help with that."

A few days later, Jon returned with several men carrying a

white upright piano, which fit perfectly at the end of the hall. "A gift," Jonathan said, "to brighten your day."

Blitz was ecstatic. "How I've missed playing!"

"It needs tuning," Jon said, "but —"

"I can do that." Blitz dashed out.

This seemed overwhelming. "Thank you so much, Jon."

"It's of no consequence. We have several. It hasn't been used in years!" He checked his pocket-watch. "I must go."

A few hours passed, then Blitz returned with a set of tools, and set to work tuning the piano, only stopping to eat.

It was late in the evening when he finished. Then he pushed the piano into place and began to play.

"Oh, my dear Mr. Spadros," Mary said. "It's perfect."

Blitz beamed up at her, and she kissed him.

The paint was chipped, and white was my least favorite color. "It needs sanding," I said to Blitz. "But it sounds wonderful."

"Well, I'll leave that to you. You did say you needed something to do," he winked, "as we're all so dull."

"Don't you know it's horribly rude to listen at doors?" But I was not at all serious. "I'm sure I'm rather dull as well." I leaned against the wall, trying to find a bit of coolness. "Do you think we can open the windows now?"

"I have an idea," Blitz said, and went upstairs.

Mary and I exchanged a glance. A laugh burst from me. "He never stops moving!"

She turned crimson, and we broke into a fit of giggles.

Blitz found a small window in the attic, which when opened, allowed the air to flow up and out. "We'll have to close the window when it storms, but this should help."

Blitz taught me how to sand the piano. After many days' work, I stained it a deep cherry, to match my beloved desk.

Blitz spent hours playing in the evenings, and as it turned out, his play was completely self-taught. "The first time I saw one, I knew what needed doing. I'll be always grateful Vig gave me the opportunity." He stopped then. "One of these days I'll get him a new piano to replace the one Mr. Roy's men destroyed."

Soon Blitz was teaching me to play better. At first, he tried to teach without sitting beside me, but eventually he saw how impossible that was. We even played together, once Amelia had left for the evening. "She's an older sort," Mary said. "I don't think she'd approve."

As the days passed, I had hour-long meetings with Mr. Pike at his office on a weekly basis. We discussed the trial, what I should say, how I should act.

"Keep your feet on the floor and your eyes ahead," Mr. Pike said. "And learn to keep yourself still. We want the jury to see you as a cultured quadrant-woman, not a Pot child."

I knew how to answer instruction: Roy Spadros taught me that all too well. "Yes, sir."

"I hope your hats are small? Like the one you wear now?"

"I sold the bigger ones."

"Then you may wear a hat in the courtroom. It makes you appear more refined. But no rings. A simple necklace is fine."

"I have no jewelry, sir," I said. "All that has sold."

"Keep your clothing dark. Not so much eye makeup, and just a bit more glow to your cheeks. Always wear a corset. And sit on the edge of your chair if you can. It keeps you alert."

Sit on the edge of the chair yet keep still. Dark clothing, light makeup. "This seems quite complicated."

"Not really, just good play for this sort of round." He leaned forward. "It's a way to gain favor with the jury. No one else in the courtroom matters. But don't look at the jury. And never react, no matter what happens. No matter how shocking the circumstance, keep a quiet demeanor. Mr. Freezout will try anything to get you to behave foolishly; you must not let him succeed. And for gods' sake, be on time. Be early, if you can. Both judge and jurors despise those who are late."

"I see."

"If you want to say something whilst the judge sits, don't. I'll have a pad and pen for you. Write your words and pass the pad to me, or put it on the table in front of my chair if I'm standing. Never interrupt. Do you understand? It's very important."

"Yes, sir."

This went on for many weeks. I found these meetings tedious, but the rides to and fro were welcome breaks from sitting at home. As time went on and the days grew hotter still, the number of people outside the barricades dropped. For hours, the only men beside them were the police officers unfortunate enough to have been assigned that duty.

Jonathan brought me the paper from time to time, this day arriving for Sunday breakfast. The Clubbs had sponsored a series of articles with my photograph and various personal facts about me. That I enjoyed walking in my garden, or playing the piano. A tale of our dog Rocket bounding into our rooms after a rainstorm.

"Master Lance said his mother wishes to portray you as a sweet young quadrant-wife," Jon said.

"As opposed to a hard-eyed harlot from the Pot." A speech by the District Attorney painted me just that way, in different words.

"When you put it that way, yes."

After Jonathan left, I thought about what the Red Dog Gang might be up to. I needed to speak with Mr. Hart about the businesses which received forged invoices supposedly from him.

Wait, I thought, this proves what I said in court. Mr. Hart received these too. Did the handwriting match?

"Amelia!"

I heard her hurry to the door. She peered inside. "Yes, mum?"

"Send a message to Mr. Doyle Pike. I must speak with him."

"At once, mum."

I no longer had the list from Mr. Hart, as my desk still hadn't been brought over from Spadros Manor. Many notes about the case also lay within my locked dresser drawer.

I loved my desk. I needed a place for it. Perhaps I might find a corner in the parlor?

Whether I missed Tony or not, I did miss my study. I missed having a work room where I might consider my cases.

Blitz and Mary lived in the far corner room behind the kitchen. That left two rooms empty, plus the large upstairs area, which I still wanted to hire out by the hour to artists and photographers.

I decided to use the room next door for my study. We were unlikely to get tenants, and I could put the space to good use.

Amelia knocked. "Mr. Pike, mum."

"Seat him in the parlor please, Amelia." Taking up my shawl, I went to the parlor. However, instead of Mr. Doyle Pike, his grandson Mr. Thrace Pike sat there, rising when I appeared.

The younger Mr. Pike was a thin man of twenty with straw-colored hair and very dark eyes. To my surprise, he'd bought a new suit! "Good day, sir," I said. "Would you care for tea?"

"Yes, madam," he replied, not looking at me.

"Is your grandfather well?"

This appeared to settle him. "My grandfather stated that he was not, and I quote, 'a messenger boy to be called across the city at will.' He asked me to attend you instead."

"Please have a seat, sir. I'll be brief."

At that point, Amelia returned with tea, which she poured. "Is there anything else, mum?"

"I'd like the room next to mine set up as a study. We can sell what furnishings need moving."

"I'll have it seen to at once."

"So my grandfather spoke true," Mr. Pike said. "You don't intend to return to Spadros Manor."

Something in his voice warned me against revealing too much. "I haven't decided as yet. But as long as I'm here, I may as well arrange the place in a manner which suits me."

"Yes, madam," Mr. Pike said, his cheeks coloring. "May I ask your urgent news?"

"Oh! Yes. Forgive me. I wished to notify your grandfather of —" How much should I reveal? This was Hart Family business. "Others than Spadros Manor have also suffered from forgery."

Mr. Pike said, "That's wonderful! Can you share any details?"

This was a mistake. "I'll have them contact your grandfather."

Thrace Pike recoiled. "I completely understand, madam. He's your lawyer, and has treated you kindly." He gazed to the side, an uncertain look upon his face. "While I'm but a clerk, and —" at this, he clearly decided not to speak further. "I would beware of placing complete confidence in my grandfather in any matter which doesn't directly influence your case."

Now this was interesting. "Whatever do you mean?"

"He's not entirely honorable in his dealings." Thrace Pike fixed his dark eyes upon mine. "He's forbidden by law and convention to share information directly involving a case, but that doesn't mean he won't share other things. Or use them to his benefit."

Very interesting. "So he has other interests? Besides the law?"

"Indeed. He owns property, businesses, has dealings with all sorts of men. Some most unsavory." Mr. Pike's lip curled in disdain. "He uses the gratitude of utter scoundrels to his benefit."

I shrugged. "He could hardly fail to come across such men in his line of work. And gratitude is a powerful emotion."

He stood. "Was there anything else you needed to convey to my grandfather, Mrs. Spadros?"

So that got a response. Mr. Pike had too much scruple for this city. "Do you like your job, sir?"

He seemed taken aback. "My family situation's improved by it." He blinked, as if remembering something. "Thank you for your payment, madam. For the documents. And for not informing my grandfather of it. And for giving it in a form we might use." He seemed humbled. "Yes. I mean, no. I don't enjoy working for him. But —" at this, he sat, leaning his elbows on his knees. "My goal is to learn. What this man does to you is unthinkable, and —"

The man's mind seemed to dart every direction. "Which man?"

"Freezout." Mr. Pike shook his head in scorn. "He's corrupted everything a man in his position should stand for. You're clearly innocent, yet he plans your death! You were right to ask who pays him." His manner cooled, and he peered at me. "I see now that I aimed too low. Bridges needs a District Attorney unbought."

He sat quietly for a moment. "My grandfather is respected. And I believe we can free you, madam, I truly do. He's selected me to be in the courtroom above all the others. If I continue to do well, with my grandfather's recommendation, I could become an Assistant District Attorney. I'd be in position to do some real good." His face took on astonishment, and hope. "I may hold the cards to bid game!" His expression softened. "And for that, I thank you."

The Selection

Blitz pronounced the bed in the room next to me better than the one they had, so we ended up selling theirs instead. Amelia had my desk brought over, and I felt appalled to see the locks broken, the papers rifled through.

I found the list of merchants who'd received forged invoices supposedly from Mr. Hart:

The Ladies' Emporium

Blind Button Dealers, Inc.

Mississippi Paper Co.

Big Bet Mining Supply

Open Stakes Trainers

I called in Blitz. "Can you find out what sort of items the Mississippi Paper company sells?"

"They sold us the packaging for the auction." He leaned against the door-post. "You need something?"

"I do." I took out a paper and pen. "I'd like to have a sign and some cards made with this writing."

When I handed the sheet over to him, he chuckled. "If they can't do this, I'll have them made up somewhere else."

I perused my lists of questions, the evidence I held. Mr. Freezout and his Red Dog Gang wanted me out of the way so they could do what they were really doing with no one the wiser.

But what could they possibly be doing? And why did they think I was so important? I was no one, especially now that I stood separate from the Spadros Family. I didn't understand how it all fit together. There was some vital clue I missed, something that would make this all clear.

* * *

The worst of the summer heat passed. While we'd had a good delay of the trial, it couldn't be avoided. So back I went.

Storm-clouds covered the sky. The guards brought me to a well-lit court hall almost as large as the one where the inquest had been held. This hall, like that at the inquest, had a second level, presumably for uppers who wished to view the trial.

The left side of the lower level was filled with men. Old and young, rich and poor, they stared at me as I passed.

On my right, Mr. Charles Hart and Jonathan Diamond sat two rows behind the railing. Others were present as well:

Tony sat at the far end of my table with his lawyer Mr. Trevisane between us, not even glancing my way as I approached. Color lay high in his cheek; from his bearing, he was both angry and deeply embarrassed.

Mr. Julius Diamond sat next to Jon with an expression on his face which could have curdled milk. The man was a Patriarch, the head of the Diamond crime syndicate. Why was he here if he didn't want to be?

Thunder pealed in the distance. Two rows behind Jon and Julius Diamond sat Alexander and Regina Clubb, as relaxed as if on a summer outing. They smiled warmly, evidently trying to put me at ease. Apparently Mrs. Clubb had forgiven me for almost breaking her arms several months earlier. I must have been out of my mind to assault an elderly woman, even if she did look twenty years younger than her true age must be.

I sat heavily. Dr. Salmon said I wasn't mad now, but I still wondered if I might have been that day.

Mr. Cesare Diamond. How to describe such a man? He stood at the front of the room to the left of the judge's seat, but casually, as if at home. He wore not the uniform of the Court, but a navy blue suit of the same color. His skin was even darker than Jonathan's, and he stood at least an inch taller.

But while Jonathan was unmarried at six and twenty, Cesare

was at least thirty, with a wife and sons, a full man in all confidence and power. This was the heir to the Diamond Family Business, and he appeared ready to take command at any time.

Cesare Diamond glanced at me as one might glance at a cockroach while in a rush to leave: noting it, yet not willing to squash the thing at present. He turned to the judge. "Since the defendant is here, may we begin?"

"By all means, sir."

Mr. Freezout said, "Your Honor, I wish to protest that members of the Four Families are in attendance."

"So noted." The judge clearly planned to ignore the matter. "Mr. Pike, do you have anything to add?"

"No, Your Honor."

Cesare turned to face the room. "I appear here as Keeper of the Court, as my brother has been recused from this case due to his long association with the defendant." He said this in the tone one might use to speak of an association with a mongrel stray dog. "Let no one question my impartiality in this matter."

This last part he said as if a matter of course.

Yet I believed it. He'd never shown me any favor whatsoever. But he'd always spoken truth. And he did heed my words when last we met, even seeming to hold a grudging respect, his behavior this day notwithstanding.

Tony's face held the tightly controlled mask he invariably took on in public. But I knew at a glance he was furious.

Cesare spoke casually, without notes. "Today we begin jury selection. You will be called to the jury-box. Each of you will be questioned by these lawyers as to your attitudes on the case before us, as well as your standing and obligations. You're not on trial; if you have a compelling reason to excuse yourself, you may speak now without penalty." He brushed a speck of lint from his sleeve. "You may be dismissed without reason being given. Don't take that as a slight on your character. These lawyers are a capricious lot." He gave a sardonic smile, and scattered laughter came from the group to the left. "They may dismiss for any reason at all, or none. When dismissed, see the clerk at the desk out front and they'll mark your name, so you don't have to return." Then he gestured to a man to his right, who held a writing-pad. "This man will call you forward."

With that, he moved three steps up to a small platform to sit at a desk, which put him a head below the judge.

This arrangement lay past an area which hadn't been in the other rooms: two rows of chairs on this side of the railing, but ringed by another railing, a small gate at its near end. The man with the pad called names, and twelve men took two steps up to take seats there.

After this, the judge read the charges against me, then asked if anyone in the room felt uncomfortable to judge a case which might lead to death. No one answered. The judge then asked if anyone felt difficulty at sending a woman to death.

This time, quite a bit squeaking and shuffling occurred, and two hands raised. I didn't dare turn round to survey the audience. "Those of you who have raised a hand may go," the judge said, and the room took a few moments to quiet as men left.

Rain drummed on the roof. The man with the pad called two other names. Only one came forward, so he called a third. This man came forward and sat.

The lawyers were introduced, and Mr. Freezout spoke first.

Each man in the jury-box was questioned, but the tone was conversational. What was their name? Where did they live? Were they employed by any of the Four Families? What did they understand about this case? Had they made any determination about whether I might be guilty or not? What did they believe about people who lived in the Pot? Did they lose money in the financial crisis, or know someone else who did?

Men were being dismissed left and right, with new ones added. We had a recess for luncheon, but I'd been brought my food in a small side room. My only company was an armed maid, who stood, face disapproving, as I ate alone.

By the end of the day, four men remained. I felt exhausted, and I hadn't done a thing but sit.

Hail clattered on the roof. The judge asked the remaining men to return the next day. We rose as the judge began to leave.

Sirens went off.

A tornado, this late in the year?

"Everyone to the basements!" Cesare shouted.

The tornadoes were monstrous on the plains outside the dome, and when one hit, smaller ones often spun off inside. So far in Bridges history there'd been no damage to the dome itself, but in the past other domes had been damaged, with catastrophic effect.

The guards shooed the four jury-men out, while the Family members, lawyers, and I followed Cesare through the judge's chambers and down a narrow stair into a wide carpeted windowless room. Elegant sofas lined the walls, and a bar and icebox stood waiting. I stayed as far from the bar as possible.

"Are the others well?" I said. "The jury-men." For them to be caught out in a storm on my account would be unthinkable.

Cesare, who stood off to my left, gave me a startled glance. Across the room, Tony's face held a bemused, cynical smile.

I looked away. *I must not let myself be drawn back to him.*

"The men have their own room, as befitting their station." Mr. Hart made this sound obvious. He stood behind me to my right.

"It would be unseemly for any member of the Court," Cesare glanced at Jon, who stood to my left, "to mingle with a defendant."

Jon's face flushed an angry red, and he turned away.

The judge seemed to have disappeared through a door in the far wall, the three lawyers with him.

"How long must we be down here?" We didn't have such luxuries in the Pot — if a tornado came, we watched for it, listened for the sirens. Yet many of the basements were flooded with fetid water, unsafe, or otherwise unusable. And there was no basement in the Cathedral that I knew of. We'd huddle under mattresses in one of the back rooms — whores and clients, children and the old — until the danger passed.

Mr. Clubb said, "We'll be informed when the All Clear sounds." Mr. and Mrs. Clubb passed us to settle near the bar.

Mr. Julius Diamond, who stood to the right watching us, came forward to shake Mr. Hart's hand. This made my earlier theory of a Clubb-Diamond alliance to exclude the Harts less plausible.

Mr. Charles Hart said to Mr. Julius Diamond, "I'm sure you

know Mrs. Spadros."

I crossed my arms. "We've been introduced." I didn't like the way he'd treated Tony in the past. "I hope all is well?"

"Indeed." Mr. Diamond glanced at Jon and Mr. Hart. "Might I have a word with Mrs. Spadros in private?"

Jon appeared surprised. Mr. Hart took it in stride. "Of course." The two took several steps towards the center of the room.

I kept my arms crossed. "What do you want?"

A counter of piano-black wood stood behind us, and Mr. Diamond rested his arm upon it. "You didn't need to take your cards off the board."

I gave a slow blink of surprise. "You read the letter."

He snorted. "Your actions were admirable, but unnecessary."

Gardena will not have me either.

"I know that now." I felt exhausted. "What do you want?"

He seemed surprised. "To offer my support. None of us want this trial. But surely you understand why it must happen." He glanced at Mr. Freezout, who stood by the bar watching everyone. Mr. Pike sat near the Clubbs, briefcase open, reading some papers.

"It must appear that no one interferes." *No witness can be tampered with, no juror intimidated.* "What a gamble you take with my life, sir. All of you."

"Oh, come now, Mrs. Spadros. Do you really believe you'll see the gallows? If it goes that far, we can have some other Pot rag who looks like you hung."

Not only was this speech insulting, but horrifying. "How dare you even suggest such a thing? This is an innocent human being you speak of!" These people were mad. "Begone with you, sir."

His eyebrows raised. "As you wish."

Jon came to me. "I don't know what you said, but I've never seen anyone speak to him in that manner, nor him react so." He grinned in delight, squeezing my arm. "Well done."

"He's a horror, Jon. He said that if I were convicted, they might have some other 'Pot rag' who looks like me hung." I dashed away angry tears. "Who thinks like that?"

"They're not good men. I feel strange saying this about my own father, but," he shook his head, letting go of my arm, "he's become estranged from me and Gardena. The old hate between Spadros and Diamond seems too much for him to renounce. That we should ally ourselves with you and Tony —"

She allied herself with Tony …? "Yet he has a Spadros grandson."

Jon slowly nodded. "Perhaps one day that will make him relent. He does love the boy, in spite of his face — and his name."

* * *

The danger passed, and we all returned home.

But the next day, I was back for another round, with another crowd of people. The same questions, over and over. I didn't understand why I needed to be present for this.

As the day progressed, people began to slip in on the right side, being kept four rows behind me by the guards. Finally, all the jurors and two alternate men "in case of illness or injury" were selected, and the rest sent home.

Since it was tea-time, I'd thought we'd leave also. But the judge gave us a recess until after tea, which I took in the small side room, an armed maid presiding.

I'd asked Mr. Pike if he might join me. He sat, saying, "It might be best to speak in privacy."

"Oh, of course." I turned to the maid. "You may leave us."

Once she had done so, I said, "Mr. Hart may corroborate the forgeries, as he's had some of his own."

"Yes, well, the request to testify probably should come from you," he said, "as the unexpected realization of **my** knowing such details might cause undue agitation."

I chuckled. "A knife at your throat, you mean."

"More likely a fist in my face." He winced. "I'm not as agile as I used to be."

"Then I shall speak with him at the first opportunity." I turned to Mr. Pike. "Do you think we got a good jury?"

"I suppose time will tell."

The Opening

When I returned, the room was full. Rows upon rows of portraits — perhaps two hundred — hung along the wall on my side of the room, stretching eight feet high. Dame Anastasia's hung there with the rest.

The judge said, "Is the prosecution prepared to begin?"

Mr. Freezout rose. "We are, Your Honor. Permission to address the jury?"

"Permission granted."

Mr. Freezout came around the table, facing the jurors. "My name is Mr. Chase Freezout, District Attorney for the Independent City-State of Bridges. On March 1st, eighteen hundred and ninety-nine years after the Catastrophe, at approximately three in the afternoon, three hundred forty-seven men, women, and children boarded Travelers' Federation Flight A26 bound for Nitivali. This priceless craft rose from the Bridges zeppelin station, above the golden fields of Clubb. Yet it never reached the Aperture.

"Why? Because at 3:47 pm, Travelers' Federation Flight A26 was destroyed by an explosion massive enough to shatter the ancient glass-work of our station, one of the marvels of the Merca Federal Union, nay, the entire world.

"This was no accident. And this is not where our story begins, rather where it ends.

"I represent the good people of Bridges, but I also represent the good people of each city in the Merca Federal Union who trusted us only to have their statesmen scattered across the countryside. As their representative, I intend to secure justice for them."

He turned towards me, jabbing his finger as he spoke.

"The defendant, born in the Pot among thieves, liars, Party Time addicts, drunkards, and whores. Brought from squalor into a decent life and raised to the highest place in her quadrant. Yet instead of a life of gratitude, caring for her home and bearing children as any proper woman would, she deliberately and with malice plotted to ruin our city. First, by orchestrating the gem fraud which sent thousands high and low into bankruptcy. Second, by exploding Travelers' Federation Flight A26, a move designed to destroy not only one ship and its people but the trust our entire nation placed on us.

"Through her position, she had access to untold wealth, which she used not to help the city which took her in but to betray it out of a fierce hatred instilled since childhood. The prosecution has dozens of letters between the fraudulent gem dealer Dame Anastasia Louis and the defendant, proving their association. The prosecution will display the very invoices the defendant used to order the parts and material used to create the explosion. Witnesses will testify that the defendant gave a package to Dame Anastasia Louis which almost certainly contained a bomb —"

The audience murmured, glancing at each other with shocked faces. Evidently they'd not heard this before.

"— removing her co-conspirator as she tried to flee the city when their scheme ended in debacle. And what better day to perform such betrayal than the Hundredth Celebration of the day which gave us our freedom from the Pot's tyranny? We have witnesses as to how the defendant rushed to the scene. Why? We maintain it was to view her dastardly handiwork, to gloat in the terror and destruction around her.

"Today we gather to honor these people," at this, he gestured across the room, to the rows of portraits, "and to secure justice for them and their families. To do that we must remove a cold-blooded killer from our midst who should never have been among us in the first place."

He turned to the jurors. "It is by law set down in the vast millennia before the Catastrophe that we chose you, the jury, to help judge this matter. We are grateful that you serve here today."

The judge said, "Is the defense prepared to begin?"

Mr. Pike rose. "Yes, Your Honor. May I address the jury?"

"You may."

As Mr. Freezout did, Mr. Pike approached the jurors. "Good men of the jury, it's an honor to speak to you today. My name is Mr. Doyle Pike. My job as defense attorney is to ensure that each man — or woman, in this case — receives a fair trial.

"The facts of the matter are not in question. Travelers' Federation Flight A26 bound for Nitivali did explode that terrible day, with three hundred forty-seven people aboard. Our zeppelin station did shatter. Yet the defense maintains that the rest of the prosecution's story is just that — a story."

The audience murmured.

"Let me introduce you to Mrs. Jacqueline Spadros." He took several steps aside, his back to the judge, gesturing to me with an open hand, and I blushed at the hundreds of eyes upon me. "She's twenty-two years old, married for four years now. A bright, lovely young woman, dragged before this court to be slandered and gazed upon. Through no fault of her own, she's been made the center of an unseemly spectacle. In a way, you might say she's the three hundred forty-eighth victim of this tragedy."

The jurors peered at me, and I tried my best not to peer back. By their faces, some did find me attractive. Some seemed disturbed by what they saw.

"So what did happen in the time leading up to the senseless destruction of Flight A26? The defense plans to show you the true nature of this abused and abandoned young woman. How she came to be brought to Spadros quadrant, placed into terrible danger, betrayed by a woman she trusted as a mother, then set up to take the blame for the crimes of others. She is far from having any motive — which we will show in great detail. Far from having reason or even opportunity to do these horrible crimes, she has a gentle heart which seeks to help, not harm.

"We will bring expert testimony in to show that these invoices — and many of the letters in question — were forgeries. We have witnesses as to her character and her friendship with the Clubb Family. Most importantly, we have witnesses describing the theft of letters belonging to Mrs. Spadros and invoices signed by her husband which provided samples of their handwriting more than sufficient to forge these documents.

"On the day of the explosion, Mrs. Spadros was on Market Center until less than an hour before the explosion, which is when she learned of the bombing. She then frantically risked her life and reputation to stop it. We maintain she is a brave young woman, innocent of all charges. We urge our District Attorney to stop the persecution of this young wife, her husband, and her family.

"You, the jury, have the most vital role here. You must judge whether a young woman is guilty of terrible crimes.

"Now, in the law, the prosecution has a very high standard to meet called the burden of proof." He gestured to Mr. Freezout. "He must **prove** Mrs. Spadros did these things. The reason the law is set this way is to prevent someone rich and powerful from forcing you to spend all your money proving you did **not** commit a crime." Mr. Pike shook his head. "He must prove she **did** do it, and this beyond a reasonable doubt. This is the standard by which you must judge.

"We must work together, you and I, to ensure no taint spoils these proceedings. So I will not speak to or acknowledge you until Mr. Freezout and I have finished presenting our evidence. It is not out of disrespect, but to avoid any appearance of favoritism. I thank you very much for your service to our city."

The judge turned to the jury-men. "Jurors, you are warned. Do not speak to anyone about what you have heard and seen today. Do not read a paper, or allow others to read a paper to you about these matters. If you happen to hear of this case from words shouted in the street, or some other way, you must by law report it to the bailiff here at once. Do you understand?"

The men nodded.

"The Court will recess until nine am tomorrow." The judge banged his gavel and rose, as did we all.

The Prosecution

The next day, the trial began. The musicians from our Queen's Day dinner each told of the argument Tony and I had, listing the Family members present. "The master was furious the Diamonds been invited," one said. "He surely didn't want them there."

Mr. Freezout said, "What happened after the dinner?"

"They went off to their parlor room. We was paid way too well for what we done. Something weren't right."

Mr. Pike questioned this man. "Did they ever speak of gems?"

"No, sir."

"So other than the fact that uppers went to speak privately, and you felt they were too generous, you saw nothing amiss."

The man's face flushed red. "Yes, sir."

The District Attorney next called several witnesses, who said the same thing: they saw Dame Anastasia carry a package, and heard her say it was from me. The widow who stood behind the gate counter said, "She was quite happy for it."

"Do you have questions for this witness, Mr. Pike?"

"I do." He rose. "What exactly did Dame Louis say?"

The woman glanced at me. "She said, 'Look at what Mrs. Spadros gave me! I'm sure it's a clock — hear how it ticks!'" I could see her shudder from where I sat. "To think it was a bomb!"

Mr. Pike seemed unperturbed. "Madam, did Dame Louis say she received it from the hand of Mrs. Spadros herself?"

"Why, no sir, she didn't."

"So it's possible she received the package from a messenger?"

"I suppose. She never did say, sir."

Mr. Pike turned to the judge. "I now plan to speak with this witness on behalf of my client."

"Proceed," the judge said.

"Madam, you stated you were behind the counter at the gate for Flight A26 the day of the explosion. Is that correct?"

"Yes, sir."

"And did anyone in this room approach your counter?"

She pointed at me. "Mrs. Spadros, sir."

Mr. Pike said, "When exactly did she approach your counter?"

"It was a few minutes before the explosion."

"Was there anything which struck you as out of the ordinary?"

"Well, I didn't recognize her at first: she had her hair down like a young girl, and she had a gentleman by the hand who I took to be her father. Also, she was quite agitated."

"Agitated?"

"Yes, sir, and out of breath."

"Did you see her do anything before this?"

"Well, sir, she came pushing through the crowd, dragging the gentleman behind. She pushed through to the front of the line!"

"And what did she say?"

"She said we had to stop the zeppelin at once. But I told her once they've taken off you can't stop them. I asked the gentleman if I might book them a flight on the next ship. But then she told me she was Mrs. Spadros and that the zeppelin carried a bomb."

Murmurs in the courtroom.

"And what did you do then?"

"Well, sir, this shocked me so I didn't know what to say. But then the gentleman said the same! So I called the bomb alert."

"Can you explain to us what a bomb alert is?"

"We call the ship and tell them of a bomb threat. They're supposed to immediately dump cargo. But they never answered."

They never answered.

"What happened next?"

"Then there was a loud noise, and the ceiling glass fell. Cut my arm badly, it did." She pulled up her sleeve to show a large white scar. "If my coworker hadn't been there I might have died."

"Did you notice what Mrs. Spadros did at that time?"

"No, sir. I never saw her again, until today."

"Thank you, madam. I have no further questions."

The judge spoke. "Mr. Freezout, do you wish to redirect?"

"Yes, Your Honor." He rose. "Madam, was the identity of the gentleman Mrs. Spadros held the hand of ever ascertained?"

"I don't understand the question."

"Did you learn what man a married woman held the hand of?"

Trying to discredit me, are you?

Murmurs filled the courtroom.

"Objection," Mr. Pike said. "Impeaching the character of the defendant."

The judge said, "Sustained. Mr. Freezout, please keep your comments civil. Madam, you may answer the question."

The woman seemed chagrined. "No, sir."

Mr. Freezout took the judge's words in stride. "And at the time, had you seen this woman before?"

"No, sir."

"So when she came up to you and said she was Mrs. Spadros, did you have any reason to believe her?"

"No, sir. That was why I didn't do anything at first. I took her to be a wild girl with a wild story. You get these from time to time. But then the gentleman spoke for her."

"So then you contacted the ship."

"Yes, sir."

"I have no further questions."

The judge ordered a recess for luncheon. I pushed past Mr. Pike, grabbing Mr. Freezout's arm. "Why are you doing this?"

He shook my hand off. "Young lady, I am not allowed to speak with you. Direct any questions to your lawyer."

Mr. Pike took my arm. "Madam, I —"

I pulled away. "No!" I turned to Mr. Freezout. "Why are you doing this?" Everyone in the courtroom stared at me. "You know I didn't do this! Who's paying you off?"

The judge returned to his area. "The jury is warned not to pay heed to the defendant's words." He turned to me. "You may neither speak to nor lay hands on the prosecution, madam. If you persist, I shall put you in chains."

I backed away, glimpsing a smirk on the DA's face.

"Someone is paying him to do this," I whispered to Mr. Pike.

"Of course, my dear," Mr. Pike said.

"He's not afraid of people knowing, either."

Mr. Pike pulled me aside. "True. But you must restrain yourself! You only make yourself look unruly." He glanced at the jury box. "They watch your every move."

The men in that box had dismay on their faces, disdain, scorn.

"You're not helping with these outbursts," Mr. Pike said. "You're just making them remember where you come from."

* * *

While we were at luncheon, an apparatus of brass and lenses had been set up, with a small lamp and a canvas screen. An elegant older woman with white hair now sat beside Mr. Freezout, a blue-eyed boy with brown hair next to her.

"Before you begin, sir," Mr. Pike said, "might I have the defendant write something, here in front of the jury?"

I had no idea what this might be about.

"Yes," said the judge.

Mr. Pike came to me, and the jury watched him closely. He held up a book. "This is a book of law," he said, "so it's unlikely the defendant has read it." He brought out pen and ink. "Madam, please copy the first three paragraphs on page 23."

So I did. Mr. Pike held up the paper then folded and placed it on a small table which lay to the right and in front of ours. The jury followed his movements with interest.

An expert in handwriting was called forth, who was questioned by Mr. Freezout as to his qualifications. The man gave a demonstration of what he looked for on examining handwriting, and how to compare handwriting to determine the author.

The man then was given the forged invoices. The man placed each into the apparatus, and they were projected upon the screen. Showing them side by side, he determined they were done by the same hand. The crowd murmured, but I needed no contraption to inform me of this.

"I have no further questions," Mr. Freezout said.

"Mr. Pike," the judge said, "you may proceed."

Mr. Pike rose. "Sir, I found your instruction most helpful."

The man seemed surprised. "Why, thank you, sir."

"Could you tell me how you came to be here?"

"I was contacted by the prosecution to evaluate these letters just prior to the inquest."

"And were you paid for this work?"

"As I always am when testifying, at standard rates."

"Very good, sir. Might I have your indulgence for perhaps five minutes, while some prior testimony is read?" Mr. Pike turned to the judge. "If it please the court."

The judge said, "Proceed."

Mr. Pike produced a paper. "I offer Exhibit 49, a list compiled by the prosecutor's office from the sworn testimony at the inquest into the destruction of Flight A26. The list compares the inquest exhibits with exhibits to be offered into evidence here in this trial."

Mr. Freezout looked appalled. "Where did you obtain this?"

"From your office, sir. My clerk was given it by your secretary. I believe it's my right as this woman's attorney to have all evidence of her supposed guilt."

I didn't know Mr. Freezout, but I'd wager the man was furious. I felt sorry for his secretary, who, after all, had only done his duty.

"So entered," the judge said.

"I wish to read this listing in order to compare the documents you've been given, sir," Mr. Pike said to the man, "with those claimed in the inquest to be forgeries."

Mr. Pike read the listing of forgeries, and behold, they matched what the man had evaluated exactly. "I find it curious that you've not been given the opportunity to examine the true handwriting of the defendant, and to compare it to these documents."

Murmurs swelled in the courtroom. The man said nothing.

"Would you be willing to do so, sir?"

"Of course."

First Mr. Pike took the page I'd just written, asking the man to compare it to a letter I wrote months before. Of course, it matched.

Then he asked the man to check it against the forgeries. At once, the man said, "Identical."

"Can you tell us how you came to this conclusion, sir?"

"By looking at them."

"I see. Would you show the Court, as you did with the others?"

The man hesitated, glancing at Mr. Freezout. "Certainly." He put my letter against the forged one.

They did look similar, but not that similar.

"You see. Clear as crystal."

Remembering Mr. Pike's warning, I wrote: *he's lying!*

"I have no further questions for this witness," Mr. Pike said. He returned to his seat, glanced at my note, and nodded.

Next, my gardener was called to the stand. Mr. Freezout said, "Would you tell the Court of the conversation you had with the defendant the week before the zeppelin explosion?"

"Yes, sir. I was mulching the flower beds when Mrs. Jacqueline came to ask me about ammonium nitrate."

"What exactly did she ask?"

"If it were good for gardens. I said yes, but we didn't use it. Spadros soil's good enough."

A few people in the audience chuckled.

"Did she ask anything else?"

"If ammonium nitrate could be used to bomb something."

Scattered murmurs.

"And what did you say?"

"I said why bother when you could buy some extra dynamite? I showed her the ad in the paper. She seemed interested, so I brought her my Pa's old book about it."

The murmurs grew louder, and the judge banged his gavel.

"I have no further questions," Mr. Freezout said.

The judge said, "Mr. Pike?"

"The defense has questions, Your Honor." He went to the man. "Did Mrs. Spadros tell you she wished to bomb something?"

"No, sir, and I feel horrible for the implication. The Spadros Family has been so good to me. I should've been dismissed for testifying in the inquest, yet since then, I've been treated well."

"Did she mention why she wanted the information?"

"No, sir."

After my gardener left, Mr. Freezout said, "At this time, the prosecution wishes to enter testimony given by the defendant whilst under oath during the inquest regarding Exhibits 1 through 41, the letters we have already certified as written by her."

The judge said, "You may proceed."

"I would like to call my wife, Mrs. Delanie Freezout, to speak the words uttered by the defendant."

Mrs. Freezout went to the stand and was sworn in.

I wrote on my pad: *Is this usual?*

Mr. Pike glanced at my words, then wrote underneath it: *They're forbidden to call you to the stand.*

Mr. Freezout said, "I offer Exhibits 50 and 51, two copies of the defendant's testimony whilst under oath." He handed one to his wife. "Please begin at the third paragraph on page two."

They began: she read my words, he read his. It was even more uncomfortable to hear than it was to experience the ordeal the first time. The letters I'd sent Dame Anastasia were coded. But I'd been sloppy, and my shame was being broadcast yet again.

Mr. Freezout said, "Thank you, my dear, you may step down." Then he said, "The prosecution calls Master Tim Keycard."

The boy was clean, his straight, light brown hair freshly cut. Work-boy's clothes hung off a painfully thin frame. He went to the witness booth and stood jauntily, a cynical look in his eye.

The bailiff said, "Raise your right hand. Do you swear to tell the truth or face the Fire?"

"Yeah, sure," the boy said.

"You may be seated."

Mr. Freezout stood. "Please state your name for the record."

"Tim, of the Keycard Cafe."

"How old are you?"

"Ten."

Mr. Freezout pointed at me. "Do you know this woman?"

The boy's bright blue eyes were hard as a man's. "No."

The judge said, "Let the record show that the prosecution indicated the defendant."

Mr. Freezout said, "Where are you from?"

"Just told ya, Keycard Cafe. Stud and Snow."

"So you live in the Spadros Pot."

"Yeah."

"Can you tell us your mother's name?"

He shrugged. "One of them whores, I reckon."

"And your father?"

The boy let out a sharp laugh. "No one got a Pa there!"

The room fell quiet.

"I asked you here today to tell us what living in the Pot is like."

Tim peered at us suspiciously. "We don't got those fine clothes ya got, but we make do."

"So how do you make do?"

"Get up around mid-day, eat whatever's left, go run some with my gang, see what we can steal. Back by nightfall, get ready for the quadrant-folk. They like they boys clean."

Gasps from the crowd.

"You mean you're —" Mr. Freezout appeared afraid to speak.

"I'm a whore, fancy man, like the rest." He leaned back, put his hands behind his head. "Been doing it since I was five. Easy money. When I get too big I'll watch the doors or shake down drunks a something." He surveyed the audience. "What's a matter? Y'all act like it's bad." He let out a short laugh.

Mr. Freezout said, "What else can you do?"

At that, the boy leaned forward, for the first time interested in the conversation. "I know people. I can get you bout anything ya want." He nodded sagely. "I been practicing with the knife. Damn good at it. And I ain't afraid to pull a trigger neither."

"You sound capable. If I wanted, for example, Party Time —"

Tim rolled back with a merry, snaggle-toothed laugh, his pale freckled cheeks pink. "Aw, that's easy! Just tell me how much."

"Aren't you worried about the police?"

"Naw," he said. "They come by all the time. Some a my best customers. But strictly business. They all know."

"Know what?" Mr. Freezout seemed genuinely interested.

"They out where they not wanted, they fair game." He drew a finger across his throat.

"Would you do it, if you had a chance?"

"Damn straight," Tim said. "Anyone would."

"So I take it you don't like the police. Can you tell me what you've heard of the First Mayor, Mr. Xavier Alcatraz?"

Tim frowned. "A gods-damned traitor."

The audience gasped.

"Master Keycard," the judge said, "I should ask you to control your language. There are women present."

The boy giggled as if that were the funniest thing he'd heard all day. "Y'oughta hear the whores talk! All right. They was right about quadrant-folk, all soft. But he was. A traitor a the worst kind. Killed our King, he did, him an them Clubbs."

"Did you hear of the gem scam?"

The boy's eyes went wide. "Oh, that was rare!" He grinned. "Any child can do fakery, but to mark a whole city?" He gave a sneering laugh. "Quadrant-folk'll believe anything."

"Well, it was nice seeing you, Tim." Mr Freezout turned to the judge. "I have no further questions."

The judge said, "Mr. Pike?"

"I have a few questions, Your Honor." He rose, went to the witness booth. "How did you come to be here today?"

"Old fancy man." Tim pointed at Mr. Freezout. "His men told me if I come here today they'd get me a place on Market Center."

Outraged murmurs. Places on Market Center weren't easy to come by. "Let the record show the witness indicated the prosecution," the judge said.

"That sounds good," Mr. Pike said. "Get anything else?"

Tim grabbed the lapels of his jacket. "These here clothes. Right smart, go for a bundle. Nice food, bath. Like a quality gentleman."

"So he's giving you quite a bit." Mr. Pike's voice turned conspiratorial. "Did he go over what you should say?"

"Objection!"

"Overruled," the judge said. "I'd be surprised if you didn't go over what to say with a witness, Mr. Freezout."

Tim said. "I ain't a liar nor a snitch, if that's what ya mean."

"Of course, young sir, not at all. I have no further questions."

The judge said, "Does the prosecution have further witnesses?"

"No, Your Honor," Mr. Freezout said. "The prosecution rests."

The judge said, "The Court will recess until ten tomorrow."

The Revelation

The next day, Mr. Pike called many of the servants from Spadros Manor as witnesses, who testified I'd been there off and on since I was a child.

He asked an old scullery maid, "What sort of mistress is she?"

"Very fair, sir. Kinder to the staff than she should be."

"In what way?"

"She praises our work, and thanks us. Us!" The woman shook her head in astonishment. "She's given us gifts, even."

"What sort?"

"We had an outing a few months back, and she gave me this necklace," she pulled it out to show. "Was one of them 'miracle gems,' and I ain't been sick once since then, sir."

"How would you speak of her character?" He asked Pearson.

Pearson said, "The highest, sir. She's only ever been concerned for the well-being of others, even the servants. When there's a wrong done, she's the first to insist on it made right."

At the recess, Mr. Pike came to me. "I think it's going well." Then he chuckled. "Your Spadros Manor will be up to their eyeballs in new applicants for servant work."

I had luncheon in the small room, and Mr. Hart joined me. The food was adequate at best, but Mr. Hart seemed in good appetite. "I remember my grandfather saying you should never pass up a chance to sit, nor a hot meal."

"Your grandfather?" The man was seventy, so … "You knew Charlie Hart? **The** Charlie Hart?"

He chuckled fondly. "Of course. I was named for him. A big

man, with a big laugh, and a good sense of humor. A brilliant mind, especially for tinkering. My Etienne got that, at least, if nothing else." The thought of his son seemed to dishearten him.

"What was it like, growing up? I mean, back before you controlled the quadrant it must have been a turmoil."

His eyebrows raised, and his lips pursed as he nodded. "It was. But we children never saw much of it. Oh, an uncle or a cousin might be hurt, but we were kept safe as could be."

"I see." But then something he said made me wonder. "You speak as if you had a large family. Where are they now?"

"The Bloody Year took them all." He peered at his plate. "I never wanted to run the Family, Mrs. Spadros. I was the youngest son of the youngest son, and I never thought I'd come anywhere near it. But — well," his tone turned melancholy, regretful. "Things seldom turn out as you thought they would."

We sat silent for a moment. I feared his reaction if I should speak. But I had to know if he would help us. "Sir, we've heard that you had forgeries as well."

He didn't seem surprised. "You wish me to testify."

"Yes, sir."

He took my hand, "I'll do whatever you need me to."

This sparked a thought. "Have you any news about Joseph Kerr? Or Josie? Anything at all?"

Mr. Hart withdrew his hand, shook his head, and sat in thought for a long moment. Then he roused himself. "Did you hear the Mayor's death was ruled foul play?"

I recalled the Mayor's face as he glanced up at me at the back of Vig's saloon the night Marja died. I frowned, confused both at the sudden change of subject and at Mr. Hart's news.

Mayor Badugi owned a chain of very popular bistros. He was both personable and well-liked. And as Mayor, he'd done a great deal to bring peace to the city.

He'd been an ally not only to the Four Families but to Bridges itself. Who would possibly want to kill him? "No, I hadn't."

He patted my hand. "Never you fret about the Kerrs, my dear. We'll find them sooner or later. I promise you that."

Once we returned from luncheon, Mr. Pike called my former dressmaker Madame Biltcliffe. Both lawyers questioned her at length about the break-in at her office and the theft of the invoices Tony had signed. Then she left.

Her face seemed very pale. And she never once looked at me. Was she still angry with me? After the things she'd said during our last meeting back in the spring, I'd felt afraid to write to her.

Finally, Jon was called to the stand.

"Please state your full name, sir."

"Jonathan Courtenay Diamond."

"And your age?"

"Twenty-six."

"Who are your parents, sir?"

"Julius and Rachel Diamond."

"Is there anything notable about them?"

"My father is a gentleman. My mother was once Apprentice to Inventor Hector Diamond, my grandfather. That is, of course, until her marriage."

Mr. Pike nodded. "And you reside where?"

"Diamond Manor."

"And are you married?"

"No, sir."

"Might I inquire as to your prospects?"

"I have no formal attachments at present."

"I see. How long have you known the defendant?"

"I first met Mrs. Spadros when she was eleven."

"In what capacity?"

His eyes flickered away. "As a playmate, I suppose."

"You would have been fifteen at the time, then?"

"Yes, sir."

"So you were more of a caretaker, then. The difference in your ages and all."

His eyes flickered away. What was he hiding? "I suppose. We only spent a short time together, here and there over the years."

"I see. And did the nature of your relationship change?"

He shrugged. "All relationships change. We have in the interim become close friends."

"At what point in time did your relationship change?"

"After Mrs. Spadros married, my sister and I called on her more frequently."

"Your sister being …?"

"Miss Gardena Diamond, also of Diamond Manor."

"And what age difference lies between you and your sister?"

"Gardena is two years my junior."

"And what is your relationship with her husband?"

Jon blinked. "I beg your pardon?"

"You've known his wife since childhood. You describe yourself and Mrs. Spadros as 'close friends.' Do you have an amicable relationship with her husband?"

Jon let out a short, relieved laugh. "Entirely. I would say my friendship with Mr. Anthony Spadros is as close, if not more so."

"I find that surprising, in light of the difficulties between your two Families."

Jon shrugged. "I'm the youngest son of seven, and have little say in the relationships between Patriarchs. I choose my own loyalties, and I'm grateful my father allows this."

"Very well. Would you please tell the Court of your other duties, besides being the youngest son of Diamond Family."

"I'm Keeper of the Court, so appointed by the Independent City-State of Bridges."

"How old were you when you received this appointment?"

"Eighteen."

"And what does the Keeper of the Court do?"

Jon glanced over to where his brother Cesare sat. "The Court's Keeper oversees the hiring of Court staff and other operations. For major cases such as this one, he provides an impartial witness to the trial, and may be asked to provide his impressions of the original case if the defendant chooses to appeal."

"Is there any other pertinent detail about your position as it relates to this case?"

Jon considered the matter. "The Keeper of the Court can't be compelled to testify unless named as defendant."

"So you could have refused to be in this chair today, even if served with a subpoena, without penalty."

"Yes, sir."

"As protected as a highborn maiden."

I expected Jon to blush, or protest, but his face turned amused.

"Yet your eldest brother Mr. Cesare Diamond sits in your seat."

"I have recused myself from this case."

"As is appropriate," Mr. Pike said. "Now, would you give us an accounting of the defendant's character?"

"Sir?"

"Well, you've known her longer than anyone we've found to testify so far. What do you think of her?"

Jon's cheeks reddened. "Um," he glanced at me, then to Mr. Pike, "I find her character entirely suitable. She is headstrong, and sometimes too fierce, but only in the defense of what is right. Underneath lies a gentle nature, easily wounded. What she most cares for is helping others. She pays no mind to convention if it would harm someone, even a servant. She believes all are equal in the Dealer's sight —"

Scattered applause, which surprised me, and some angry murmurs, which did not.

"— and has ever advocated for improvement to the city. I feel honored to have her friendship."

I glanced back. Thrace Pike seemed transfixed, as if having some revelation.

"Thank you, sir. I only have a few more questions. We've heard Mrs. Spadros was ill. Would you know the nature of her illness?"

Jon's face turned stricken, and he looked to me. I nodded reassuringly. He bit his lip, then took a deep breath. "I do."

"If it wouldn't distress you too much, sir, would you share your impressions of the matter?"

He looked to me, and I nodded. Mr. Pike and I had planned this; Jon did just what we'd hoped. "She tried to take her life."

Gasps filled the room, and the judge banged his hammer. "Order," he said. "Order in the court."

Mr. Pike said, "Can you be more specific, sir?"

"Mrs. Spadros has become exceedingly distressed by the events leading up to this time. She turned to drink. When she learned she would be on trial for the murder of her beloved friend Dame

Anastasia Louis, who she still mourns —" at that, Jon faltered. "Her grief became too much to bear. She poisoned herself."

The room fell dreadfully silent.

"I'm truly sorry to have reminded you of such a time," Mr. Pike said. "And is Mrs. Spadros recovered, in your view?"

"The doctor says so," Jon said, "but it was very close."

"I have no further questions."

Neither did Mr. Freezout, for which I felt grateful. It seemed to take something out of Jon to speak, and his face seemed drawn when he returned to his seat.

* * *

As my carriage returned me, people lined the streets. Some women clutched handkerchiefs, others flowers. The men seemed grim, or refused to watch. A few held mocking smiles.

Police filled the street for a full block before my house. Their main task seemed to be the handling of parcels. Boxes full of envelopes sat on the curb near the barricades, bunches of flowers lay about, and several leashed dogs were led to and fro.Ten feet along both sides of my front stair and walkway, bouquets stood on end, packing the area even out to the street. The aroma of flowers hung thick in the humid air.

Blitz opened the door.

"What's all this?" I said.

Amelia rushed up. "Mum, the news." She handed me a copy.

I followed her to my room, which was full of flowers. Tea had been set, and I settled on my chair to read.

THE LADY OF SPADROS:

Grief "Too Much To Bear"

Childhood Confidante Tells All

In a stunning courtroom revelation, Master Jonathan Diamond said Mrs. Jacqueline Spadros "poisoned herself" after being charged with the death of Dame Anastasia Louis, who he described as "her beloved friend, who she still mourns."

Master Diamond, Keeper of the Court and "close

friend" to the Spadros heir and his wife since childhood, appeared in distress as he described the events. According to his testimony, Mrs. Spadros became "exceedingly distressed" at the death of Dame Anastasia, turning to drink. He stated that "her grief became too much to bear" when she learned she would be tried for her friend's murder.

All this ... was for me?

"There's been cards and letters, mum. Parcels, too. The police have dogs sniffing them — the safe ones they bring here." She left, returning with a box. "I'm sorry to have opened them, mum, but —" she glanced away, "some you don't want to see." She gestured to the parlor, which held a large basket of shredded mail.

"Thank you, Amelia." However did she know?

It must have shown on my face, for she said, "I know how men are, mum. And some women, too. If they have chance to kick someone when they're down, they will." Anger crossed her eyes. "I made note of them, for Mr. Roy's attention."

I chuckled at that, although I doubted he'd take much interest on my behalf. Since Tony and I first met with Roy's enemy Charles Hart, Roy had left us to our own devices, to make us see we needed his favor. So far as I could tell, it had worked: Tony was listening to Roy again. "What do these people say?"

"Other than the vile things scoundrels usually say to women?" Her face grew thoughtful. "That this is a play by the Families to sway the city on your behalf."

"I faked almost dying to escape the gallows?"

Amelia shrugged. "You're rich beyond their wildest dreams. Plus, you're from the Pot, and away from the Manor, which to some makes you an easy target."

An explosion outside rocked the room.

Startled, I let out a scream, and I clutched the arms of my chair, my heart pounding. A bit of plaster fell.

Amelia sighed. "They found another one."

The Testimony

The courtroom was full when I entered the next morning. The two rows behind the railing were cordoned off with a wrist-thick red rope. But Jonathan Diamond and Charles Hart weren't there.

Doyle Pike sat twisted away from me, his arms over the railing, conversing with Mr. Thrace Pike and several other clerks. I went along the near end of the table to sit beside him.

A few moments later, Mr. Trevisane and his men entered. Mr. Trevisane sat next to me; his men sat in the row behind.

A man with thick black hair entered next. His eyes were like Mr. Hart's, but this man had a flatter, rounder face. His associates all resembled Mr. Charles Hart in some way: red hair, or the way they moved, or the shape of the chin. The first man shook hands with Mr. Trevisane and sat beside him, leaving a seat open. The others sat along the row behind.

The third group had to be Clubbs: golden or brown hair, some going to gray, blue-eyed, lean and tanned. Their leader sat at the far end of the table, the rest sitting behind.

I glanced at the upper level: Roy and Molly Spadros sat there.

It didn't take an Inventor to deduce who might testify today.

Mr. Pike twisted back around. "Are you prepared to testify?"

I'd felt moved by both the flowers and the explosions, prone to sudden tears. But I steadied myself. "As prepared as I might be."

Doyle Pike grinned his alligator grin. "Good girl. We may not get to you today, but we should be prepared in either case."

The bailiff announced the judge, who strode in.

The first witness called was Alexander Clubb.

Mr. Clubb was a tall, handsome man, by any estimate at least as old as Mr. Pike. But Mr. Clubb's back was straight, his walk definite, his eyes clear. He looked a prematurely graying man in his middle fifties, which of course was absurd: he had daughters older than that.

After the swearing in, Mr. Pike began. "Would you state your full name for the record?"

"Alexander Clubb."

"And you live where?"

"Clubb Manor, near the zeppelin station."

"And your family?"

"I have eight daughters and a son still living."

"Very good, sir. Are you acquainted with the defendant?"

"In a most general sense, sir."

"When did you first meet?"

"I suppose it must have been when she was a girl. Perhaps fourteen? She visited my daughter often."

"Would you consider her a friend to your family?"

Mr. Clubb turned to me, his eyes full of compassion. "I would."

This statement, in light of all that had happened, surprised me.

"What is your relationship with the Spadros Family?"

Mr. Clubb gave Mr. Pike a warm smile. "Since the kindness of Mr. Acevedo Spadros I to my father Mr. Johnny Clubb, our Families have held firm alliance these hundred years."

Far from the truth, but good enough. We'd never been formally at war, but sharing a border there'd been skirmishes, and their Family lost as many in the Bloody Year as anyone's.

But this man knew Johnny Clubb! I stared at him in awe.

"I wish to congratulate you on your yacht launch this spring."

"Thank you, sir."

"Was the defendant there that day?"

"Why, yes. She appeared to enjoy herself."

"And the day was peaceful?"

"Indeed."

"Who was in attendance?"

"All the Family heirs and their wives. My family, of course."

"I see. Any particular reason you invited the heirs?"

"To be honest, younger people tend to enjoy such parties more than the older set." He gave a knowing grin, and many chuckled.

"I've asked you here today about a package shipped on Flight A26 the day of the zeppelin explosion. Do you recall the matter?"

"Why, yes. My son asked me to arrange a shipment for him."

"Did he tell you the nature of this shipment?"

"He did."

Mr. Pike turned to the judge. "Mr. Clubb has agreed to testify on condition of leniency for both himself and his son."

The judge nodded. "You may continue."

"Mr. Clubb, what did your son tell you?"

"He wished me to add a person to a shipment of persons from the Pot to a factory in Dickens."

"These persons were being shipped? With the cargo?"

"Yes."

"So you were engaged in trafficking."

Mr. Clubb seemed unperturbed. "You might put it that way."

"Did you know who this person he wished to ship was?"

"No."

"You never asked?"

Mr. Clubb shrugged. "I did; my son said he didn't know, only that he'd been asked to assist."

"Did you ascertain the name of the person requesting this?"

"Miss Gardena Diamond."

Gasps filled the courtroom.

"I see. I have no further questions."

"Does the prosecution have questions for this witness?"

Mr. Freezout hesitated several seconds, peering at his notes.

"Mr. Freezout?"

The District Attorney twitched, glancing up at the judge. "No further questions."

Oh, Gardena. I'd gotten her into this mess. What would she do?

Mr. Pike said, "I offer into the record Exhibit 52, the transcript of a sworn deposition by Miss Gardena Diamond, who testifies under oath on condition of immunity. In it, she states she was asked by the defendant to arrange the shipment of a person to Dickens. The person to be shipped was unknown to her."

I blinked, surprised. Whilst technically true …

Hmm, I thought. We might all survive this.

The judge said, "In the interest of time, I'll allow it, provided that the prosecution agrees with your summary."

Mr. Pike handed the paper over to Mr. Freezout, who read it over. "I agree, Your Honor."

"Well, then," the judge said, evidently surprised at Mr. Freezout refusing to argue the matter. "So entered."

Mr. Pike said, "The defense calls Mr. Anthony Spadros."

The audience chattered as Tony came up, was sworn to truth, sat. The scar on the right side of his face had healed over the months, and was barely noticeable. He had his emotionless public mask firmly in place, and didn't so much as glance at me.

"Would you state your full name for the jury?"

"Anthony Spadros."

"Thank you, sir. And your occupation?"

"I'm a gentleman."

"And the sole heir to the Spadros Family?"

"I am."

"And you are married to the defendant?"

"Four years now."

"What are your duties as heir to the Spadros Family?"

Tony didn't flinch. "I oversee the management of Spadros Family properties throughout the quadrant."

"And do you have help in these matters?"

"I have men at each property who report to me, but until recently, financial oversight was mine alone. At the urging of my wife, I hired an accountant to help with record-keeping."

Mr. Pike nodded. "That seems wise, sir. When the accountant examined your books, what did he find?"

"Bills for purchases we had not authorized. Each merchant submitted invoices which I had neither written nor signed."

"So these were forgeries."

"Yes, they were."

"I see. And how many of these forged documents were there?"

"Seven. I asked my wife to assist me in learning what these purchases might mean."

"You asked your wife to do this?"

"She has a keen mind, and often understands the importance of matters which I do not. I would be foolish to ignore such an ally."

Murmurs throughout the courtroom.

"Our District Attorney has thoughtfully provided these invoices for us," Mr. Pike said, "so we're aware of their contents. But what interpretation did you and your wife make as to the meaning of these purchases?"

Tony's eyes flickered to Mr. Trevisane. "Whoever purchased these items meant to create an explosive device."

The audience murmured.

"Yet we didn't know what they meant to bomb, or why."

"Do you recall the theft of letters from your wife?"

"I do, as I testified in the inquest."

"Did you determine who stole these letters?"

"My butler informed me three kitchen maids stole them."

"What investigations have been made as to this matter?"

"My butler keeps record of all letters, as does my wife. My wife took over the matter to see if any other letters were missing."

"And what did she determine?"

"She was seized by the Court before she was able to complete her work. But we surmised that these maids both stole letters from her desk and intercepted her incoming mail."

"Thank you, sir, that will be all."

The judge said, "Mr. Freezout, do you wish to cross-examine?"

"I do." He faced Tony. "Do you love your wife?"

Tony froze. "Without doubt."

"So you would put a favorable interpretation on her actions."

"I endeavor to speak true, as I have sworn here today."

"Did **you** come to the conclusion that those who wrote these invoices planned to create an explosive device, or did your wife?"

Tony stared straight ahead. "We discussed the matter and came to that conclusion together."

"I see. And did the idea that your maids intercepted her incoming mail come from her, or did you decide this together?"

Tony's face went blank for an instant. "I don't recall."

"Sir?"

"It was several months ago."

"But your impression?"

"Objection," Mr. Pike said. "Asked and answered."

"Sustained."

Mr. Freezout seemed put out. "Mr. Spadros, you say your wife was taken before she might complete her examination of your butler's records. Is that correct?"

"Yes."

"And she's at one of your properties, rather than at her home?"

For an instant, Tony's face softened into amusement, then his mask returned. "The property is hers; she was in the midst of renovating it —"

"Yes, we know the story the defense has concocted —"

"Objection," Mr. Pike said. "Might the prosecution allow the witness to **answer** before defaming the defense?"

"Sustained," the judge said, his tone amused. Then he frowned at Mr. Freezout. "You are warned to keep your questioning civil."

"My apologies, Your Honor," Mr. Freezout said. "So your wife was renovating her apartments and now there she remains under guard. How do you feel about this matter?"

"Objection," Mr. Pike said. "Relevance?"

"Sustained," said the judge.

"Oh, well," Mr. Freezout said. "Then I have no further questions. But I reserve the right to call this witness in rebuttal."

"So noted," the judge said. "Mr. Spadros, you may step down."

Mr. Pike said, "The defense calls Mr. Charles Hart."

Mr. Hart lumbered forward and was sworn to truth. He sat in the narrow armchair with difficulty.

"Please state your full name for the Court, sir," Mr. Pike said.

"Charles Paigow Hart II."

"And your occupation?"

"A gentleman."

"And you're the Patriarch of the Hart Family?"

"As I'm the oldest member, I suppose so."

"And your residence?"

"The Hart Family has lived on the top floor of the racetrack since my grandfather captured it during the Coup. "

"And what do you occupy your time with, sir?"

Mr. Hart smiled in amusement. "I'm seventy years old. I like to ride, and paint landscapes, and watch my horses run. I play with my grand-daughter. I'm a bit too fond of eating," he patted his belly. "But I like to bake from time to time — as a hobby."

"Very well. The Court has invited you here today because we learned that you've had problems with falsified invoices."

The audience murmured.

Mr. Hart sounded surprised. "Indeed we have."

"Your Honor," Mr. Pike said, "I offer Exhibits 53 through 57, invoices for purchases allegedly made by the Hart Family."

"So entered."

Mr. Pike had Mr. Hart read each one, then passed it for the jury to examine before placing it on the small table. The items were strange: women's clothing, makeup, wigs of various colors and styles, horse training, blank business cards.

The cards, of course, were probably the ones the Red Dog Gang used to stamp their mark on. The wigs and makeup reminded me of Dame Anastasia's theatrical disguise book. Did the scoundrels mean to disguise themselves as women?

"What interpretation did you put on these items?"

Mr. Hart said, "We didn't know what to make of them. All we knew is that we didn't order them, so we refused to pay."

"Thank you, sir. Your Honor, we have no further questions."

"Mr. Freezout, do you have questions for this witness?"

Mr. Freezout rose. "I do." He hesitated for an instant. "When was your first formal introduction to Mrs. Spadros?"

Mr. Hart's eyes moved to the side. "I was first formally introduced to Mrs. Spadros at a Grand Ball several years ago."

"Does this — acquaintance — change your testimony?"

"Not at all."

"I have no further questions for this witness."

"Mr. Pike," the judge said, "would you care to redirect?"

Mr. Pike glanced at Mr. Trevisane. "Yes, Your Honor." Going to Mr. Hart, Mr. Pike said, "I'd like to clarify something you said earlier. You were first formally introduced to Mrs. Spadros at the Grand Ball several years ago. At that time, did you converse?"

"No."

"Did you have any dealings with her?"

"No."

"When was the next time you met her?"

"At the next Grand Ball."

"And did you converse then?"

"No."

"Were your meetings thereafter similar?"

"Indeed."

"When did this series of brief introductions end?"

"At this past Grand Ball."

"What happened?"

"I greeted Mr. Anthony Spadros and his wife. Later, I asked Mr. Spadros for permission to dance with his wife. When I returned Mrs. Spadros to her husband, Master Jack Diamond accosted us and was removed by his brothers. Mr. Spadros invited me to sit with them, which I did briefly, then left. That was all."

"I see. Yet you've sat here in this courtroom every day since these proceedings have begun. Why is that, sir?"

"I wished to offer support to Mr. Spadros and his wife. I've been unjustly accused in the past; I know how frightening it is."

Mr. Pike turned to the judge. "I have no further questions."

* * *

After luncheon, Tony sat in the upper box beside his mother. Mr. Hart had returned to his usual seat behind me, yet Jon was nowhere to be seen. The writing expert's contraption was set up again, but a different man was called to the stand. This man was perhaps fifty, yet fit, with round spectacles and a bow-tie.

"Sir," Mr. Pike said. "Can you tell me your qualifications?"

"I've worked in forensic handwriting analysis for twenty-seven years with the Federal Forgery Department in Hub."

I felt a shock. The Families let one of the Feds into Bridges?

Mr. Pike said, "Have you visited Bridges before?"

"No, sir."

"Do you recognize anyone in this room?"

"You, sir, and your clerk there," he pointed to Thrace Pike.

"So you do not recognize the defendant."

"No, sir. I have never seen her before today."

"Thank you. Are you being paid a fee for this service?"

"I am not. I'm here on assignment from the Federal Bureau at your request. We're always glad to help in cases involving interstate affairs such as this one."

"The defense is grateful for your help. Now," Mr. Pike went to the small raised table and took up the paper with my handwriting upon it. "By your request, I have here Exhibit 58, a known sample of the defendant's handwriting. We have letters the defendant asserts are in her hand, plus invoices and a letter asserted to be forgeries. How would you care to proceed?"

"I will examine the defendant's handwriting first," the man said. "Your Honor, may I step down to use the machinery?"

"By all means," the judge said.

So the expert stood, going round to the brass contraption while everyone looked on, I for one quite interested. He examined the paper, then used the lighting to display it on a screen. "When I first see a paper, I look for the basic lines of it. Does the author write at an angle, and if so, how much? How are the letters formed, and how do they connect? Are there any unusual spacings, uniquely shaped letters, or flourishes? We must first understand the original to note the signs of forgery."

He peered into a magnification glass. "This was copied."

The audience murmured in surprise.

"Yes, sir," Mr. Pike said. "Indeed it was."

"May I see another example of her handwriting?"

One by one, my letters were given to him, and he pointed out the ways each letter was like the copied text. He was neither an attractive man nor particularly charismatic, yet he had the audience's full attention.

"So in your opinion," Mr. Pike said, "Are Exhibits 2 through 41 and Exhibit 58 by the same person?"

"Yes, I would say so." He moved my copied page to one corner of the top of the screen, one of my letters beside it. "Now, may I see the disputed texts?"

Mr. Pike moved the stack of my letters aside, then brought the second stack to the expert. "We now refer to Exhibits 42 through

48, the disputed texts, as compared to Exhibits 2 through 41."

"On the face of it, these two sets look similar. Both by a woman, with similar ink, and likely the same brand of pen." He pointed to a curve. "But this mark on Exhibit 42 shows hesitation, and here the angle to cross the 't' is off by a full five degrees when compared to the texts by the defendant." He pointed to a 't', "Look at the curl up at the end of the 't', which is only seen in the disputed document. The writing starts and stops at odd places as well," he pointed to each place, "which is characteristic of copying. You see this in the text Mrs. Spadros copied, yet not in the letters she alleges are hers."

"So this is how you could tell that her first text was copied."

"Yes, it's quite simple. There's an ease to the writing when one pens from the heart, which isn't seen in copied work. But even so, here —" he pointed at the paragraphs I'd copied.

"Let the record show that the witness indicates Exhibit 58." The judge gestured to the expert. "Proceed."

"Look at the angle of the vertical lines in the copied text, then compare it to the defendant's natural writing."

Mr. Pike said, "The witness compares Exhibits 58 and 14."

"In Exhibits 2 through 41, and in Exhibit 58, the defendant writes in a more upright fashion. In Exhibits 42 through 48," he laid them out one by one, "the vertical lines are slanted," he produced a protractor, measuring on the projected image, "to six degrees. In the second group of texts, note the darker starts and finishes, and how many times the pen is lifted. This is classic for someone focused on the form of lettering rather than the content."

"Now," Mr. Pike said, "what is your professional opinion as to the writer of the disputed documents?"

That sent the man into some thought. "With copied work, it is very difficult indeed, as the person is trying to match another's work. A woman, of some education and skill at writing. A good eye, and a remarkably steady hand. Yet even so, you can see in Exhibit 46 how her hand shakes here," he pointed, "and here. This is often seen when attempting to simulate another's writing."

"So tell me, sir," Mr. Pike said, "in your professional opinion, are Exhibits 42 through 48, the invoices asserted to be forgeries, all in the same handwriting?"

"It's difficult to be certain. But I would say yes."

"And is this handwriting the same as Exhibits 2 through 41, letters demonstrated to be by Mrs. Spadros?"

"Certainly not."

More murmurs, and the judge banged his gavel.

Mr. Pike said, "What would you say if you were told another handwriting expert stood in this very spot and asserted under oath that all these documents were created by the same hand?"

The expert hesitated. "I would say he's mistaken."

"You're most charitable," Mr. Pike said. He produced Mr. Hart's invoices. "I wish you to compare Exhibits 53 through 57," Mr. Pike turned to the jury, "the invoices Mr. Hart brought us earlier, with Exhibits 42 through 48, the invoices Mr. Spadros has alleged to be forgeries."

The man peered at them through his magnification devices, and you could have heard a pin drop. Finally, he straightened, displaying a invoice upon the screen. "All the invoices show the classic signs of copying, including the signatures. I find it curious that here," he pointed, "and here, this second set of invoices show the same curl up at the end of the 't' as the alleged forgeries do."

"The witness refers to Exhibits 54 and 56," the judge said.

Mr. Pike said, "In your opinion, did the same person produce both sets of documents?"

"I could not say with any certainty, sir, but it does seem likely."

Mr. Pike said, "Would you examine one last document for us?"

"Of course."

"I'd like you to look at Exhibit 1," Mr. Pike turned to the jury, "a letter to Dame Anastasia Louis. Is this letter by the defendant?"

The man peered at the document. "I would say not."

Shocked murmurs, and the judge banged his gavel.

Mr. Pike said, "How did you conclude this, sir?"

"In Exhibit 1, you see similar deviations from the defendant's writing as seen in the other disputed texts: the curl-up of the 't,' the six degree angle on the uprights." He pointed to each place in the letter. "Plus all the other signs of copying are present."

"So in your opinion, would you say that the same person

produced Exhibit 1 as produced the other disputed texts?"

"It's impossible to be certain, sir, but it's very likely."

Oh, Anastasia. Tears filled my eyes; I blinked them away.

"Have you seen any of these documents before today?"

"No, sir."

Mr. Pike said, "I have no further questions for this witness."

"Mr. Freezout," the judge said, "any questions?"

Mr. Freezout looked up from his writing, and to my surprise said, "No further questions, Your Honor."

We recessed for tea, which I took alone in my small side room, an armed maid guarding. After I finished, Mr. Pike came in. "They'll be calling you next. I'm going to ask upsetting questions, Mrs. Spadros. They may be very upsetting. But I want you to answer everything exactly true." He peered into my eyes. "Do you understand? You must speak true in all things I ask. It's vital."

"So you don't want me to say what we planned?"

"No, I've changed my mind. Only speak true," he smiled, patting my hand, "and it will go very well." He got up and left.

I sat pondering why he changed his mind. But I trusted him, at least for this. In spite of what Thrace Pike had to say about his grandfather, Doyle Pike had done exceptionally well for me.

When called, I returned into the grand chamber, was directed to the witness booth, and swore the oath to speak true. I glanced at the back of the hall: as at the inquest, there stood Jack Diamond!

Jack Diamond appeared as always: head shaven, dressed entirely in white, meeting my eyes with a level gaze of his own.

Fear gripped me, yet also despair. Would this Red Dog Gang stop at nothing to torment me?

Eleanora vowed Jack didn't take David. But Jack had to be a conspirator. How else could they get into his factory? How else could David have been held there for so long?

The hate this man had displayed towards me and my father over the years flashed before my eyes. Why would Jack Diamond be present in this courtroom on this day, but to cause me distress?

But the questioning had begun; I willed myself to focus, forced my feelings aside. I would get only this one chance to show I was someone worth letting live.

The Mother

As at the inquest, Mr. Pike asked my name, where I was born, and so on. "Mrs. Spadros, would you tell us how you came to be in the Spadros Family?"

"I was brought to Spadros Manor as a young girl of twelve."

But then he began to ask things not asked before:

"And how did this happen? You lived in the Pot, madam. Surely you weren't suddenly transported there."

I didn't particularly wish to speak of this. Why was he asking? How much should I tell? I didn't look at him. "Sir, I — I was sold. By my father. To the Family."

Gasps and murmurs. Mr. Hart flinched, setting his jaw.

"At age twelve."

"Yes, sir."

"What did he receive in return?"

"Sponsorship into Spadros quadrant. He owns a liquor store on Third Street."

Jack Diamond's eyes narrowed, his jaw set.

"I see. So was this arrangement agreeable to you?"

"Sir?"

"Did you wish to visit Spadros Manor? Were you happy?"

"No, sir. Not at all."

Horror spread across Tony's face.

Mr. Pike paged through some papers. "According to your testimony at the inquest, you returned to your home most nights."

"Yes, sir."

"And you never knew when Mr. Roy Spadros would send men

to fetch you."

"No, sir."

"Did they speak kindly? Did you go willingly?"

"No, sir. I hid. But they always found me. It would be different men, and they treated me roughly. I felt terrified."

Mr. Pike turned, pacing the room. "So you, a twelve-year-old girl, were sold by your father, brought to a place against your will, then sent home, only to have strange men seize you at any time."

"Yes, sir."

Mr. Freezout said, "Objection. Of what relevance is this?"

The judge said, "Mr. Pike?"

"I wish to establish that Mrs. Spadros might have had reason to hide her activities, even from this court. She **is** charged with perjury, is she not?"

"Continue then, sir," the judge said.

Mr. Freezout didn't look happy with this at all.

Mr. Pike continued on as if nothing had been said. "And when you came to Spadros Manor, were you treated well?"

I considered this. "Looking back on it, yes. Well, mostly."

"Mostly?"

"Well, sir, I came from the Pot. I'd never had a bath before, and thought they tried to drown me. I'd never eaten with utensils. I didn't know how to read, or do anything they thought proper. I didn't understand what to do, and when I did wrong I was beaten." I swallowed. "That's why I hid. I didn't want to go back."

The room was quiet, and a flood of emotion came over me. I met no one's eye, determined not to cry in front of these people.

"And when you did go there," Mr. Pike said finally, "was there anyone in particular who looked after you?"

"No, sir, it was always someone different. I think they were told not to be kind to me."

Murmurs in the courtroom.

"So you were there unhappily for many years."

"Yes, sir."

"Where was your mother in all this?"

Tony's head shot up. I'd never told him about Ma. Roy always implied she was dead, and I thought it best to let Tony think she was, if only to protect her.

"I went home to her every night, sir." I remember her tears the night Air died, her anger at my dalliance with Joe.

You stupid girl! We could have gotten you out of there!

When I considered the matter logically, her behavior became clear. "I don't think she felt she had any choice but to let me be taken." How she must have suffered, never knowing if I'd disappeared because Spadros men took me, or if I was seized by some scoundrel! "She never spoke of it."

"Let's discuss your relationship with Dame Anastasia Louis."

Anastasia. I glanced at her photo on the wall with the rest and took a deep breath, trying to remain calm, not to cry. "I met her at my engagement party, sir. Over a hundred were in attendance, yet when the betrothal was announced, no one would speak to me."

"Because you were from the Pot?"

"I suppose they thought me unworthy." And looking back, I suppose I was. "Then she came forward and was kind to me." A wave of grief. "I'll never forget her for that."

"She lived close by, did she not?"

"Yes, sir, only a mile away." I chuckled at that in spite of my misery. "We were next door neighbors, yet a mile away. It seems odd to say it."

Scattered chuckles and some quiet chatter. The judge banged his gavel, and the room quieted.

"So, Mrs. Spadros, did you continue to return home after this?"

"No, sir. I haven't been back since I was sixteen."

"Do you keep contact with your mother? Friends? Family?"

"I was forbidden to return. I haven't dared contact anyone."

Mr. Pike sounded surprised, quite believably so. "Haven't dared? Were you threatened?"

"Yes, sir, Mr. Roy said that if I tried to return he'd ..." I glanced up at Roy, suddenly frightened. He gazed back at me, a placid expression on his face.

"He'd what?"

You must speak true in all things I ask. "He'd burn the Cathedral with everyone in it, even the children, should I set foot in the Spadros Pot again."

The room sat in stunned silence, then erupted in confused anger as people cried out, then began to argue with each other.

"Order," the judge said. He banged his gavel several times, and the room became still.

"This must have been terrifying."

"It was, sir."

"Once you were living here in the quadrant permanently, became married, did you have many friends?"

"No, sir. None would call. I was shunned on the street."

"So they were rude?"

"Not with my husband nearby. They curtsy and smile, but when he leaves, harsh words begin. Cruel words that refined women shouldn't speak."

"Like what?"

"Like what has been spoken every day by the rough men outside as I walk to this courthouse. Words I never heard from the worst scoundrels in the Pot. It has shocked me to hear these words from quadrant-women."

And I would remember, if I survived.

"So it sounds as if Dame Anastasia was your only friend."

"In Spadros quadrant. Of course, Jon and Gardena have been kind to me —"

"You mean Master Jonathan and Miss Gardena Diamond?"

"Yes, sir."

Mr. Pike paused a few seconds as he ambled about. "Did Dame Anastasia know about your heritage and birthplace?"

"Yes, sir, and about how I came to live here."

"And as I can see by the inquest findings, and the evidence our esteemed District Attorney has gathered, you and she not only called on each other but wrote each other frequently."

"Yes, sir."

"Did you ever have concern about your — pardon me, let me go back a bit. Was your husband aware of your birthplace?"

"He was, sir, but not —" I glanced at Tony, taking a deep breath, "not that I was sold. He was only twelve himself at the time, and the subject never came up later."

Surprised murmurs.

"So I imagine you found Dame Anastasia, an older woman who, as you say, was kind to you, a replacement for the mother you were no longer allowed to see."

This took me by surprise. "Yes, I suppose."

"And did you confide in her about your trials at Spadros Manor? Your treatment by the other women?"

"Sometimes. I didn't wish to complain, sir. Now that I see the benefits of living here I appreciate them. But we did speak of it."

"So she was not only a friend, but a confidante."

"Yes, sir."

Mr. Freezout sat with his arms crossed, a sour look on his face.

"So if she asked you to help her, you would."

"Of course!"

"I see. And did she ask for your help?"

"She did."

"What was the nature of that help?"

"She gave me a list of men and asked me to inquire as to why they hadn't paid their debt."

"Why would she ask Mrs. Spadros for this? Surely a lawyer would be a better choice."

"She claimed she was bankrupt, and wished to move from Bridges to a place where she could live more simply."

Murmurs filled the courtroom. The judge banged his gavel.

"So she told you she had no money for an attorney? Why did she think you might be able to help?"

I glanced at Tony. "Um, sir, I had secretly helped other women before. She knew this and thought I might be able to assist her."

"So you had a secret business of aiding other women." He put his hand to his chin. "But the other women despised you."

"Not uppers, sir. Widows, women impoverished. I often had connections which were helpful."

"So you conducted this secret business without your husband's knowledge."

"Yes, sir."

"Why? Were you afraid of him?"

"I feared he might not approve."

"Any other reason?"

"I feared Mr. Roy might take offense."

"By this you mean Mr. Roy Spadros."

"Yes, sir."

Murmuring in the courtroom.

"And what might Roy Spadros do to show his offense ...."

Stunned gasps filled the chamber.

I wasn't sure what to say. "What's your question, sir?"

"Has Roy Spadros ever hit you?"

That seemed obvious. "Many times, sir. But only when I deserved it."

Mr. Hart froze, and I wasn't sure what his expression meant.

"I see. So you ran a business of helping other women, kept secret from fear of your father-in-law taking offense. And Dame Anastasia Louis knew of this."

"Yes, sir."

"Did she offer any payment for your service?"

"She gave me her signature necklace. It seemed much too great a payment at first, but it turned out to be false. And she gave me the deed to some apartments."

"The ones you renovate now."

"Yes, sir."

"So what did you do to help her?"

"Well, I directed her to you, sir."

Mr. Pike turned to the judge with a smile. "As I testified before the inquest." He faced me. "Did she help you in other ways?"

"Yes, sir. She was one of the connections I spoke of."

"You've testified that you corresponded frequently. When you wrote regarding your — clients? Is that the right term?"

"Yes, sir."

"Did you write plainly?"

"No, sir. We used a code, so if a letter were to be lost or stolen, no reputations would be harmed."

"I see. Very wise. So when you wrote about a client, or some other secret matter, you did so to protect others."

"Yes, sir."

"So what did the letters entered into evidence here discuss?"

"A man has caused harm to me and my husband. I was trying

to learn more of him."

"And what was his name?"

I glanced at Jack Diamond. "Frank Pagliacci." But Jack didn't react to the name.

It wasn't him, mum, I swear.

"What sort of harm did Frank Pagliacci cause?"

"He followed us, did harm to our men." Tony's pale sweating face that night flashed before me. "Must I speak of it?"

"Of course not. So these letters were an attempt to learn about him. Why?"

"Why?"

"Why did these need to be encoded?"

"To protect myself, sir. No one knew of my business. I tried to keep the fact of this man harming us secret as well."

"Why?"

"My husband didn't wish it to become known."

"So you were trying to gather information for your husband, and protect your husband's good name from being dragged into a scandal which a ruffian had caused."

I watched Jack as Mr. Pike spoke: no reaction. "Yes, sir."

Mr. Pike turned to the chamber. "When you came here to stand before the inquest, had you ever been in a courtroom before?"

I focused on Mr. Pike. "No, sir."

"Did you know anything about what was expected of you?"

"Only what our lawyers said. I did everything they asked to the best of my ability."

"Did you know you had to speak true?"

This was upsetting. "I did, sir, but —"

"But what?"

"I feared to expose something which my husband commanded me to keep secret." Murmurs filled the hall. "And I feared to expose Dame Anastasia to further scorn and censure."

"Why would Dame Anastasia be scorned or censured?"

A sob burst from me. "Because Frank Pagliacci was her lover. She **never** told me, even though she knew he'd harmed us. But he's a villain! At the end he terrified her. She wouldn't even tell me where she was going, in case he should seize me. He knew she meant to flee, and I believe he killed her and all those people to keep her from betraying him."

"Oh, dear," Mr. Pike said. "Yet you protected her even so." He glanced at the clock then turned to the judge. "Might we have a ten minute recess?"

The judge banged his gavel. "We will return in ten minutes."

We rose as he left, and I was escorted into the small side room. Mr. Pike followed. "You're doing very well, my dear. I particularly liked the part about your husband commanding the matter kept secret. That should stir a great deal of controversy." He chuckled. "Does a married woman have higher duty to the court than to her husband? I can see the editorials now … "

I wiped my eyes. "I'm trying. But I fear I won't survive much past this trial. Already men who've split from the Spadros Family plot to kill me. That is, if Mr. Roy doesn't kill me first."

"But I thought he pardoned you."

"He told his men they couldn't kill me. That doesn't mean he won't." This was a fact Tony seemed not to understand. Roy knew about Roland, so I became disposable. Roy now had an even greater lever on Tony than I might ever have been. I wished Jon and Gardena had never brought the boy into Spadros quadrant. "Excuse me, sir." I entered the windowless Ladies' Room, an armed maid at my side, as much to be alone as anything.

Then I saw the blood.

The Delay

"I'm indisposed," I said to the maid. "I have spoilt my dress."

"Wait here." She left, locked the door, then returned several minutes later with supplies. "I've notified your lawyer, who will notify the court." She helped me clean myself and rinse my petticoats, placing them into a black linen bag, then several more armed maids arrived. "We'll take you out the side way. Your coachmen have been notified."

"What time should I return?"

"Court's been adjourned, mum."

"Adjourned? But I can just bathe, change, then —"

"Your attorney will take care of everything, mum," the woman said. "In these cases, they allow a one week recess —"

"A whole week?"

"Yes, mum. It's all been taken care of."

I spent the rest of the day in my room, fuming. Damn this womanly affliction! Damn the men who enforced such rules! I wanted the trial to be over!

But after a day or so, I realized perhaps the delay was best. As Mr. Pike predicted, the newspapers were fat with editorials, letters to the editor, and — in the *Golden Bridges* — speculation as to what the jury might be thinking.

Was this man Pagliacci the true murderer? Or was this a ploy by the Families to keep one of their own from hanging? Why was this the first time the man's name had been mentioned? Why had he not been questioned? Some of the letters expressed anger at the

District Attorney for bringing my case to trial while this man — who seemed to have far more motive — roamed free.

But Mr. Freezout didn't remain idle. From all accounts, the man never slept, giving interview after interview throughout the city. "There is no man registered in Bridges by this name, and I believe the report Mrs. Spadros gives to be complete fiction. It appears the Four Families will stop at nothing to defend their Pot rag, even smear the memory of a dead woman."

This quote sparked no little outrage at using such language — and at the *Bridges Daily* for printing it, where women and children might read. "We'll read the *Golden Bridges*, Mr. Editor, should we care to be confronted with this sort of trash!"

Others applauded Mr. Freezout for his "candid speech": "Call a spade a spade, and this one's spoilt, from what I hear."

It surprised me that the *Bridges Daily* would allow either quote to be printed, but the next day an editorial appeared from Mr. Paul Blackberry himself:

> It is the duty of all proper and competent news-reporters to publish the truth. Our esteemed District Attorney shows his colors, and we do not hesitate to display the words of a man who aspires to the hallowed Hall of our city. Since the day our First Mayor stood his ground against aristocrats and monarchs, the Office has been reserved for men with high character and noble calling. It is up to you to decide whether this man — and those who stand with him — deserve such honor.

And I thought I was good with the knife!

But this delay did give me some time to think. Amelia and Mary wouldn't let me help with anything other than an occasional "this is how you do something" from Amelia, who seemed to feel it a personal affront that I knew so little of what she considered womanly accomplishments.

I cared little. Raised by whores and bouncers, my father a ruined assassin, dragged to Spadros Manor to be taught how to kill people and run their criminal enterprise. What did they expect? That I would smile and simper like some display wife? I might be sought after for my portrait, but I had my own plans.

Like finding this woman who murdered Marja.

Remembering what Mrs. Clubb told me about her proved difficult at first. I'd been drunk, after almost dying from alcoholic withdrawal. I believe I was hearing things which weren't there.

And before I fled Spadros Manor, I was drunk every minute, or as close to such as I might become, just to escape from my life.

My thoughts drifted to Tony, but I forced worry aside. His mother Molly would take care of him. And if not, surely Sawbuck would. Tony was no longer my responsibility.

I lit a cigarette, taking a deep drag, blowing out pain, loss.

Mrs. Clubb said she had a witness that a woman calling herself Black Maria pulled the trigger on Marja that night. Sawbuck suspected her name was Maria Athena Spade — that is, if this "Black Maria" wasn't trying to frame that poor woman too.

I hadn't yet heard back from Mr. Paul Blackberry, the *Bridges Daily* editor. But if anyone could find information, it was the Clubb Family, who had an extensive network of spies and informants. I wrote to Mrs. Clubb, sending the letter through Amelia so the police might not open it.

Amelia and Mary spent the week making rosewater from the roses, small lace sacks of potpourri from the rest, and bundles of kindling from the stems. It was the perfect answer to the outpouring of flowers we'd received. Mary found several cases of perfume bottles — glass with glass stoppers — for a penny a case!

I turned one over. "Here's why." A diamond shape — the cut gem shape, not the Holy Symbol the Diamond Family took for their own — was embossed upon the glass. Inside the diamond were the initials DAL.

Dame Anastasia Louis, her mark.

"Well, at least she helps us now, mum," Mary said soothingly. "We'll give these to the neighbors as apology for all that's gone on. Any leftovers we can sell." She shrugged. "At least we won't run out of rosewater."

The Exposé

The day to return to court came, and I was told not to appear before luncheon. When I went out my front door, more crowds than usual were at the barricades. On the drive there, many lined the street shouting, just as they did that first day. The closer we got, the more people there were, all shouting in anger.

What had agitated them?

I entered through the side door. Mr. Doyle Pike met me in the small room. "I hope you're well?"

"For days now. You quadrant-folk have some strange rules."

He chuckled. "I suppose so." He glanced at the armed maid, a stout unsmiling woman of perhaps sixty. "Might we have a moment in private?"

She left, and I said, "I presume I'm to speak again today?"

"Yes," Mr. Pike said. "Try to find an opportunity to," he glanced at the corner, "bring up the matter we discussed. Hopefully, he'll give you an opening." He was obviously afraid our discussion was being overheard. "And take care when exiting. The mood outside is unpleasant."

"Oh?"

He grimaced. "I asked for more guards outside. We may need to bring you out of the side door, if matters look bad."

This seemed alarming, but it would be many hours in the future before we left. "Whatever you feel best, sir."

I waited several more minutes in the room alone before a knock signaled the time for my return to the witness chair.

Jonathan and Mr. Hart sat behind the small railing. Jon looked tired, thinner, and I wondered where he'd been the past week.

Every member of all the Four Families barring children sat in the balcony: the Hart and Clubb women, their husbands. All the Diamond men and their wives. Even those Clubb granddaughters who were of age sat there with their husbands. Tony was there, face pale. Roy and Molly Spadros sat beside him.

Yet Jack Diamond was absent.

But instead of the compassionate faces from a week ago, the lower level seethed with rage.

What happened?

Someone whispered in Mr. Doyle Pike's ear. Mr. Pike's face turned outraged. He demanded explanation from his grandson, Mr. Thrace Pike, who appeared astonished, unable to give answer.

"Mr. Pike?" The judge snapped. "Are you ready to proceed?"

Doyle Pike twitched. "Your Honor, may we approach?"

"Counsels may approach the bench," the judge said.

Mr. Freezout looked surprised, but came forward as well. The three men had a whispered discussion which lasted some time.

The audience and jury, at first curious, became restless, then began to talk amongst themselves. Finally, the two lawyers returned to their seats.

The judge banged his gavel, then turned to the jury. "Jurors, you have been forbidden to read any newspaper, nor allow the news to be spoken in your presence. This stricture holds. If you read or allow anyone to read news to you during this trial, you will be charged with misconduct and contempt of court. If you happen to hear any news whatsoever, whether about the trial or the defendant, you must not only report it at once, but must consider it hearsay, unworthy of your attentions. You may not form an opinion of the defendant or come to any decision on her guilt until you have heard all the facts presented by these men. You are not to discuss this case with anyone or make any investigation. You must only pay heed to what is said by these lawyers and these witnesses in this room. Do you understand?"

The men in the jury box blanched. "Yes, sir," they said, yet one looked away.

"Madam," the judge said to me, "please remember that you are still under oath to speak true."

"Yes, Your Honor."

"The defense may proceed."

Mr. Pike rose. "Mrs. Spadros, I hope you're well."

"I am, sir."

"Can you tell me what happened on the day of the explosion?" Giggles ran through the room amongst those, I gathered, who were at the inquest. "Please limit yourself to the relevant facts."

"Yes, sir. I got in my carriage to meet with Miss Gardena Diamond. My butler came with a letter from Dame Anastasia."

"Is this the letter?"

"Yes, sir."

"I offer Exhibit 59 — a letter from Dame Anastasia Louis to Mrs. Jacqueline Spadros."

"So entered," the judge said.

"Now would you read it for us, madam?"

"My dear Mrs. Spadros:

"I must leave in haste. You'll hear many things about me once I'm gone; I suppose most of them are true. I was a foolish old woman who should never have trusted Frank Pagliacci. I helped him. I loved him. But he has no love for anyone but himself.

"Although the charade with the Doctor was Frank's idea, I gave you the case so you'd take the necklace. Dismantle it at once and sell the gems to one of my appraisers. Please don't hesitate; do it now.

"Your fondest wish has always been to leave Bridges. If you sell the gems in the next few hours, you should have more than enough money to do so. That will make this whole debacle worth it.

"I truly am fond of you, and I wish you well.

"All my love,

"Anastasia, Dame Louis

"PS. Thank you for the clock. Such a heavy package for its size! I'm most intrigued. I will follow your instructions and wait to open it until we have passed through the Aperture."

Mr. Pike said, "What were your impressions of this letter?"

"I felt perplexed. I gave her no gift. And I believed her necklace to be real. I didn't understand why she would want it destroyed. And she didn't write our usual words we used to assure the other that the letter was genuine."

"So you weren't sure it was from her."

"No, sir. But I also felt afraid. If someone threatened her enough to make her leave Bridges in haste, was she in danger? If she'd been given a package, what was it? I didn't yet consider that it might be a bomb, but the whole matter felt wrong."

"So what did you do?"

"I asked my driver to take me to the zeppelin station so I might talk with her and see this package."

"Did you go to the station?"

"My men told me they had strict orders from Roy Spadros —"

A horrified look crossed Roy's face. Had he really not thought through the implications?

"— not to go into Clubb quadrant before the Celebration."

"So they took you to meet with Miss Diamond."

"Yes, sir."

"Where was this?"

"At the Diamond Women's Club."

"Did you remain there?"

"No, sir, we'd already planned to go to Market Center."

Both Gardena and Tony had fear on their faces. Which made me sad, because I'd never betray their son.

"Why did you plan to go to Market Center?"

"Miss Diamond was being blackmailed."

Gasps filled the room.

"The blackmailer said to go there. She planned to meet her brothers on Market Center so they could catch the scoundrel. But she was afraid, and had begged me to go with her."

"I see. Do you know why she was being blackmailed?"

"I'm not entirely certain, sir. It was a highly personal matter, one too close for her to relate to me, I suppose."

"But you did ask, I take it."

"I did. But knowing now what I do, her answer couldn't have been true."

"What is it you know now that you didn't before?"

"The timing, sir."

"In what way?"

"According to her, the blackmail involved an incident many years in the past. There seemed no reason to blackmail her on this matter now. Yet our meeting with the blackmailer was timed so that I might not meet with Dame Anastasia before she got onto the zeppelin. I believe the blackmail a diversion."

"I see. So did you catch the blackmailer?"

"No, sir, only a man of feeble mind carrying a briefcase. He knew nothing of the plot, and seemed distressed when caught."

"What did the briefcase contain?"

"Dame Anastasia put that necklace she always wore in a lock-box and gave me the key. The briefcase held a picture of the lock-box, but open, with the necklace inside, and a paper with the word 'boom'."

Chatter filled the courtroom; the judge hit his gavel.

"What interpretation did you put upon these items?"

"I felt sure the package she mentioned in her letter was a bomb. Dame Anastasia loved clocks, so I reasoned that when she heard the package ticking, she assumed it to be a clock."

"Had you ever given her a clock before?"

"Yes, sir, long ago."

"But you knew you never had given her anything recently."

"That's correct, sir."

"Very well. What did you do then?"

"I told Mr. Cesare Diamond of my fears —"

Cesare, who'd been reading from a ledger, jerked upright, horror on his face.

"— and he directed me to their carriage. The carriage-driver dropped her brothers at the bridge while I went to the zeppelin station." At this, I felt grieved. "But I got there too late."

"Witnesses claim you were dressed as a young girl, with your hair down. Why were you dressed in this manner?"

I smiled at the memory. "I knew I must get to the gate. It was of the utmost urgency if I were to save the ship from destruction. Yet eighty yards and many hundreds of people stood before me. A young girl can take actions a grown woman cannot."

"We have testimony from the woman at the gate that you tried to warn her, even after she ignored and dismissed you."

Melancholy swept over me. "I felt sure the package contained a bomb. I wish I were wrong."

"I have no further questions at this time," Mr. Pike said.

"Mr. Freezout," the judge said, "do you have questions?"

Mr. Freezout smiled, but it was unpleasant. "I do."

"You may proceed."

"You were brought to Spadros Manor numerous times as a child, on direct orders from Roy Spadros. Did he ever say why he brought you there?"

Mr. Pike had a slight frown on his face. I said, "He did."

"And what did he say?"

"He said he wanted me to help my husband if needed."

"Did he specify in what way you were to help?"

"No, sir."

"What training did you undergo to be able to help him?"

"He taught me about the Family Business."

"You mean, what the Spadros Family does for a living."

"Yes."

"I see. Were you taught to fight?"

I glanced at Roy, but his face showed nothing. "Yes."

"What methods of fighting did you learn?"

Mr. Pike sat frowning, as if he'd completely missed something important. I said, "I was taught to shoot, to fight with my hands, and how to use a garrote." I almost mentioned the knife-fighting Josephine Kerr had taught me but that wasn't what he asked.

Scattered murmurs.

Mr. Freezout must have sensed this, because he asked, "Can you use any other weapons?"

"I learned how to fight with knives when I lived in the Pot."

Tony stared at me, mouth open.

"I see." Mr. Freezout glanced at a paper on his table. "Mrs.

Spadros, when did you learn that Dame Anastasia was involved in a scam against the city?"

"A week prior to the explosion."

"How did you come to learn of this?"

"Certain things she told me I later found to be untrue. I became suspicious. She avoided me. So I began to investigate her."

"In what way?"

"I made inquiries at her factory. I learned her gems were false."

"Did you do anything then?"

"No, sir, I didn't think anything of it. But it did make me wonder what else she lied to me about."

"How did you feel when you learned she had formed an attachment to a man who caused your Family harm?"

"I felt hurt, sir. Betrayed. Yet I couldn't contact her."

"And the first time you learned of this was on receiving this letter, the day of the Celebration?"

"Yes, sir."

"Witnesses say they saw you with a man at the zeppelin station. Who was he?"

"One of my husband's men, sir, as I said at the inquest. The men called him Morton."

"What was your relationship with this man?"

"He was my husband's man, tasked with my protection."

"And you had no … other relationship?"

"Objection," Mr. Pike said.

"Sustained," the judge said. "Mr. Freezout, you have been warned of this once in this courtroom already." He turned to the jury. "You are to disregard Mr. Freezout's tone and implications." He turned to the District Attorney. "Proceed."

Mr. Freezout said, "How often was this man Morton tasked with your protection?"

"Occasionally, sir. Generally, when I travel within Spadros quadrant, I only have my coachmen with me. This day I traveled into Diamond, so this man came along."

"How did you get into Clubb quadrant?"

"The Diamond carriage-driver took me in, sir."

"And did he take you all the way to the station?"

I glanced at Mr. Pike, who nodded. *Speak true in all things.* "No, sir. I saw a train leaving the island, so we got aboard."

"And this man Morton accompanied you."

"Yes, sir."

"So let me recap: you'd just learned that Dame Anastasia allied herself with a man who'd harmed you and your Family. Yet we're to believe you went to all this trouble to save a woman who betrayed you? No one else of any importance to you was on the zeppelin. Why go to the station?"

This was my chance. I stared at him, feigning shock. "No one of any importance, sir? My **mother** was aboard the zeppelin!"

The room erupted. I thought Tony might faint, his face grew so pale. The judge banged his gavel. "Order!"

The jurors had varying reactions: I saw shock, reddened eyes, anger and sympathy, but also disgust and cynicism.

The bailiff cried, "Order! We shall have order here!" He slammed the butt of his thick staff into the floor, but the level of noise only increased.

Boos and curses filled the room. The man who'd turned away before shook his head and spat.

The judge raised an eyebrow, gesturing to the bailiff. The bailiff gestured to the guards, who dragged the man over the railing.

The bailiff raised his shotgun and racked it. The audience, rather than quieting, became outraged. People threw things at me! Both lawyers and their retinue ducked under the tables. Crouching behind my chair, I peeked out at the spectacle.

The bailiff calmly took out a whistle and gave a piercing blow. The Court guards shouted in unison, moving backwards into a crouch to point their rifles at the crowd.

People screamed, hiding under the pews. The guards pulled many out in turn, putting them into handcuffs and dragging them to the back wall. A brass bar was attached there, and agitators were chained to it.

All the while, the judge banged at his gavel.

The room quieted.

The judge said, "Those of you detained are charged with contempt of this court and sentenced to thirty days in the Prison, your board assigned to your quadrant. Those of you living on Market Center will be responsible for your board. If you or your quadrant does not pay, you will not eat. You are also fined thirty cents, payable immediately. If you cannot pay, your property down to your clothing will be sold to pay for your crime."

The people, many of whom worked for a few pennies a day, gaped at the judge in horror.

"You, sir," the judge said to the juror who spit, "are charged and sentenced as the rest. First alternate, take his seat, please." The judge peered at the floor. "We will take a thirty minute recess so the room may be cleansed."

Armed maids hurried me to the small room. Tony, Jon, and Mr. Hart stood waiting. All three said at once, "Are you well?"

I almost laughed in spite of it all. "Their aim was poor."

"Thank the Dealer," Tony said, pulling me into his arms. "I'm so sorry, Jacqui. Gods, I never knew your mother even lived."

This was awkward. I extricated myself. "Roy made you believe she was gone. It seemed best not to contradict him."

Tony's face darkened. "My damned father." He scoffed, shaking his head. "Every time I think I've plumbed the depth of his horrors, something new emerges."

I said, "What's happened? People seem so angry. And Mr. Pike said the mood out front was unpleasant."

Jonathan said, "Gertie Pike has betrayed you."

I stared at him. "What?"

Mr. Hart said, "Mr. Blackberry refused to print it, but the story's on the front page of the *Golden Bridges*. She claims your auction to help the poor was a sham, the money has entirely gone to your attorney, and no one was aided but you. The people outside are in near riot."

I went to a chair and sat. "And the fact it wasn't in the *Bridges Daily* makes people feel it must be true. Why would she do this?"

But I knew. The woman had never left the Bridgers in her heart of hearts, and in her outrage at my deception likely felt this exposé the only way to bring the truth to light. "Mr. Pike must be furious." Now I understood the discussion with the judge earlier.

As if summoned, in walked Mr. Pike, who seemed surprised to

see so many in the room. "Pardon me for intruding," he said, "but I have need to speak with my client."

"Of course, sir," Mr. Hart said, and the three left. But Tony glared at Mr. Pike.

Why should Tony dislike him so?

Mr. Pike sat across from me. "So you've heard the news."

"Yes."

"This is bad. I begged the judge to declare a mistrial, but he was quite candid. The Four Families won't have it."

"Why?"

"I don't know. Perhaps they mean to secretly intervene. Perhaps your husband plans to renounce his position as heir and leave Bridges with you."

Would Tony do that? He'd spoken of it when angry at Roy, but I wasn't sure I'd go with him.

No, I never would. Me out of the way was exactly what the Red Dogs wanted.

This was no different than the concoction of Mr. Hart's which Jon put forth, and much less attractive an offer. In a strange city, with a man I didn't love, so much hurt and mistrust between us? I shook my head. "I don't think that would happen."

The Families told the judge not to stop it. They told Mr. Pike not to stop it. Why? What could they be planning?

"You saw how people reacted, Mrs. Spadros. This was exactly what I feared. They neither trust nor believe you." His tone turned angry. "My grandson's wife has seen to that. And the jury must all twelve doubt your guilt for you to walk free. All of them."

All of them. It seemed too great a thing.

"Mr. Freezout offered his deal again."

"I leave in disgrace and betray everyone."

"But you leave alive. Isn't your life worth something?"

I'd gone too far. I couldn't go back. I wouldn't take Mr. Freezout's deal then, and there was no reason to offer it now other than to get me out of the way.

It seemed as if he had me.

But I would rather hang than let the people who murdered Marja, Anastasia, and so many others walk free. "It is. But I can either let him do this, or I can fight him." I put my hand on Mr. Pike's, gazed into his ancient gray eyes. "We can fight him, Mr. Pike. I didn't do it. And the people who did do it stand mocking."

Mr. Pike sat staring towards the table for several seconds.

Then he took on a determined demeanor. "I've never had an innocent client, Mrs. Spadros, but you've certainly come close." He rose, a new energy about him. "Let me see what I can do."

They called me in shortly thereafter. I wasn't brought to the witness chair, but instead to my seat at the table. The room was silent this time, subdued.

Mr. Pike stood. "Your Honor, for the second time the defense moves for a mistrial. The defendant cannot and will not receive a fair trial in Bridges. I move to relocate to a new venue."

The judge said, "Motion denied."

"On what grounds?"

The judge hesitated; the jurors froze. "Lack of jurisdiction."

Mr. Pike's eyes narrowed. A slight, cynical smile flashed past. "Very well."

Nice move, Mr. Pike.

The jurors' faces became thoughtful, considering themselves — nay, their wives — in my position. They'd seen the earlier exchange and wondered at it. They'd seen the rage directed at a woman. Then to hear that twice now Mr. Pike's pleas to move to a different city were denied …

Several of the jurors watched me. Heat rushed to my cheeks, and I looked away.

"Mr. Freezout," the judge said. "Before we were so rudely interrupted, you were cross-examining the defendant. Do you have further questions at this time?"

"No, Your Honor, but the prosecution wishes to ask for a continuance on rebuttal."

"On what grounds?"

"The prosecution has reason to believe the defendant's mother is **not** dead —"

I gaped at him in disbelief. No one knew Ma was alive but a very few people, most of them in the Pot.

"— and we need time to find her."

The jurors faces were grim.

"We've spent more than enough time on this case." The judge hit his gavel. "The Court will recess until ten tomorrow. If you believe this woman is alive, you have until then to produce her." He rose, as did we all.

People began to file out. When the door opened, a faint roar came from the front of the building.

Jonathan Diamond took my arm across the small railing and spoke to Mr. Pike. "We'll go out the side door."

Jon moved me to his left arm as we hurried along. Guards armed with revolvers moved to position themselves around us as we went through my small side room and down the narrow passageway beyond.

A guard pushed past to open the door: a navy blue and silver Court carriage sat perhaps six feet away.

It all happened so fast.

We stepped clear of the door. A motion to our right: a familiar-looking man, a gun in his hand as he turned.

Right towards Jon!

I lunged towards Jonathan. "No!"

Not even looking at me, Jon shoved me hard with his left hand as he drew his revolver, ducking away to his right, and shot. The man fell, blood spraying behind his head, a bullet-hole under his chin where it met his neck. I hit the ground, stunned.

People ran towards us. A guard lay beside me, shot in the upper chest, gasping. Hands lifted me.

"Get horsemen," Jon said.

I was pushed into the carriage. Jon got in beside me, closing the door as we drove away. I peered out of the back window: dark shapes lay on the ground.

A knock came at the door. "Come in," Tony said.

One of Tony's men entered. "Sir, about the coat."

"That was one of Tony's men!" Sawbuck did say the man ran off with the other rogues. "I never did anything to him. Why would he try to kill me?"

Jonathan pulled the curtain shut behind me. "I'm sorry to shove you down. I couldn't risk him hitting you."

"Where did you learn to shoot like that?" I don't think I could have ever shot so true, not surprised as we were.

He smiled, tucking a curl of my hair behind my ear. "Lots of practice," he whispered. "And a few close calls." He peered out of the side window.

The horsemen around us cleared the frenzied crowd away as we went. The carriage shook as rocks hit the side. One came through the window, and we shrank back at the broken glass.

Tony's own man tried to kill me.

Jon said, "You're not safe at your apartments."

"But you can't mean to leave my staff without protection!"

"They're safe enough as long as you're not there," Jon said. He reached up to the brass speaking tube. "Take us to the Manor."

"Yes, sir," the driver said, his voice sounding tinny.

"Jon, I told you, I'm not going back to Spadros Manor!"

Jonathan shook his head. "I'm bringing you to Diamond Manor. We have the best security in the world."

The Heir

The crowd thinned as we galloped past the government buildings, and we crossed into Diamond quadrant without stopping. The curtains were closed, so all I saw were glimpses: black brick buildings, silver-wood siding, white-painted wrought iron lamp-posts. Our outriders called out, "Make way for the Court," and carriages pulled aside to let us pass.

Those on the sidewalks glanced up as if this happened every day, going on with their discussions, purchases, and promenades.

Jon said, "I'm sorry you're visiting under such circumstances."

I turned away from the window with a fond smile. "I've always wanted to see your home." But then, I felt a sudden alarm. "Will Jack be there?"

"No. He's at our Country House." He gave me a fake smile. "You'll be safe as can be."

"Jack was there! When I testified last week. Where were you?"

Jon patted my hand. "A short trip, that's all."

There must have been fifty Diamond men surrounding the white stone Manor, all armed, none looking at us. Apparently someone had sent word ahead of us: Gardena met our carriage, thrusting a navy blue cape in. "Put this on."

I did, covering my head and hat with the hood. The three of us went down a long front path, up a short flight of steps, then across their wide porch and inside.

Their butler, an elderly man dressed precisely like our butler Pearson back at Spadros Manor, escorted us upstairs and to a guest room which faced the back of the Manor. "Your rooms, mum," he said, bowing.

I said, "Very nice, thank you."

He gave me a startled glance.

"That'll be all," Jon said, entering the room behind us.

Once the door closed, Gardena grasped my hands. "Did they hurt you?" Then she stared at my left arm. "You're bleeding!" She turned to Jon, demanding, "How did this happen?"

I felt no pain, but my left sleeve felt wet, the fabric torn. Blood lay on my fingers. "Jon pushed me down when the man tried to shoot me. He saved my life."

"You must sit," Gardena said, "I'll call for the doctor at once."

"Dena, it's just a scrape." Once they both left, I let her maids take off my boots and help me into a short-sleeved dark purplish-blue house dress of soft cotton.

My left arm was scraped and bruised, and it stung as the maids cleaned and bandaged it. Once they finished, I settled into the padded wing-chair. They brought tea on a dinner-tray next to my chair; I sipped it, grateful for the moment's silence.

Their guest room had white walls, the Diamond Family symbol endlessly embossed upon the white ceiling. The furnishings were of ebony-stained wood, with eggshell white coverlets. White lace curtains let in the slanting light of late afternoon.

Gardena knocked. "Are you well? I thought I'd check on you. I had to get Roland settled. All the commotion distressed him."

"I'm well. Please sit." She pulled up a chair and did so. "Has someone sent word to my staff? They must be alarmed at all this." Then fear struck. "Please tell me Tony's safe. If they shot at **me** —"

"He's well, Jacqui. That was Jon's first thought when we arrived. He sent his own men." She put her hand on mine. "Anthony's safe. And he knows you're here."

I blinked back tears. "I've treated him so horribly, Dena."

At that, she leaned over, put her face in her hands.

I said, "Why won't you have him? What has he **done** to you?"

Gardena scoffed, her fingertips pressed to her forehead. "Jacqui, he's your **husband**! Doesn't that mean anything to you?"

I leaned back, confounded. These people were so blind, unable to see what lay right before them. "I don't care about these quadrant-ways. I know you care about them. These are your ways. But look at the reality! Tony loves you. You love him. You both love your son. By all rights, you should be together. This whole thing makes no sense."

A sudden melancholy came over me. "I never truly consented to marry him. But I've learned to care for Tony, sometimes, as a brother." A younger brother. When he wasn't saying cruel things to me. "I felt forced to hide everything I was from him so as not to die! He thinks he loves me, but he doesn't know or understand me at all." It seemed hopeless. "He won't let me go, no matter what I say, will he?"

"Jacqui, he loves you. More than he ever loved me. He fell in love with the idea of a person, with the exterior, with how I made him feel. Yes, he has great passion for me. I was his first love. But there is, as you say, the reality, and wish as he might, he can't change that. I don't think that even if he defied his father and asked for my hand the night we dealt our son into the world my father would have allowed it. My father hates and fears his. Julius Diamond was taught to hate the Spadros Family from birth, and he would never give me to Roy Spadros to be treated the way you've been. Not even Roland can change that."

My arm throbbed. If Roland couldn't change his mind, what could I do? "What'll happen now?"

"I suppose," she said, "you'll return to court tomorrow."

* * *

Several hours later, a physician came to call, asking many questions yet never touching me, instead having the maids remove my bandage and move my arm about. He pronounced my arm unbroken — which I could have told him — and gave instructions for changing the bandages in the future.

I hoped they didn't pay the man much for that.

Dinner was brought to my rooms, along with a round table and chairs. The whole arrangement filled the room. Gardena, little Roland, and Jon joined me.

Roland seemed quite excited to see me, expressing great interest in my story of his Uncle Jon saving me from the villain.

"Your uncle is quite the marksman," I said. "When you get old enough, you should practice shooting as often as possible if you want to be as skilled as he."

This thrilled him no end. "Is he better than my daddy?"

"At shooting? I'm afraid so. But your daddy has many admirable qualities, which you'll see when you know him better."

He pondered this. "My tutor says I'm a mix of two Families."

I smiled, but wondered about teaching a four-year-old such things. "You're Master Roland Spadros of Diamond Manor —"

Jon and Gardena gave me sharp, alarmed glances, full of shock and fear.

"— and you can become whatever you choose."

Roland seemed confused. "My name is Roland Diamond."

"That's your other name, " Gardena said quickly. "But you have a secret name," she gave me a 'what the hell are you doing' glare, "that no one must know."

"I do?"

"Yes," Jon said quickly. "It's a very special name, because you're a very special boy."

Roland pondered this. "I'm going to be quite the marksman."

"Very good!" I took a drink from my water-glass, heart pounding, wishing it were wine. "What do you like doing best?"

"Digging in the mud for fish worms."

"Do you like fishing?"

"Grampa does," he said. "I like digging the worms. The mud feels squishy."

"I'm sure you do him fine service."

He blushed, shoveling mashed potatoes in his mouth.

I turned to Jon and Gardena. "I'm sorry," I whispered.

Gardena took a deep breath, fanning herself, eyes closed. Jon nodded with a relieved smile.

I'd received no invitation to join the Family for dinner, nor had Mr. Diamond come up to see me.

I was their guest, and injured. Not to at least inquire as to my health was … shall we say, unmannered. "Is your father well?"

Jon kept his eyes on his food. "They're both well. And the rest. My brothers have their own homes and families. And my parents wished to dine alone tonight."

"I never had dinner in a bedroom before," Roland chimed in. Jon and Gardena's cheeks both reddened. "Except when I got the chick pox." He giggled. "That was itchy!"

"I'm sure it was." Melancholy swept over me. Dining with a Spadros Pot rag must have been too much for Julius Diamond. I asked Jon, "What time must I be ready to leave for court?"

Gardena smiled warmly, my indiscretion apparently forgotten. "Never fear. We'll have you there in plenty of time."

After dinner was cleared away, Gardena took Roland to ready him for bed. Jon and I went downstairs to sit on their back veranda, and he read to me while the shadows lengthened.

Far off at the front of the Manor, a doorbell rang. Jon kept reading aloud, but I heard two men having a discussion.

As their voices grew louder I distinguished them: Julius Diamond and his son Cesare.

Jon glanced up at me, then returned to reading his book.

Footsteps approached.

"Why is she here?" Cesare said to Jon. "Are you mad?"

"It's a pleasure to see you too," Jon said.

Cesare growled, disappearing into the house.

I rose, following him. "Sir, I must speak with you."

He didn't answer, so I hurried up, grabbing his arm. "Wait —"

He faced me, flinging my arm off. "Don't touch me, Pot rag.

"I must speak with you."

He stopped. "What do you want?"

"You were there when the briefcase was opened. You know I knew nothing of the bomb until then. Please, you must testify."

His voice dropped to a furious whisper. "You dare not only to lay hands on me, but to tell me what I must do in my own Manor?"

"I'm asking you to tell the truth." What would sway him? "I know you see me as less than nothing. But you know I didn't do this. You claim to be impartial then prove it! If you fail to speak when you could do so, you support those who wish me dead."

This threw him into intensive thought, and I could hardly breathe. Jon approached, face concerned, but I shook my head, willing him to say nothing.

Cesare said, "I will testify. But in return, answer me true. Why would my brother go into Spadros quadrant?"

"Which brother?"

"You know very well which brother. Jack. Why would he go into the Spadros slums? Why was he at that woman's home?"

"Why don't you ask him?"

Cesare spoke through gritted teeth, "You damnable Pot rag wench — I did! His answer made no sense. If you want **anything** from me, you tell me right now."

*Why **did** he go there?* "I'm not certain."

"Well, what do you think?"

What did I think? I'd feared Jack Diamond more than anyone in the world. I wanted him dead, or at the very least, gone.

But Eleanora said it wasn't him.

And if he had a traitor in his own factory, that might explain how they were able to keep David there for so long.

If Jack Diamond didn't kidnap David Bryce, who did?

Cesare said impatiently, "Well?"

"I think someone has framed him."

Cesare's eyes narrowed. "Come with me."

I followed him to a room I took to be his study. "Leave it," he said when I tried to close the door, so I did. He pointed to a chair. "Sit down."

Jon appeared at the doorway.

Cesare glared at him. "What do you want?"

"May I join you?"

"For gods' sake," he said, exasperated. "Do you think I mean to seduce this thing?" He gestured at a chair. "Very well."

Jon sat beside me.

Cesare sat behind the desk and spoke to Jon. "Did you know about this?"

Jon turned to his brother. "I've thought so for a while now."

"And you never said anything?" Cesare scoffed in derision. Then he said to me, "Tell me everything."

I rose, outraged. "How dare you scoff at this man! Jon has been my most faithful friend — he just saved my life! Twice now he's saved it. I will not hear such disrespect, especially from a man who hesitates at helping the innocent."

This took Cesare aback. "My apologies, madam."

"Apologize to him — it was him you insulted. This is your youngest brother, not some ruffian."

I glared at Cesare and he at me. Then Cesare let out a breath and turned to Jon. "I apologize."

Jon said nothing, but the set of his shoulders told me this was not the first time he'd been insulted so.

Cesare said to me, "Now would you tell me what in the Fire is going on?"

I'd tell this man everything when Hell solidified. But I did tell him the basics of my investigation into David's disappearance: the descriptions of the men who had him there in the Diamond Pot, how the boy's mother identified the man in white as the one who came to their home — twice, the stable-man's description of the two who stole the carriage, the man who'd been accused of blackmailing shopkeepers in Spadros quadrant in the gem scam.

The entire time, Jonathan stared at me, mouth open, eyes wide.

When I was done, Cesare looked ready to spontaneously combust. "Who dares slander a Diamond heir?"

He seemed to be asking me, so I shrugged.

"And now it seems I must recuse myself as well!" He put his hand to his forehead. "You'd best never need me to stand in for you again, Jonathan."

An awkward silence fell.

I said, "So you will testify?"

Only his eyes moved. He peered at me a long time. "Yes," he said. "I believe I must."

The Power

Later I lay in bed but I didn't sleep.

Cesare didn't believe Jack would do this.

Gardena became outraged at my even suggesting it.

Jon — his own twin — knew nothing whatsoever about it.

Was Jack Diamond even involved at all?

Had I been part of framing an innocent man?

Not innocent, I thought. Jack Diamond had been implicated in dozens of murders, the victims tortured, mutilated. He had the worst reputation possible, as horrifying as that of Roy Spadros himself. Perhaps even more so.

Surely some of what was said about Jack was true. And he'd threatened me more than once, in front of witnesses.

Yet here I am, in Diamond Manor.

Jon won't let Jack harm me, I thought. The shooting kept repeating in my mind. The hole in the Spadros man's neck. The spray of blood.

Moonlight came through the lace curtains. I shivered, but I wasn't cold. This was just like Tony's attack by the Red Dog Gang in January. If these rogue Spadros men — the so-called 'Ten of Spades' — wanted me truly dead, they would have **all** been there.

It was another distraction.

I sat up. Wait, I thought. Could these rogue Spadros men be in league with the Red Dog Gang?

This seemed concerning.

I lit the lamp beside my bed. The writing-desk across the room had a fountain pen and paper. I sat up in bed, using a book as a backing for my paper.

Rogue Spadros Men "Ten of Spades" — defied Roy, shot at Tony & Sawbuck & one tried to shoot me. Distraction?

<u>Red Dog Gang</u>:

Frank Pagliacci — cad, scoundrel, kidnapper, strangles young men. Wears brown. Not smart. Very good looking.

Man In White — in his Forties, dark of skin, shorter and heavier than Jack Diamond. Likes to make mischief.

Someone had gone to great lengths to blame Jack Diamond for the Red Dog Gang's crimes. But to be so bold as to impersonate him? That game could turn fatal if Jack ever caught up to the man.

Then something occurred to me: Master Blaze Rainbow (the man I first knew as Morton) knew Frank Pagliacci. He also knew Jon, Gardena, and their father Julius. Surely Morton would've said something to Jon, or Cesare — or at the very least Julius — if he'd seen Jack with these men.

This was the biggest clue pointing towards Jack's innocence in this matter. How could I have missed it?

I continued my list:

Gardena's blackmailer — dark of skin, supposed to wear brown. Same man? More distraction.

Zia Cashout — Outsider. From Dickens? Has red hair. Left Feds. In love with Frank.

That gave her a motive to want Dame Anastasia dead.

Black Maria/Birdie/Death Card/Maria Athena Spade? — porcelain skin, black hair, very pretty, wears red. A Secretary? Shot Marja. The Clubbs have a witness.

Whatever her real name, Black Maria's motive wasn't clear. Did she kill Marja on orders? Or had they some personal connection?

Group of six men — attacked Tony (distraction?), stole

Party Time, kidnapped our Associates. Spadros rogues?

No, I decided. If those had been Spadros men, Crab surely would have said so when Tony questioned him back in January.

District Attorney Mr. Freezout — wants me gone, wants information on the Families. Running the Red Dog Gang?

Lots of distraction, I thought. But why? What did Mr. Freezout really want? What vital task required **me** out of the way?

As far as I knew, if Mr. Freezout was **not** with the Red Dog Gang, he had no real motive to want me gone. He might have a grudge against the Spadros Family, or perhaps all of the Families. But at most, this trial would remove what everyone thought to be a barren unworthy wife.

Remorse, shame, and grief struck me then, but I pushed the feelings away. Giving Tony an heir would have solved nothing.

I had to focus. What made me so important? Why was Freezout really doing this?

It had to be money or power. No other reasons made sense. You didn't risk your life and the lives of your loved ones to three generations by attacking one of the Families for some misguided sense of honor. Well, unless you were in a Family yourself.

Did he need support to become Mayor? Mayors had been assassinated before — surely he couldn't believe that becoming Mayor would keep him safe.

Then something else occurred to me: Who ran against Mr. Freezout? I couldn't recall.

I put the list, pen, and book aside — being careful not to spoil the white coverlet — and wrapped my arms around my knees.

This was most odd. The Families always supported one or more candidates — it was a game to them. There were "get out the vote" campaigns for their Family's candidate, with bribes and treachery even extending upon Market Center. These schemes were planned months in advance.

None of that was happening. Why?

Did the Families **want** Freezout to win?

* * *

The morning paper's headline:

Assassination Attempt!

Mrs. J. Spadros Attacked Outside Courtroom

My goodness, I thought. This made it sound much more — and somehow less — exciting than it really was.

The spray of blood from behind the man's head came to mind.

I didn't particularly want to read about my own experience, so I scanned further. The Court had set up barricades on Market Center, and was searching anyone coming within two blocks of the Courthouse for weapons.

Mr. Freezout gave a rousing speech decrying violence, vowing to make the city "free of the ruffians who control our quadrants."

He dared say this? These words astonished me. Someone very powerful backed this man. But who? Who would have grudge against me, in particular? If it were Jack, why, he had me here. But he hadn't so much as set foot in the house, so far as I could tell. If it were some other Family member, they were defying their Patriarch in the most outrageous way possible.

The Clubbs had zero motive to want me dead. In fact, they — at least Lance's parents, and I daresay Lance himself — had a sharp interest in my staying alive so I might persuade Gardena to accept him. Could there be dissension in the Clubb ranks?

Charles Hart seemed to be an entire ally. His wife had taken a dislike to me under the mistaken impression, it seemed, that I wished to be Mr. Hart's lover. Could she have planned this?

I pondered this for a while. I couldn't understand this motive. But I supposed it might be possible.

The Spadros Family had the most at stake. Tony didn't want me dead. Roy likely wished to save me for his "entertainment" once the trial completed. The "Ten of Spades" seemed to focus on Tony and Roy more than making any sincere attempt on my life.

I had to be careful of them after the trial, assuming I survived. What better way to bend Tony to their will than to seize his wife?

And the Diamonds had made great effort to keep me alive, although Mr. Julius Diamond had yet to acknowledge my presence in his home.

I felt confounded. Who in Bridges had more power than the Families? Who was unafraid of them?

A gasp burst from me as a horrible thought came: could Mr. Freezout be a secret Bridger?

The Bridgers were a fanatical religious group which believed the illegal drug Party Time was the means to Hell. They were in no way powerful, in fact, most despised them, but they had no fear of anyone, it seemed, including the Four Families.

If Mr. Freezout were a secret Bridger, Mr. Blackberry or the Clubbs would have sniffed it out by now. Perhaps the Bridgers were paying him. But where would they get this sort of money?

I recalled Gertie Pike's betrayal. Could she be in league with the Red Dog Gang too?

"Nonsense," I murmured. Mr. Freezout likely used her ill-advised outburst for his own purposes.

A knock. "Jacqui," Gardena said, "are you well?"

"Come in," I said. "What are you doing here?"

She closed the door. "Mr. Hart arrived late last night —"

Interesting.

"Roland woke, and came to my room. He left his toy there. I brought it to him just now, and I heard you gasp." She sat beside me. "Are you well?"

"I am. But disturbed at these attempts to kill me."

She gave me a quick hug. "I don't blame you. I remember how terrified I felt when I learned Roy Spadros threatened to kill me."

"What? When did this happen?"

"When I was a girl. My mother took me to Italy for a year to get away from here. I was fifteen. Well, fourteen. My birthday was on the steamship."

Roy Spadros threatened a fourteen year old girl? "Why would he threaten you?"

"It was after Daniel died. We went to war. Remember?" Her face grew somber. "I didn't learn of the threat until we'd been in Italy some time. I overheard my mother telling someone why we couldn't go to Milan. The Spadros Family has people there."

"I had no idea."

Gardena sighed. "But now, looking back on it, it makes sense."

"What does?"

"Why my father feels as he does."

"I don't understand."

"Just from things he's said. He believed that Tony was sent by Roy Spadros to violate me."

"What? That's absurd! Why?"

"For attacking Spadros quadrant in the first place. I think Roy said something to make my father believe his revenge would come later."

"To make him afraid." That piece fell into place. "Roy Spadros loves anything which makes others afraid. He thrives on it." Then a thought came to me: Was Roy allowing this trial simply to make me and Tony afraid?

"Jacqui, what is it?"

I shook my head. "There are too many players, too many motives I know nothing about. What's their true end game? We haven't seen it yet. It can't be just to get me out of the way."

A maid knocked. "It's time for your bath, mum. Your dress is cleaned, mended, and ready."

Gardena nodded, not looking at the woman.

"Thank you," I said.

The maid gaped at me, stunned.

I rose. "Excuse me, if you will, Dena."

I once thought of this whole thing as a puzzle I didn't have all the pieces to. But now it felt as if a crowd played poker, each with different motivations, with different aims.

One played for spite. Another, for cash. A third planned to cheat, perhaps kill the rest if discovered.

The only thing I knew was that until I learned who was playing in the first place I was in terrible danger from them all.

The Relationship

Jonathan and I rode to the Courtroom together that day, and to my surprise, Cesare Diamond rode with us. A huge crowd stood along our route from the Diamond bridge, but quiet, watching our curtained carriage pass. Many wore black armbands, or the symbol of the Spadros Family on their hat or coat.

Cesare snorted quietly, smirking.

Why did this man ride with us? "Perhaps you have something to add, Mr. Diamond?"

"It's all very amusing, how it's playing out."

"Why was Mr. Hart at Diamond Manor last night?"

Cesare smiled knowingly. "However might I answer this? I wasn't there."

I sighed, turning to the window. I wasn't going to get answers from this man.

Cesare crossed one leg over the other. "He came to offer a bribe in return for my father's influence upon me. Which would have made no difference." He spoke as if he considered his father's wishes irrelevant. "Since I'd already decided to testify." He shrugged. "But Mr. Hart didn't know that."

I laughed. "So you took his offer anyway." How audacious! "Whatever might he have offered?" Was Mr. Hart truly so besotted with me as to offer up his entire quadrant to save my life? It seemed incredible. He claimed he wanted to be friends, but everything about him spoke of his intimate regard.

"Why, an alliance, of course. We almost had one," his eyes flickered to Jon, "long ago, but matters intervened." He leaned back. "But now, we have alliance with both Hart and Clubb —"

And I now realized why the Diamonds helped me.

They had as much stake in Gardena marrying Lance as the Clubbs did.

"— and Roy Spadros can do nothing about it." When Cesare spoke Roy's name, I shuddered at the hate in his voice.

And I recalled what Gardena said in the past: Cesare thought the Clubbs were too dangerous to ally with. What changed?

Something major had happened to sway this man.

Yet I knew Gardena: if Cesare tried to pressure her into marrying Lance, she wouldn't do it.

I smiled. This might be the best thing which could happen.

* * *

On entering the courtroom, I went straight to Mr. Pike. "Cesare Diamond's agreed to testify."

"Oh? That's the best news I've heard today."

"He's up to something," I said. "Be wary."

Mr. Pike let out an amused laugh. "My dear, anyone with an ounce of sense is wary of Mr. Cesare. He's more formidable than his father ever was." His eyes took on a distant look. "Reminds me most of old Mr. Caesar, grandfather to Mr. Hector."

So Cesare's great-great-grandfather. "You remember **him**?"

"An infamous and remarkable man. I met him once, when I was a law clerk. I was younger than Thrace there," he paused, considering, "and he as old as I am today. Or perhaps older — well, at least that's how it seemed. As cunning as Mr. Cesare and as mad as his young brother Jack. Utterly ruthless." Mr. Pike shuddered. "Sit down, my dear. I must prepare for today."

Instead of sitting, I turned to survey the room. Armed guards stood two rows back facing the spectators, which had left the four rows in front of them empty. Even so, this meant that most of the spectators could only see the judge and any witnesses, and the ones closest could only see the guards. In spite of this, the crowd sat quietly. I glimpsed many with the black armbands and Symbol of the Spadros Family.

Thrace Pike sat in the row behind his grandfather, face flushing when our eyes met. Shame and anger radiated from him, and I imagined his encounter with Gertie the night before was most unpleasant. How could he continue as a law clerk when his wife undercut his work in such a spectacular way?

Tony, Roy, and all the Families sat in the balcony behind me. Tony didn't look at me, nor did anyone else up there.

And I felt daunted. Tony always looked to me.

But what did I expect?

Disheartened, I sat, eyes burning. I'd ruined everything, and for the first time in my life, I felt I not only had no control over what was going to happen to me, I had no way to make it better. Joseph Kerr was gone, all my hopes and plans with him.

Many witnesses came forward that morning: a carriage driver who picked up a dark-haired woman from the Spadros poorhouse on Lance Clubb's orders. A dock hand at the station who led the group of people to be smuggled into the zeppelin's hold, testifying on condition of immunity. He remembered a dark-haired woman with brown skin amongst them.

A dock hand who helped load the cargo, his upper arm now in a cast, also remembered her. Mr. Freezout had grilled all these men relentlessly, asking if they'd been paid to say these things. To everyone's surprise, this last dock hand said yes. "A man came to me after the explosion, said he'd pay my doctor bill if I told what happened." The man — brown haired, tall, good looking — sounded decidedly like the descriptions of Frank Pagliacci.

Mr. Pike then re-questioned this man. "Do you mean to say that when this man paid you that it changed your testimony?"

"Why, no, sir. I'm grateful to him for paying me, but it was only the truth. I recall her plainly: she was quite beautiful. Looked a bit like Mrs. Spadros there."

Mr. Freezout's eyes narrowed, but he said nothing.

The judge said, "Any further questions for this witness?"

Mr. Pike and Mr. Freezout said, "No, Your Honor."

So the man left.

Mr. Pike said, "The defense calls Mr. Cesare Diamond."

Mr. Freezout made a choking sound. But Cesare's name had been on the witness list almost from the beginning, and the DA could say nothing against it.

A stunned silence, and all eyes went to where Cesare Diamond sat. Cesare nodded to his right, and there stood his father, who came forward to take his seat. Cesare moved to the witness stand. There he was sworn to speak true, and he sat.

Mr. Pike said, "Will you state your full name for the Court?"

"Cesare Eléwénjewé Diamond."

"And your profession?"

He sounded offended. "I am a gentleman, not a tradesman."

Several of the jurors stiffened at his words, faces set.

"And your parents?"

"Mr. Julius and former Apprentice Rachel Diamond, of Diamond Manor."

"I see. So you are heir to the Diamond Family, then."

He didn't hesitate. "I am."

"Do you have any other title?"

"Until a few moments ago, I was Acting Keeper of the Court."

"But you are no longer?"

"The Keeper of the Court cannot testify to the same case he supervises. I recuse myself, and my father acts in my stead."

"Tell me about the relationship between the Diamond and Spadros Families."

Cesare leaned back, surprise on his face. "Acevedo Spadros betrayed my ancestor Caesar Diamond during the Coup. In reply, Caesar Diamond ordered the murder of Acevedo's younger brother. Since then, we have been at war."

"I see no battles in the street today. Is there reason for this peaceful coexistence?"

"There has been a cease-fire." This seemed to make Cesare uncomfortable. "Nine years now."

"But you are technically still at war."

"Yes."

"We have testimony regarding the relationship between the defendant and your brother Jonathan. Can you enlighten us as to the relationship between the defendant and any other brothers?"

"I beg your pardon?"

"Your brother Jack, for example."

Cesare pursed his lips and gave the tiniest shake of his head. "I don't speak with my brother often. From what I've observed, he has an intense hatred of the defendant's father."

"Can you elaborate?"

Cesare's gaze dropped to the railing before him. "My brother is obsessed with the death of a manservant whom the defendant's father murdered." Cesare took a deep breath. "I've heard him threaten to kill the defendant's father."

Murmurs in the audience.

"What does young Master Jack do for a living?"

"Objection," Mr. Freezout said, exasperated. "Relevance?"

Mr. Pike said, "Your Honor, I believe the relationship between Jack Diamond and Jacqueline Spadros to be highly relevant."

The judge said, "Overruled."

Mr. Freezout's face turned sour.

Mr. Pike turned to Cesare. "Please answer the question, sir."

Cesare let out a breath. "Master Jack Diamond is a gentleman."

"Does he bear other titles?"

I snorted quietly. *Mad Jack, Black Jack ....*

"Keeper of the Prison," Cesare said.

"Ah," Mr. Pike said. "Keeper of the Prison. So this **is** relevant." He turned so the jurors might see his face, giving them a wry smile. "Now, sir, have you ever witnessed Master Jack and Mrs. Spadros together in any sort of conversation?"

Cesare's cheeks reddened. "I have."

"When was this?"

"At the Grand Ball. This year."

"Can you tell the Court what happened?"

"I stood across the room. Jack shouted loudly enough to overcome the orchestra. He rapidly approached the defendant and her party, which included her husband and my brother Jonathan." He glanced away. "Men had to restrain him."

"So it was unpleasant."

"Yes."

"I won't ask you to speculate on the effect this scene — of the Keeper of the Prison attacking her husband and friends — might have on a 22-year-old woman whose father has already been threatened by him." He glanced at the jury. "So we'll move on.

What is your personal opinion of the Spadros Family?"

Mr. Trevisane, who sat beside me, rose. "Objection. Are we to encourage slander?"

"Sustained," the judge said.

"Ah," Mr. Pike said. "So even the attorney for the Spadros Family agrees that your opinion may not be a positive one."

Cesare glared up at where the Spadros Family sat. "His assessment is likely correct."

Mr. Pike turned to gesture at me. "What is your assessment of the character of the defendant?"

Cesare's eyes narrowed. "May I speak frankly?"

"As you always do," Mr. Pike said.

Cesare hesitated, and I think he felt sure he walked into a trap. To his credit, he proceeded. "I dislike her heartily. She is rude, undisciplined, and coarse. She is unfit for quadrant society and merely mimics the social airs and graces of her betters. I thoroughly disapprove of her being given this opportunity of trial, which is reserved for decent folk, not members of the Pot." He almost spat the words out at the end.

Scattered applause.

"So you're not impartial to her case, then."

Cesare blinked. "I suppose not." He said this as if coming to some realization that shamed him.

"Then it's good that you've been offered the opportunity to recuse yourself."

A few surprised murmurs came from the audience.

Mr. Pike turned to the judge. "I presume my motion to declare this a hostile witness will be acceptable to the Court."

"Indeed," the judge said. "So make note."

"Mr. Diamond, would you tell us what happened the day of the zeppelin disaster? Please begin where you believe it relevant to this case."

"A week prior, my sister told me she believed herself the target of blackmail. The reason she was being blackmailed is not relevant to this case. She wished me and four of my brothers to accompany her to Market Center to apprehend the blackmailer. When she arrived at the meeting place, the defendant was with her."

"Was this your intent?"

"No, and I expressed my disapproval at including that," he shuddered, "creature with us."

"Very well, sir. Please continue."

"The defendant became offended and asked to leave, but my sister insisted. During the conversation, I mentioned another item which I have now learned may be relevant."

"What item is this?"

"Several weeks before, my sister had asked me to secretly arrange the shipment of an item with Master Lance Clubb."

"Did you inquire why this item needed to be shipped secretly?"

"Perhaps 'secretly' is too strong a word. My sister asked that I tell no one else the item was to be shipped. I got the impression she didn't want my father to know about it."

"I see. Were you aware of the contents of this item?"

"Not at the time." He hesitated several seconds. "I later learned that the defendant's mother was the item to be shipped."

"So your sister asked you to help smuggle the defendant's mother out of the city within cargo."

"As it turns out."

"And did you make these arrangements?"

"I did. My understanding was that Master Clubb would speak with my sister as to the particulars."

"I see. And at that time, was there any reason Master Clubb might speak to your sister?"

"I beg your pardon?"

"I presume they'd been introduced."

"Ah. Yes. Master Clubb had asked to court my sister, and permission was given."

"So they might speak on private matters without impropriety."

"Indeed."

"So you spoke with Master Clubb to make arrangements for this — item — to be shipped."

"I did."

"Let's return to the day of the disaster. You mentioned the shipment of this item. What was the defendant's reaction?"

"She seemed to have clear knowledge of the item being shipped but was appalled by the timing."

"What exactly did she say?"

"Something to the effect of 'so soon?' It was my impression that the defendant thought it would take longer than it had, and that this was not to her liking."

"I see. What happened then?"

"A man fitting the description of the blackmailer appeared, holding a briefcase. My brothers apprehended the man. We went down to meet them."

"You brought two women into the presence of a scoundrel?"

Cesare seemed taken aback. "I couldn't leave them there unattended!" Dismay crossed his face. "You're correct; the man could have held a bomb. It never occurred to me."

"I'm sure you did the best you could, sir. What happened when you met them?"

"The man knew nothing of the blackmailer. He held a briefcase. I believe the defendant has described what lay inside."

"What were your impressions upon opening the briefcase?"

"Mrs. Spadros obviously had information I didn't. She came to the conclusion that the zeppelin was to be bombed, and appeared desperate to get to the station. My impression was that she wished to prevent the zeppelin from taking off."

Loud murmuring, and the judge banged his gavel.

"Did you come to a different conclusion?"

"Once we reached the bridge, I considered that perhaps the **bank** was the target, and sent men to evacuate the premises. I don't know if the bank officials heeded the warning."

"As it turns out, they did." Mr. Pike turned to the judge. "I have no further questions for this witness."

The judge said, "Mr. Freezout?"

"No questions for this witness, Your Honor."

"Mr. Pike, do you have further witnesses?"

"No, Your Honor. The defense rests."

"Does the prosecution wish to call witnesses in rebuttal?"

I froze. Surely he hadn't found Ma.

"No, Your Honor."

"We will recess for luncheon," the judge said, "then we will resume at two." He banged his gavel, and rose.

I ate in the small side room, with only a stern armed maid in attendance. I wasn't sure what would happen next.

Mr. Pike came in a half hour after I'd finished eating. "The District Attorney has two chances to sway the jury," he said. "No matter what he says, say and do nothing. Make no grimace, stifle any laughter. Do you understand? He'll try to make you look a horrible creature." He patted my hand. "You've done very well. Just a few more hours to go."

"Thank you."

At this, Mr. Pike's head bowed. "No, thank **you**. I'd almost given up." He smiled to himself. Then he raised his head. "But you've helped me. It might sound strange, but you have."

I didn't really understand, but said, "I'm glad to be of service. Does that mean a reduction of what I owe you?"

He let out a short, amused laugh. "Good try." With that, he left me wondering in all seriousness how I might have helped him.

The Closing

When I entered the courtroom, nothing had changed. The courthouse was full. The portraits of those killed in the disaster were displayed just as they had been the entire time. But there was an air of anticipation in the room I hadn't felt before then.

District Attorney Chase Freezout rose. "If it may please the Court, may I address the jury?"

"By all means," the judge said.

Mr. Freezout pointed at the portraits. "We're here to secure justice for two hundred fifteen law-abiding, decent quadrant-folk — men, women, and children —"

So he's decided to ignore the "Pot rags," I thought.

"— slaughtered by a cold-blooded murderess." He gestured toward me with an open hand. "Born in utter squalor, raised by villains, thieves, and whores. Taught to steal, to lie, to run scams precisely like the one we've experienced. Trained to kill from the age of twelve by Roy Spadros himself. Recall her own words: she can kill with a knife, a gun, a garrote, with her own hands if need be. She seduced her way to the side of the Spadros Family heir —"

"Objection," Mr. Pike said, not even bothering to rise.

"Sustained," the judge said. "Mr. Freezout, you're to keep your remarks civil."

"My apologies, your Honor," Mr. Freezout said, clearly unrepentant. Then he turned to the jury. "She had access to the vast Spadros Family fortune, a perfect set-up for someone with clear motive to ruin us."

"Now, the defense would claim she has only the purest desires.

'To do what is right,' as Master Diamond put it. Yet what would someone from the Pot believe to be right? They believe themselves betrayed by their city. They're trained to murder law officials if they get the chance. Our First Mayor, a traitor. Our people, targets for theft and worse. The Clubb Family? The people who 'killed our King.' As the old tales say, 'from the mouths of babes.' This sort believes these vile words from the day they're born. Can there be any doubt as to her intentions?

"So she had undeniable motive to do this crime, no matter what fiction she spins about her mother. While the defense has given us much circumstantial evidence, there is no real proof her mother was on that craft, only that the defendant says she believed it to be so. I believe this to be another means of enticing you to free her.

"And so we come to her true plan: to destroy our city. Her first step was to destroy our merchants. We have testimony — from the mouth of her own lawyer here in this room — that she asked him to dun jewelers who balked at selling these fake gems. The place and time to strike the most powerful blow, one designed to cripple the city? At the zeppelin station, at the Celebration which marked the 100th anniversary of the Alcatraz Coup.

"So she made ready, covering her tracks. Forgeries, lies, alliances with people with the misfortune to trust her. Each murdered. It's unfortunate that we won't have the opportunity to get justice for those young men strangled —"

This time, Mr. Pike did rise. "Objection!"

"Sustained," the judge said. "Mr. Freezout, Mrs. Spadros is not charged with the deaths of those men, and you know it! If you impugn her character again in this courtroom, I shall have you charged with contempt." He turned to the jury. "You are not to heed any of the prosecution's last statement. There is neither allegation nor proof that Mrs. Spadros had a single thing to do with those men's murders. Understood?"

The jury-men nodded, eyes wide.

"Mr. Freezout," the judge said, "you may proceed."

"Very well," Mr. Freezout said, unruffled. "We've provided expert testimony that the handwriting on the invoices matched the defendant's handwriting. Invoices shipping tons of explosive material on the zeppelin. We have a letter from the defendant admitting she gave the package we suspect contained the bomb to Dame Anastasia. We have numerous witnesses testifying that Dame Anastasia told them the package was given to her by the defendant. We have the defendant's own witness — a man of unimpeachable character — stating that she knew there would be an explosion. Why? Because she planned it. She hurried to arrive in time to gloat over her handiwork. Then when questioned about it, she lied to the inquest. This is a fact.

"So now you must decide what you believe. You must decide whether the lives of two hundred fifteen innocent men, women, and children should be avenged. Or whether this cold-blooded enemy of Bridges, with the means, the motive, and the opportunity to kill without mercy or remorse should be unleashed upon this city to wreak more havoc. I trust you will do the right thing, and find the defendant guilty on all charges."

The judge said, "We will take a twenty minute recess, then resume with the defense's closing statement."

I said to Mr. Pike, "How **dare** he accuse me of anything to **do** with killing those men!"

Mr. Pike put his hand on my shoulder. "That judge never becomes angry in court! The outburst unnerved me, yet Mr. Freezout took it in stride." Mr. Pike shook his head in astonishment. "I've known Freezout since he became a law clerk, and I've never seen him like this. Our District Attorney bears all the signs of a man with nothing to lose."

* * *

Twenty minutes later, the judge returned.

"Your Honor," Mr. Pike said. "May I address the jury?"

"Proceed."

Mr. Pike stood, approaching them. "Gentlemen of the jury —"

Most of the men were not technically gentlemen: they held no property, and were only merchants, or perhaps even simple day-wage workers. But they sat up, startled, and appeared gratified by the respect and honor given.

"— as I mentioned the last time I spoke with you, by law I have been forbidden to address you directly since the trial began. I was not permitted to acknowledge you on the street, to respond when you greeted me in the hallways, or even to shake your hand. And for that, I apologize. It's my most difficult duty as lawyer," he gave them his alligator grin, "because I love to talk."

Some of the jury smiled, and many in the audience chuckled.

"There is good reason for such formality: to ensure that no taint, no dishonor falls upon the proceedings here. Why is this important? Because a young woman's life and future is at stake. This good and honorable man," Mr. Pike gestured to the judge, "is named as judge over this room, yet today each of you must also judge this matter. You have a sacred duty from tradition held long before the Catastrophe to speak your honest truth."

He gave the same open-handed gesture Mr. Freezout had given me, yet his tone was kind. "You've met Mrs. Jacqueline Spadros. She came to these quadrants as the young Miss Jacqui Kaplan, a small, frightened girl of twelve, ripped from her mother's arms at a moment's notice to be thrust into a strange world.

"But she was not treated kindly. She received harsh words and blows at the hands of Roy Spadros and his staff. She was shunned and scorned by the gentlewomen of Spadros quadrant.

"Through no fault of her own, this young woman has been raised to the center of a feud involving the very Family who claims hold of both Court and Prison."

The jurors looked uncertain, and the audience murmured.

"She's had to balance the commands of her husband and her need to protect herself, both from her enemies and her own Family. And so in desperation, she turned to outside employment.

"But as scandalous as it may be, that's not why she's on trial."

A few of the jurors nodded.

"Years of living in Spadros Manor under its kind tutelage —" this last, said with a tone of irony, "— has not dimmed her true nature."

Some of the jurors had wry smiles, others glanced up warily to where the Spadros Family sat.

"We've heard testimony from both high and low of her compassion, her fierce determination to help others and do what she feels to be right. I don't believe there's any doubt as to that.

"We've been asked to examine the source of the false gems circulating the city, the speculation on which has caused such upset. But other than the fact that Dame Anastasia Louis befriended Mrs. Jacqueline Spadros, and that Mrs. Spadros invited Dame Anastasia to her home in return, our District Attorney has provided little evidence that Mrs. Spadros knew about the matter until well into it.

"And no matter what her crimes might have been, Dame Anastasia is not on trial."

Scattered murmurs.

"Now there are many who say that the three Families who came to dine with Dame Anastasia this Queen's Night did so to plot against the city. Since none of us were present, we have no idea whether this is true. The prosecution has provided no real evidence to help us decide. But let's suppose that this is true: that three of our Families plotted to destroy our city's merchants, using Mrs. Spadros as their dummy. What benefit could the Families gain by ruining our merchants? Would it not rather benefit those who wish the rule of the Families ended?

"But it matters not whether one Family man, one entire Family, three Families, or all of the Families tried to harm this city. Why? Because none of the Families are on trial here."

Several in the jury put hand to chin, glancing aside.

"We've heard the District Attorney insinuate that this young woman is guilty merely because of where she was born. If every one of the many tens of thousands living in squalor deserve death for their unlucky birthplace, does he advocate the same brutal fate King Polansky Kerr meant for your ancestors?"

A man shouted, "They deserve it!" Many in the audience behind me gasped in horror, yet some applauded.

Mr. Freezout was on his feet. "Objection! Impugning the character of the prosecution."

"Overruled," the judge said. I imagined he wasn't too pleased with Mr. Freezout's insinuations about my character up to now.

Mr. Pike turned to the jurors, as if he spoke to only them. "Our District Attorney plays on your hate, your jealousy, your distrust, your contempt. But you have been chosen out of many hundreds of others for your better nature. Your higher mind. Your willingness to carry out the sacred duty I spoke of earlier."

Some of the jurors straightened, others gave a slight nod.

"The horrifying way our ancestors were treated, some of whom still live today, can never be countenanced. Ever. But no matter how heinous the crimes of those who lived in the Pot 100 years ago," he then emphasized each word, "the Pot is not on trial here."

The audience fell silent.

"We've heard testimony as to the matter of the invoices, and the letter to Dame Anastasia Louis which was found at the station. Now, I know the prosecution has an expert who claims these were from her, while my independent expert claims not. You," he pointed at the jury, "are the only judges in this matter. You must judge which expert you found more reliable."

The jurors glanced at each other.

"Perhaps you may be thinking — as the prosecution asserts — that Mrs. Spadros acted from bitter resentment for the destruction of her home. Yet which makes more sense? That a young woman resentful of matters which occurred before her birth would hatch an elaborate plot which murders the two women she loves most? Or that there's another culprit yet unchallenged?"

He let the words hang there for several seconds.

"So this brings up the question: why was **she** put on trial, when there is reasonable question of at least one man — and a woman forger — who might have done these things?

"Mrs. Spadros has no training in finance, no knowledge of gems. There's no evidence she bought or sold a single stone. She gained no benefit from Dame Anastasia's scam. What possible motivation might she have had to cause the financial crisis? Even if she hated Bridges with passion, causing a **financial** crisis seems low on the list of things one might consider doing."

This threw many of the jurors into thought, their gazes turned inward.

"Could this young woman really have done the things she's accused of? Each day holds but four and twenty hours in it. Is this

— in your estimation — a woman with the sheer time to run a household with several dozen servants, conduct business, destroy the economy, **and** blow up a zeppelin? The idea is preposterous."

A few people in the audience behind me chuckled.

"If she truly wanted to destroy the Clubbs — who by all accounts call her friend — why not bomb their yacht launch?"

Gasps filled the air, yet he spoke over them.

"In one stroke, she would have not only murdered all four Family heirs but wiped out the entire Clubb Family. Surely such a cunning revolutionary as our esteemed District Attorney claims her to be would yearn for this sort of bold action."

This gave me a shock. It seemed so clear. Why had the Red Dogs **not** done this? What was I missing?

"Our District Attorney persists in claiming she was at the zeppelin station for nefarious reason. And yet we've heard a great deal of testimony corroborating her claim: that she learned of the bombing less than an hour before it occurred, risking her life to stop it." His words became precise. "She defied a direct order from Roy Spadros to save **them**," he pointed at the rows of photos across the room, "from death."

A masterful move! I felt deeply impressed. He couldn't stop the portraits from being displayed, but he could use them.

Mr. Pike clasped his hands behind his back. "And yet here we are, determining whether this brave young woman should die. Why? Surely our beloved District Attorney knew many of these facts in advance. This is the man who aspires to lead us as Mayor, a man with generations of wealth and the full might of the Bridges legal system behind him. Surely he knew all this.

"These are the precise questions you must answer: Did Mrs. Jacqueline Spadros do any of the crimes she's charged with? And if so, which of these did she do? If you truly and firmly believe that this 22-year-old woman murdered 215 quadrant-folk, killed over a hundred of her own people, and concocted the financial ruin of Bridges, then so be it. But in truth, this abused and abandoned young woman is the 348th victim of this tragedy.

"You must search your heart to ensure you have no reasonable doubt in the matter. Her life rests in your hands. If you have the slightest unease as to the truth of her guilt, you must vote to set her free. If there is a question in your mind as to whether there could be another who committed these crimes, you must vote to set her free.

"The District Attorney will urge you to condemn this young woman. He will appeal to your anger, your hate, your pity for the victims' families. But we are not a lynch mob, gentlemen. We're a court of law, and if we let emotion blind us to the truth then no one is safe from baseless accusation.

"Thank you for your time and attention to this matter."

When he returned, I whispered, "You did very well, sir."

Mr. Pike whispered, "Mr. Freezout must speak once more."

The judge said, "Does the prosecution wish to make rebuttal?"

Mr. Freezout stood. "Yes, Your Honor." He addressed the jurors. "The defense would like you to believe several things which we know to be false. One: that someone youthful and outwardly-attractive could never commit a crime. Two: that overcoming harsh and unfair treatment somehow negates the training of childhood. Indeed, in this case, being taught to hate quadrant-folk combined with brutal treatment would lead to even greater hatred. Three: that this defendant, who lied in the inquest, has such high character that she would never stoop to stealing, lying, or killing. Four: that because the defense believes committing a crime is unlikely, the defendant didn't do it.

"We must stand on evidence, good sirs, not belief, not attraction, not flattery —"

A few of the jurors twitched.

"— not convoluted arguments, and certainly not pity for the defendant. Have pity rather on," he pointed to the portraits, "all these men, women, and children who lost their lives at the defendant's hand. Take pity on the families ruined through her fraudulent gem scheme.

"The last thing the defense wishes you to believe is that you must be absolutely certain the defendant is guilty, or you must set her free. This is not true."

The jurors appeared confused.

"Every item of life is uncertain. If for example, you lay abed in a windowless room for a day, rising at midnight, would you judge that the sun failed to rise? No! Because although you did not see the sun rise for yourself, you understand the forces of nature. You have the testimony of witnesses that the sun did indeed rise. You feel the heat of the summer day which still lingers. You know that up to this point, the sun has always acted according to its nature. Are you absolutely certain the sun rose? You cannot be: you did not see it. But when you rise at midnight, you weigh the evidence and find overwhelming proof that yes, the sun did rise."

The jurors nodded, their faces thoughtful.

"And so it is here. We will never **know** if the defendant did the crimes she is accused of. We were not there. Yet our job is not to know. Our job is to look at the evidence and judge: did she do these things? We understand the forces in the defendant's life. We observe her nature, and understand that people, like the sun, act according to that nature. And so it is here. We have testimony that the defendant did indeed give Dame Anastasia the package that undoubtedly killed these people. That she shipped the explosives which caused the zeppelin's entire destruction. You feel the effects of her actions all around you. If the evidence proves that the defendant did these crimes, you must find her guilty."

The jurors' faces turned grim, and my heart sank.

"I thank you for your time and consideration. The fate of the city rests in your hands."

The Verdict

The jury was escorted to a room to spend the night and consider the case. But before that, the judge warned them that although this might be difficult, they needed to deliver a clear verdict in the morning.

The guards made me wait until everyone had filed out of the room. When Mr. Pike and I approached the front steps, Cesare stood facing away, a host of reporters around him. "I didn't testify for Anthony Spadros, his wife, or anyone else. I'm a man of honor, and the truth needed to be told. No matter what my opinion of Mrs. Spadros, or the damage to my reputation, to refuse to speak true would be a miscarriage of justice."

"So you believe her to be innocent?"

"Entirely. And it's despicable that she be here at all, not to mention alone, without husband or family by her side. The Spadros Family has treated her shamefully by refusing to allow her to see her loved ones —" He turned aside, then collected himself. "It surprises me not. Dishonorable betrayers all. Good day, gentlemen." He continued on without another word, the reporters hounding him all the way to his carriage.

I stood stunned at his words in my support. Mr. Pike said, "My dear, I think we've won. Of course, there is the matter of the jury. But no matter what they say, you'll not be hanged. The people won't allow it."

"What alternative is there?"

"The Prison, of course."

Where Jack Diamond ruled. Jack might not have kidnapped

David, but he'd shown no sign of lessening his hate towards me. "If I don't win free, I'd prefer the gallows."

Mr. Pike patted my arm. "Then we'd best go home and pray."

So I did. Blitz, Amelia, and Mary met me at the door. Mr. Hart had sent a dozen red roses, which I put on my dresser. Whatever Roy might say about Mr. Hart, he'd been there at the trial more than anyone.

"Come sit with me a while," I said to them. So we sat in the parlor and had tea. After a while, Blitz began to pace the room. Amelia did needlepoint, and Mary read aloud from the Holy Writ.

I took pen and ink and drew a picture of my mother as I remembered her, to bring with me should I go to the Prison. Would they take me from the courtroom at once? Or would I be allowed to return home for my things?

I remembered those grim-faced men in the jury, and my heart sank. I'd be taken at once, I felt sure of it.

I'd always feared a cage, and my entire life since Air died had been one. At least I'd be free of this last cage soon enough. "Do I have anything black? I should wear black to go to my death."

Blitz said, "Are things really that bad?"

"Worse," I said. "I might miss the clean death of the gallows to face Jack Diamond instead."

Amelia began to weep. "Oh, mum," she said. "I don't want you to die. Especially not like that. You've been so good to us all." Mary took her into her arms and held her as she wept.

"No," I said. "I'm no good. I lied and cheated. I schemed and plotted. I've caused the deaths of most everyone who loved me."

Oh, Tony, I thought. *Will they make you watch?* That would surely kill him. I said to Blitz, "I fear what my husband might do should I be taken."

Blitz leaned both hands on the back of the sofa behind Mary, nodding, his face concerned.

"If they kill me, sell these apartments and give the money to the poor. I should never have lied about the auction." Grief overcame me, and I put Ma's picture aside.

The three came to me then. Blitz knelt before me, taking my hands in his. "You won't be alone tomorrow. We'll shutter the house and come with you."

"Will they let you?"

Blitz smiled at that. "I'd like to see them try and stop me."

I couldn't eat. I couldn't sleep. I found myself at the window as the sky lightened, recalling those horrible days at Clubb Manor in the early hours of the morn, when I felt so frantic for Joe.

Was he with some other woman now?

If he were alive, he must be, I thought. He could never deny himself anything, it seemed, not even for me.

What did I do to make him feel he'd lost me? I couldn't think of anything. I remembered standing in terror watching the horror in Tony's eyes at seeing Joe and I together.

I should never have let myself care for Tony, I decided. I should've followed Joe out of the window right then and there.

Joe must have thought I'd return to Tony when I didn't follow. Did he stand outside the window waiting, hoping I'd appear?

When I never came to him, did he give up?

If only I could see Joe, talk to him, I could make it right.

But it would never happen. The whole city searched for him. At the time, I wouldn't have wanted him to risk his life even if he regretted what he'd done. But I vowed that if I did survive this day, I'd try to learn where he went.

Perhaps the support my quadrant had shown me on Market Center might stay Jack Diamond's hand for a few months, so as not to cause an uproar. I might be able to learn something.

Soon Amelia came in with my tea and toast. It felt ironic, drinking my morning tea as if I'd ever lie with someone again. But its bitter taste was the only thing my mother could give me, and so I felt that in a way she sat with me that day.

After I drank it, I fell to the floor and prayed, not that some miracle would happen, because I never believed in those. But I prayed that the Dealer would help me to play this terrible round with honor. I would not faint when the verdict was read. I would go to my fate with dignity, face Jack's knife without crying out. He would not get the satisfaction of seeing my fear.

I would make Roy Spadros proud.

That thought entirely confounded me. Why should I care about what that scoundrel thought?

But as I lay upon the floor, I couldn't help but feel this to be true. For better or worse, Roy Spadros — that cunning, sadistic old man — had raised me to be who I was that day.

I sat in my chair, wiped my face. What did this mean?

I didn't know, but it explained my urge, in spite of everything, to return to Spadros quadrant after I left Tony, even though it likely meant death.

Amelia bustled in. "Mum, you haven't eaten a thing. And you didn't eat dinner either. You don't want to faint in the Courtroom. Here," she spread some jam on the cold toast, "eat something. Read your post. That should cheer you."

The post had been opened, as they'd been doing for weeks now to spare me the daggers. But these were all good wishes. And I trusted these people; I no longer needed to hide from them.

Notes from Vig, from little Tenni, even one from Madame Biltcliffe. "I deeply regret our last words, cherie, and I hope you'll forgive them. I do still love you, and wish you only the best."

There had been nothing to forgive. She saw better than anyone who I was, and had the courage to say so. I set the pile of post aside, wiped my tears, and forced myself to eat. I wouldn't give these people who plotted to kill me the spectacle they hoped for.

Amelia got me bathed and in my house dress, sat me in front of breakfast, got me into my charcoal dress, but I felt numb, in a daze. "Oh," she said, "you need a necklace." I faced away from the mirror; she'd been doing my hair. She rummaged about. "Oh, this is lovely! We must have missed it for the auction: I never noticed it before." She hung a heavy pendant around my neck, but I hardly took note of it, trapped as I was in my thoughts.

Roy Spadros raised me. But I wasn't like him. Was I?

We piled into the curtained carriage. There might have been a riot outside for all I cared. I recall there being many more with Spadros markings on the way to the Court, but at the time it made no impression. All I knew was that I rode to my death.

I'd seen the jury-men, their grim faces, the way they wouldn't meet my eye. What else could their judgment be? I was a Pot rag, and no truth could keep those men from punishing me for rising to the place they coveted.

I wasn't afraid anymore, not really. Perhaps the Dealer did give me some small strength that day. As I stepped from the carriage, the shouts of the crowd meant nothing. I truly didn't hear them. The door lay before me; I stepped through.

The spectators fell silent as I entered. The guards brought me to my seat, and I surveyed the balcony as Blitz, Amelia, and Mary took seats behind me. Tony stood there, in the front row, his face pale in his emotionless public mask, and Roy Spadros — the man Tony believed to be his father — stood next to him.

Roy's cold pale eyes met mine, and he gave a slight smile, a small nod.

I stood there so stunned I couldn't move. Coming from Roy, this was high praise shouted.

"Are you well, Mrs. Spadros?"

Mr. Hart stood beside me on the other side of the small railing, and took my hand.

A sudden panic struck that Roy might see his most hated rival speak to me. But it wasn't terror on my own behalf, but that Roy might attack this fat old man who'd done so much for me.

But Mr. Hart smiled. "Come now, my dear — all will be well. Turn round and sit. They await you to begin."

I turned round. The judge sat up in his place, the jury had filed in, and all eyes were on me. Cheeks burning, I sat.

I didn't dare look at the jury-men. A golden bird sat embossed upon the front of the high box the judge sat in: the seal of the Merca Federal Union. *From Ashes We Rise*, it said, and those words brought me encouragement.

"Mrs. Spadros," Mr. Pike said, "stand up."

Had the judge spoken? I stood, gripping the sides of my dress to keep my hands from shaking.

A man spoke, and they tell me it was the leader of the jurors. But I focused on the golden bird, not breathing. "We the jury find the defendant, Jacqueline Kaplan Spadros —" he paused, and I thought, why hesitate? It must be bad. "Not guilty —"

I have to admit I don't recall what he said next, because, as fate would have it, I did faint.

The Scheme

When I opened my eyes, Jon gazed back. I touched the side of his face. "You're not Jack."

He smiled as if quite amused. "No, my love," he whispered. "I'm not Jack."

Tony pushed past Jon, out of breath. "Oh, gods." He shoved my chair back, leaning over me as he knelt, taking me in his arms. "Are you hurt?"

"I don't think so." I surveyed them. "They said I'm not guilty?"

Mr. Pike peered over from across the table. "They cleared you of it all. Congratulations."

Was this a dream?

Tony retreated; Mr. Hart bent over me, grabbing me under my arms. "Up you go." With one smooth motion, Mr. Hart lifted me completely off my feet as if I were a child then set me steady. "You are one lucky young lady."

I laughed then. *Lucky.* I regarded all these men who'd helped me. "Thank you. All of you."

Tony's cheeks reddened, and he turned away.

Thrace Pike came up to us. "Did you hear? The scoundrel's gone and won himself Mayor."

I glanced around the half-empty hall. I'd completely forgotten the election was yesterday. "Let's get out of here." I took Jon's arm, feeling unsteady; Tony and Mr. Hart followed.

The front porch was empty but for police and guards of the Court who stood at intervals along the walls. Police waited along both edges of the wide stair, one at each step, simply watching. At the bottom of the stair, reporters stood frozen, faces ashen. Behind them, the crowd stared in horror.

In the center of the wide steps, Mr. Alexander Clubb and Mr. Julius Diamond stood casually, as if having a conversation. A few feet away, Mr. Roy Spadros was giving the new Mayor Mr. Chase Freezout the beating of his life.

I gasped, appalled.

"Who paid you?" Roy's pupils were wide, his cheeks flushed, his black gloves covered in blood. Holding Mr. Freezout's white hair in one fist, he punched Mr. Freezout in the face with the other. "Who paid you to perform this outrage?" His eyes narrowed. "You will speak, if you wish to live."

Mr. Freezout's eyes widened in terror, jerked to the left, and his head followed. Judith Hart stood with her son Etienne at the bottom of the stair. At Freezout's glance, she sneered, then fixed me with a glare of pure hate, her eyes flickering to my chest.

I put my hand to the necklace I wore — the one Mr. Hart had given me!

I stared at her. Mrs. Hart paid Mr. Freezout to persecute me? Why? Why could she possibly hate me this much?

Roy laughed. "She hates him as much as I do."

I glanced back at Mr. Hart, who stood motionless, staring in his wife's direction. His face, if anything, held sadness.

Mrs. Hart's face held nothing but hate as she looked between us. Did she think him to be my lover? "Wait," I called, intending to straighten this matter out at once.

But Tony took my arm. "Let her go."

"But Mr. Hart isn't —"

"Let it go," Mr. Hart said. "Just — please, let it go."

Roy stripped off his bloody right glove; knuckle-dusters gleamed silver in the midday sun. He glanced at me. "A Midsummer's gift from Molly."

Mr. Diamond began to laugh as if this was the funniest thing he'd seen in a long while. He held out his hand. "You're all right."

Roy stripped his other glove off and threw the pair at Mr. Freezout. Then he took off his knuckle-dusters, slipped them into a pocket, and held out his hand.

So Julius Diamond and Roy Spadros shook hands as the reporters took pictures: the first time a Spadros and a Diamond had shaken hands in front of the cameras since — well, ever.

Roy kicked Mr. Freezout as the new Mayor lay groaning on the steps. "Take this filth away."

The police dragged Mr. Freezout off, presumably to fetch a doctor. Blood was splattered over the steps where he once lay.

"You did well, Jacq," Roy said. "It went exactly as planned."

Julius Diamond nodded. Charles Hart winked. Alexander Clubb smiled at me. I stared at them all. "You four **planned** this?"

Roy said, "How could we do otherwise? The only way to expose these people was to let this farce proceed." He glanced up at Mr. Hart with disdain. "Figures."

"I don't know what you have against each other," I said to Roy, "but this man has been at my side through this entire ordeal."

"Time has only made him viler than he was." Roy spat on Mr. Freezout's blood. "You'll change your play when you learn the truth." He stalked off, Mr. Clubb and Mr. Diamond following.

I turned to Mr. Hart. "I don't understand."

Mr. Hart said, "Nothing you might say will sway him. He only wishes to cause upset at a time when you should be happy."

At the time, this made sense. It was Roy's character. "However did you work together?" The whole matter seemed astonishing.

Mr. Hart smiled. "Your husband has been of great service."

Tony helped set up this ordeal? Went between them all to plan it? I didn't know what to think. "Well, then," I said, gazing at the blood on the stair, "it's time we left."

Tony said, "Might I have a moment with my wife?"

With that, everyone withdrew, murmuring "of course."

Tony took my hands. "I'm sorry not to be there beside you. The lawyers felt —"

"That it would appear best if I stood alone. Yet you allowed it, facilitated it." I felt bitter. "It was all a play. Like everything else."

"What? How can you say that?"

"You abandoned me, Tony, leaving me without one word of aid or comfort. When I needed you most, you weren't even there!"

"I abandoned **you**?" Tony's face hardened. "You have no right.

I've been shot at, lost my reputation, put Gardena in danger, all for you. And this after you abandoned **me**! After everything we've been through together, you betrayed me! Ugh, I can't ever get that image from my mind of you and that — I hardly can call Joseph Kerr a man for what he's done —"

"How dare you?" I shook off his hands. "If this was all some scheme to lure me back to Spadros Manor, you've failed miserably. I would rather die than return to a cage."

Snow began to fall. Tony's face held shock and dismay as I left him standing beside Mr. Freezout's darkening blood.

* * *

The afternoon papers were most amusing:

Mayor Freezout Humbled!

Roy Spadros Beats Mayor: Police Do Nothing

The *Golden Bridges* asked: Does Roy Spadros Rule Bridges?

It certainly seemed so, especially in the days to come. It was only after Mayor Freezout's death a few years later that everyone learned that the doctors had only given him a few months to live.

The jury-men were interviewed. "That girl should never have been tried," one said. "It was clearly a set-up."

Another said, "I wasn't convinced she did it. And I didn't like that Freezout either."

"They should leave these Pot rags alone," a third said, "not drag them into the quadrants. She didn't even know what a bath was! How could she do all these crimes?"

And on and on. Insulting, horrifying, yet whatever their reasonings, here I was: alive and free.

To celebrate, Jonathan and I went to my apartments with Blitz, Mary, and Amelia, and cooked dinner together.

"I've never cooked a thing in my life," Jon said. "We weren't allowed in the kitchen, even as children, except on rare occasion." He found the various items fascinating. And he even sat at table with my "servants," though it took some doing to get Mary and

Amelia to sit with us.

The two women kept saying, "Are you sure you wish this, sir?" until Jon began to laugh.

"Sit down, please," he said. "This is your home, not mine."

Amelia burst into tears, falling on her knees beside him. She grasped his hand. "Thank you so much for your kindness, sir."

He smiled at her. "It would please me if you joined us, Mrs. Dewey, but I don't wish to cause distress."

That got to her. "Oh, no, of course, sir. Not at all." She wiped her eyes with her apron, stood up, and curtsied. "I'm sorry, sir. Forgive me for speaking out of turn."

I laughed. "Sit down, Amelia, the food grows cold."

After dinner, Jonathan and I sat in the parlor. He took my hands in his. "I almost lost you this year, Jacqui. So I've made a decision: I'm not leaving the city again without you."

"Will that cause trouble?"

He smiled, but didn't meet my eye. "No. Not at all." He looked me in the eye then. "You said that you were alone. As long as I live, I don't want a day to go by that you feel alone."

Amelia brought in a package. "This just arrived, mum."

Jon stood, hurrying to her. "I'll open this outside. Just in case."

I said, "I suppose we should get a bomb-sniffer of our own."

"Oh," Amelia said, as if she never considered more bombs might arrive. "A letter came as well." Her face flushed red. "I'm sorry, mum, I opened it before seeing it was from Mr. Anthony."

What could Tony possibly have to say to me?

Jacqui —

Since the first night I laid eyes on you, all I've wanted most was to be your King of Hearts. But I see now that you consider me The Fool.

I won't trouble you again. You have been hurt beyond imagining, but my dearest hope is that your hurt is not beyond mending. I wish you only happiness.

Your servant,

Anthony Spadros

I stared at the page.

You have been hurt beyond imagining.

I won't trouble you again.

Pain squeezed my heart. *Oh, Tony … I never meant to hurt you!*

I took a deep breath, let it out. I couldn't let myself feel for this man. I couldn't go back, not after everything that'd happened.

I slowly tore Tony's letter in two, placing the halves on top of the unlit fire. Then I lit the pieces, watched them burn.

The nightmare was over. I was free.

Jon returned with the opened package, and we sat together on the sofa. Inside were my business cards and a wall sign:

Kaplan Private Investigations

Discreet Service For Ladies

Jon said, "So you truly mean to go on with this?"

"I do. The first case I intend to take is my own!"

"Your own?"

"Yes. I intend to learn why I was framed. Why your brother's being framed." Jack Diamond was a despicable scoundrel who'd probably be the death of me. But as Mr. Pike said, even scoundrels deserved justice. "Why this Red Dog Gang used Mrs. Hart and Mr. Freezout this way."

The beating the Mayor took told me he was not the mastermind I thought him to be, but a low card, easily cast aside. Mrs. Hart was ruled by hate, manipulated into staking the round.

No, someone else was in charge of this scheme, and I intended to find him. "And when I find them, Jon, I intend to kill them."

~~ This ends Chapter 4 of the Red Dog Conspiracy ~~

The Ten of Spades

Part 5 of the Red Dog Conspiracy

Coming October 2019

Be careful what you wish for ...

After nearly eleven years trapped in the Spadros crime syndicate, 23-year-old private eye Jacqueline Spadros is an independent woman, free to run her investigation business.

But her problems are only beginning.

Deeply in debt, Jacqui is in danger from both the rogue Spadros men calling themselves "The Ten of Spades" and the ruthless Red Dog Gang — who may be one and the same.

Jacqui is determined to find Black Maria, the key to the identity of the Red Dog Gang's secretive leader. To survive long enough to do that, she needs a paying case.

The one she finds may be the one which kills her ...

Acknowledgments

Any novel is a team effort. I'm grateful to Andrei Cherascu for his initial read-through, and to Julian White, Lenka Trnkova, and Tasha Reese for beta reading. Thanks to Kit Compton for her help with and insights for the legal portion of the book, as well as to the Legal Fiction Facebook group in answering my many questions about felony trials.

I'd also like to thank Anita B. Carroll for cover design and Erin Hartshorn for editing and proofreading.

Thanks also go to my street team, The Commission, without whom this book might not have made it into your hands.

Special thanks to my Patrons, whose monthly financial donations help make this possible:

Melissa Williams

Michaelene Alston

Julian White

Cristina

Eirlys Evans

Rachel Heslin

Phoebe Darqueling

Dave Kobrenski

Follow the Red Dog Conspiracy on Patreon

patreon.com/red_dog_conspiracy

About The Author

Patricia Loofbourrow is a writer, gardener, artist, musician, poet, wildcrafter, and married mother of three who loves power tools, dancing, genetics, and anything to do with outer space. She also has an MD. Heinlein would be proud.

You can follow her at:
- Her website JacqOfSpades.com
- Twitter @Jacq_Of_Spades
- Tumblr red-dog-conspiracy.tumblr.com
- The Red Dog Conspiracy Facebook page.

Note From The Author

Thanks so much for reading *The King of Hearts*. If you liked the book, please contact me, or leave a review where you bought this!

www.ingramcontent.com/pod-product-compliance
Lightning Source LLC
Chambersburg PA
CBHW050512190726
48284CB00003B/790